Dedicated to all my favourite independent women.
My mum Morwenna, my sisters Julie, Merryn and Imogen,
and my daughters Betsey and Primrose.

No Regrets

Tabitha Webb

ONE PLACE. MANY STORIES

HQ
An imprint of HarperCollins*Publishers* Ltd
1 London Bridge Street
London SE1 9GF

www.harpercollins.co.uk

HarperCollins*Publishers*
1st Floor, Watermarque Building, Ringsend Road
Dublin 4, Ireland

This edition 2021

1
First published in Great Britain by
HQ, an imprint of HarperCollins*Publishers* Ltd 2020

ISBN: 978-0-00-843104-4

MIX
Paper from
responsible sources
FSC™ C007454

This book is produced from independently certified FSC™ paper
to ensure responsible forest management.

For more information visit: www.harpercollins.co.uk/green

This book is set in 11.3/15.5 pt. Bembo

Printed and bound in Great Britain by
CPI Group (UK) Ltd, Croydon, CR0 4YY

Tabitha Somerset Webb is a fashion and lifestyle designer. She lives in Hampshire with her husband Gav, and her two daughters Betsey and Primrose. *No Regrets* is her debut novel.

@tabithawebbuk
tabithawebbuk
www.tabithawebb.co.uk

CHAPTER ONE

Stella

'Shit! Shit!' Stella cursed under her breath as she struggled to wrangle her two-year-old, Rory, into the lurid orange foldaway seat of the supermarket trolley. One of his legs was wrapped over the handle and a pudgy arm was trapped beneath; a second arm was caught in the brake handle; a second leg was wedged into the seat mechanism. There seemed to be a final additional limb she couldn't account for; in it he gripped a long-melted and now leaking bag of gold chocolate coins. As she struggled to unravel Rory's multiple limbs, her caramel Celine Micro-Tote bag, a perk from her former career, slipped to the ground and spilled its contents across sticky, germ-varnished vinyl flooring. She cursed again, louder this time. She was not having a good day. Actually she'd been having a bad week. Since at least Monday, her life had been a mess. Since the call from the credit card company. The call she was going to return as soon as humanly possible. Tomorrow, maybe.

'Sorry!'

She was blocking traffic, blocking every other mother's access to wholesome produce, messing with their minutely choreographed schedules. One tutted, another coughed, as they stepped over, around, and between the spilled contents of her beloved Celine.

'Sorry! I am so sorry!'

A line of pastel-wearing young mothers – picture-postcard yummy mummies, who wafted in to complete their effortless weekly shop – and their pale celery-sucking progeny had formed; the clean-mouthed, rosy-cheeked children perched upright in their foldaway seats nibbling contentedly on gluten-free, dairy-free snacks as they were chauffeured along well-trodden and orderly paths through the aisles. Her own trips followed a less precise agenda. As if to prove the point, Rory began to screech. Stella knew from experience that she had about ten seconds until the whole supermarket witnessed her motherhood failure. Panicked, she quickly wrestled her snot-faced, chocolate-smeared child out of the seat and plonked him into the body of the trolley. He stopped screaming, sitting in open-mouthed disbelief at his demotion. His jaw began to wobble in preparation for another outburst, so she squeezed the contents of an almost liquid chocolate coin into Rory's open fist, which he immediately shoved in his mouth. Ignoring the filth on the floor and happy she was wearing her trusty Pineapple Studios sweatshirt (it was Thursday so she definitely hadn't been wearing it for more than three days – OK, three and a half), she used her forearm to sweep together the pile of lipsticks, chapsticks, moisturisers, hand sanitisers, used wet wipes, tampons, chewed toys, painkillers and belly-fluff into a pile.

Anxiously checking on Rory, she saw that he'd had enough of licking chocolate from his fingers and had moved onto the seat. Someone with tanned shoulders and a solicitous smile was standing beside the trolley.

'Let me,' she said, and pulled an industrial pack of wet wipes from her South American, hand-crafted Inca shoulder bag. It was the Van Nesses' nanny. Stella had met her, briefly, probably at the school gates. Without any fuss, and most importantly without objection from Rory, starting from the mouth and working outwards down each limb, finishing with the handle of the trolley, she cleaned every chocolatey surface. 'There. Who's a clever boy?' She ruffled his hair and passed the handful of dirty wipes to Stella. 'There, he no longer looks, how do you say, as happy as a pig in shit?'

Stella laughed at the unlikely phrasing and the Spanish accent. She couldn't remember her name, but she knew it had something to do with chocolate.

'Thank you. I'm... err... Stella.'

'Yes, I know.'

Stella stared at her, waiting for the shoe to drop, but the girl just stared at her, all big green eyes, Mediterranean skin, and electric red lips pressed into a cheeky smile.

'I don't remember your name.'

'I know.'

Her lips parted, revealing a smile that would have been a dental hygienist's dream. Stella could smell suncream: shea butter and banana with a hint of vanilla.

'I'm Coco. I work for the Van Nesses.'

'Yes. Of course. I knew that. Yes. Lovely to see you again, Coco. I love that top on you. Is it Tom Williamson?'

'This? I don't know. I borrowed it. I love the colour.'

She flicked at one of the yellow spaghetti shoulder straps.

That colour. That yellow colour, like a field of sunflowers, held such happy associations for Stella. It was exactly the same colour as the bridesmaids' dresses she and Ana had worn for Dixie's wedding. She still had a photo of the three of them: Dixie dressed in an embarrassing pink, like a prom dress, and Ana and herself, Dixie's sun-kissed, smiling, co-conspirators. The marriage itself was obviously a catastrophe, but the wedding was as wild as any she had ever attended. There was still a gossip embargo on at least half the stories from the after-party. They would have been about Coco's age back then, and Stella had been as young and hot and self-assured as Coco was now. She missed that feeling, but had she ever really been *that* hot?

'Aren't you cold in that?'

Coco laughed carelessly and pulled a hoodie from her bag. Stella caught a lemon scent.

'Yes, a little. But it's spring. It's so important to get sun on the skin, don't you think?' She lifted her forearm and stroked the taut, satin flesh. Tiny blonde hairs stood up from the bronzed skin. Stella shivered. She stopped herself from comparing the tanned arm of the 25-year-old Spanish au pair with the pock-marked, UV-damaged epidermis of a 40-year-old mother of two who hadn't had a shower or changed her clothes in about four days.

'Lovely to see you again, Coco. How are the Van Nesses? I haven't seen Penelope in weeks.'

'Oh, they're marvellous. Mrs Penelope Van Ness is on a retreat in Goa.'

'How amazing! Well, lucky her. Say hello from me. Come

on, Rory. Let's try and get this horror show over before your halo slips.'

Rory's eyes followed Coco as she laughed, oggling her as if she were chocolate-coated. Stella watched as she leaned down and kissed him. First on the forehead and then on the lips.

Stella had to stop herself slapping the girl away. The lips. Too much. Yuck.

'He likes you. Very unusual.'

'Kids love me. They know that I love them unconditionally,' she said with great seriousness.

Eugh, thought Stella. Another new-age hippy lost in fantasy fairyland.

'Yes, I'm sure that's it. Lovely to see you, Coco. I'm sure I'll see you again.'

She hurried her trolley and child into the fruit aisle as Rory tried to lean around her to grin at Coco.

'I hope so. I'd like that,' said Coco.

As they rounded the piled pyramid of potatoes, Rory lost sight of her and began to wail. Stella squeezed another coin into his mitt and began to surround him with food that he might – God willing – one day eat: carrots, celery, cucumbers, clementines. All the c-words. Rory sat himself down amongst the piling rainbow of fruit and veg and found himself some chocolate to lick from a receipt he'd found in the bottom of the trolley.

As she passed in front of the chilled dairy section, she caught a glimpse of Coco's bare brown back in the biscuit aisle. She was filling her basket with Hobnobs, chocolate digestives and ginger creams. In addition to the yellow spaghetti top and the soft, grey lemon-scented hoodie (no doubt left in her bed by some 20-year-old surf instructor) now draped over her shoulders, she was wearing white trousers, spandex, whose stretch, when she reached down for a packet of Oreos, revealed she required no additional support or protection. Stella regretted her choice of tatty pink Sweaty Betty jogging pants, pants that had never broken into a run.

Stella ducked out of sight, not wanting to be spotted and forced to endure more conversation, but she couldn't resist peeking back around the Kettle Chips installation to see what else she'd put in her basket. Three pot noodles. A box of raisin bran. A litre of vanilla ice cream. Another litre of ice cream, mango. Her posture was exemplary: her neck curved and proud like a ballerina; her shoulders square, arms and back toned, and Stella watched as, without hesitation, she bent at the waist to grab a loaf of brown bread and then four tins of red beans from the lowest shelf.

Stella swept a family pack of Kettle Chips into the trolley from the handy display and caught sight of her own clothing choices. On the front of her sweatshirt were tea and coffee stains, some splotches of grease, and she could now smell, not lemon, not shea butter, but instead, fish. Also she was wearing her mother-in-law's hand-painted wellington boots. In fairness, they'd been nearest the door, and given there was a 50 per cent probability of rain on any day she was heading to the Common, they had felt like the sensible choice. But now, seeing Coco in all her wholesome, winsome, youthful vitality, she felt a soul-crushing shame and regret. Shame at her declining standards and regret that she'd never be able to bend from the waist and retrieve anything ever again from a bottom shelf. Instead she reached down to a lower shelf to retrieve some honey-roasted peanuts.

'Stella? What *are* you doing down there?'

It was one of those shrill, Sloaney voices that expands to fill every space. It was the way, when her life was at its toughest, that Stella imagined her own voice sounded. It haunted her. She quickly grabbed an assortment of pumpkin, linseed and chia seeds, and a selection of pulses, and lobbed them into the trolley around Rory, trying desperately to hide the multipacks of mini-chocolate bars and super-sized chocolate treats, and the value pack of Kettle Chips. She knew there was fresh fruit and veggies somewhere under there.

Olivia Oysten-Taylor was wearing white. Of course. Not a normal white, but the kind of white that only exists in adland. She'd also gone for a sporty look.

'Olivia. How wonderful to see you. You look superb. Like Billie Jean.'

They air-kissed.

'I recognised you from behind immediately!'

From behind? thought Stella. What does that mean?

'You remember Rory?'

Olivia leaned down close to him.

'Why did I think he was called Tom? Lovely name, Tommy. So English.'

'Tom is his brother. He's in primary school.'

'Aren't you a handsome boy? Too adorable. Are you going to grow up to be a successful man like your lovely father, Jack?'

'Jake.'

'Of course. The lovely Jake.'

'How is Rups?' She loved to say his name. Rups, what kind of a name was Rups for anything other than a teddy bear. 'Is Rups well?'

'Fabulous. We're just buying a little place in Vermont, a little autumn getaway. It's just so hard to find somewhere fun to vacation in the fall, don't you think?'

'Yes, so true,' said Stella, aware that Rory was getting himself into a state again. He was chewing on the foil casing from one of his disappearing coins, half of which was drying into the fringe that Stella now saw desperately needed cutting.

He reached out a friendly hand to try and touch Olivia's precisely made-up face. She recoiled as if the smears of chocolate were toxic, not the harmless residue of a milk chocolate treat.

Stella wished she'd worn her sunglasses. If people stopped recognising her, she'd stop having these awkward and disturbing encounters. It was the one of the major issues with living in Wandsworth – you could never pop to the shops without the risk of bumping into someone you knew, which meant you were always supposed to make an effort when you left the house, even if that meant squeezing into the Sweaty Betty leggings she'd bought five years ago, just after Tom was born, and, until that week, never worn outside the house.

Rory was burbling, gleefully wiping his fingers on his jacket.

This did not concern her. Long ago she'd learned to dress her sons in dark clothing to disguise their chocolate issues.

He screeched something that she understood as 'coin', but might have been anything. He could have been giving detailed feedback on her failings as a mother.

'Shh, sweetheart,' she whispered. She gave him a carrot, which he threw to the floor.

'Strong-willed, isn't he?' said Olivia. She looked pristine. Perfectly applied lipstick. Eyebrows carefully etched in. Oh for goodness' sake, she was even wearing an actual tennis skirt.

'Hmm. Where are you off to looking so fabulous?'

'I have found the most sublime tennis instructor. He's a dream. He was on the tour back in the Nineties. French. Immensely talented.' She mimed a feeble double-handed backhand. 'Do you play?'

'Tennis? Not any more. Not since I twisted my knee skiing in Klosters in '97. I just can't do all the sports any more. I have to prioritise.'

She reached towards an upper shelf for something beige and organic-looking. Quinoa. She smiled at Olivia as if she knew exactly what it was, and how best to prepare and serve it.

'I really must keep moving, Olivia. Tom's been asked to try out for chess club and I don't want him to be late for Cantonese lessons.'

'Ah ha, sáisáugāan hái bīndouh a.'

Stella looked blank.

'Oh darling, it's Cantonese. It means have an auspicious day. I always help Felix with his homework.'

'Of course,' Stella laughed. 'Blye-blye.'

Olivia looked confused. Stella didn't wait to explain that she was making a racist joke.

'We must have you all round for Pimms and a play date. Just as soon as it gets a little warmer.'

'We must, but I'm going back to work soon. It's going to be so hard to fit everything in.' It was the first lie that came to mind.

'Oh, what were you? Were you in PR?'

'I was a journalist. Fashion and celebrity.'

'Really, a journalist, fashion *and* celebrity.' Did her gaze flit disdainfully to Stella's stained and smeared casual sportswear? 'How wonderfully *now*. Were you vlogging? What is a vlogger? How exciting. Anyway, you *must* come over. We've got a new nanny and she makes the most divine sugar-free fairy cakes. Felix and Quentin and Sebastian and Honor just can't get enough. We could see if she has a recipe for chocolate cake for little Ror-Ror. We've redone the whole garden with a gazebo and a water—'

'Yes. Yes. We must—' Stella waved as she left, ducking down to improvise a finish to Olivia's invitation in a whisper to Rory: '... water buffalos and long-tailed egrets, a flock of flamingos, and a gigantic sign saying, *Motherhood is not a competitive sport*. You're right, Olivia's a bitch. We *never* have to see her again.'

Heaped around the chocolatey boy were layers of food products: wholemeal, wholegrain, certified organic through to seeds and pulses, then layers of confectionery and snack food, and at the very bottom, out of anyone's reach and now compressed and distorted by the weight of junk, a medley of fruit and veg, mostly bruised by Rory and soon to be inedible. She really had to do something about her diet. She reached down for a jar of Nutella and felt something weaken in her back. A disc. God no, not a disc, not now. With a groan, tentatively, she pulled herself upright, and couldn't help recalling the effortless fluidity of Coco's bottom-shelf manoeuvre: Tuladandasana-Nutella, balancing stick with Nutella. Now there was a smart and specific goal she could set for herself. One day she would retrieve a jar of Nutella from a bottom shelf without the threat of total spinal failure. More yoga, she promised herself. Or maybe Pilates. She would do some research she decided; no point in making rash decisions.

Perhaps she should be buying more seeds and legumes? (She must look up 'legumes'; they sounded so Whole Foods.) She searched the shelves for more seed-like products and immediately felt better. If she just bought a selection of 'good' foods – natural foods, lentils, wild rice, pine nuts, sunflower seeds – she could figure out what to do with them later. They would look good in her cupboard, and just the thought of buying them made her feel thinner. As far as she knew, there wasn't a diet plan in the world that didn't advocate seeds – perhaps she could roast her own in the oven and then put them in an old jam jar to snack on? This was definitely a possibility. She was sure she'd seen Victoria Beckham wandering around with some seeds and it seemed to work for her, even after four designer kids and two successful careers.

Rushing through the aisles, she kept an eye out for Coco, and another for Olivia. What a shame, she thought, that nowadays her friends were more like Olivia, not interesting like Coco? Coco might frankly be a bit weird, but Olivia… Olivia was everything she didn't want to be, but was terrified she was becoming, but she also envied her. Thank god she still had friends like Ana and Dixie to keep her sane; sharing the chaos of their lives helped her convince herself that she wasn't losing her mind, or wasn't losing it alone at any rate.

She didn't see Coco again, but Olivia, her back to Stella, fortunately, was paying for some bottled water at the six items or less counter when she saw to her delight that Rory had at some point managed to wipe four of his chocolate-covered fingers down the back of Olivia's tennis skirt. The chocolatey stripes looked like shit in the bright lights of the supermarket. As if she'd run out of paper and used her hand before wiping it clean on her blue-white tennis kit. Her moment of joy was interrupted by the cashier.

'Sorry, love, can you try it again?'

'What?'

'It's not working.'

'Oh, it must, surely.' She felt the heat rising to her face and sweat begin to press through the pores across her top lip. She remembered with shame the unreturned voicemails from Barclaycard.

'Wait, sorry. I've another,' she tried to laugh. 'Too many holidays, isn't that the way?'

She found her personal bank card, and prayed to all the gods of organised family finance that she'd left some money in there.

'That's fine.'

The beads of sweat began to dry and Stella found consolation and distraction in the memory of Olivia's stained whites.

'Good lad, Rory. You'll go far.'

Stella was still giggling at Rory when she emerged from the supermarket into a downpour. The oppressive darkness of the low clouds, the ubiquity of water all around them, filled her with blood-chilling dread and she promised herself that she'd return the calls to Barclaycard. For once, she knew that this cash-flow issue was probably not her failure. The Barclaycard was paid from Jake's account. A wave of anxiety connecting the Barclaycard issue to Jake's recent moodiness stopped her in her tracks but she shook it off and began to load the SUV while Rory grinned and proudly showed her his two newly minted chocolatey panda eyes.

'Joker,' she laughed as he screamed on being separated from his trolley.

CHAPTER TWO

Ana

'So, are you ready, Rex?' called Ana, her long, dark hair dripping down her caramel back as she stepped out of the shower into their tiny mirrored bathroom. 'Are we really going to do this? I really want it to be the right thing, for both of us, I don't want you to feel... trapped.'

She scrunched her hair dry, wrapped herself in the towel, and padded into the wood-panelled Seventies galley kitchen where Rex was drinking a coffee.

'Not that I have any idea where we'll put it,' said Ana, looking around their postage-stamp-sized studio flat. 'I must water that plant.' In the window of the kitchen, a spider plant, overflowing with hanging clones, was miraculously dehydrating. Weren't they like cockroaches? Able to endure a nuclear winter, but not a Battersea spring. Part of Ana's training for adulthood, and eventual parenthood, was built around a progression: the goal being to firstly keep a plant alive for longer than six months, then graduate to a pet and if both are still thriving 12 months later, a child. The spider plant was still alive. Her cat, Boris, a half-feral tabby, had moved out a few months before. Rex insisted he must have been run over, but Ana knew he was still alive: on more than one occasion she'd seen him hiding behind the bins. He'd pretended not to know her.

'I told you before, Ana, if it's what you want... what you need, then let's do it. I will be there every step of the way.'

'Really?' she smiled shyly. 'Even though it's meant to be as stressful as divorce or losing a parent?'

'I just don't want to be like those people who become so obsessed with having a baby they can't think about or do anything else. That terrifies me. If it's meant to be, it will be. If not, we can buy a boat, sail the world, live the dream.'

'You don't like boats, Rex. You don't even like the water.'

'Actually I don't like fresh water, hurts my contacts,' he laughed, his blue eyes sparkling. 'I just love you. And if it's you and me forever, then I will still be a very happy man.' He threw his half-drunk coffee into the sink and headed for the door, attempting to pass her.

'Aren't you forgetting something?' she asked, dropping the towel to the floor. A breeze rippled over her, goosebumps all over her nakedness; her nipples stood out. She worried her nipples were too long, but no one had complained, yet.

'Oh god, are you ovulating now!?' He enveloped her breast in his hand. 'The perfect handful.' He pinched her nipple between the knuckle of index and middle finger.

She felt down between his legs and took him in her hand. 'More than a handful mustn't be wasted.' She laughed as he outgrew her hand. 'Isn't this just the best way to start the day? You telling me you'd rather be at work?'

Ana was worried they weren't having enough sex. She always worried she wasn't having enough sex, and now that their sex had a purpose, was part of her life plan, part of the having-to-do because if she didn't do it now, she might never be able to do it, she was terrified it might become a chore. A good man was hard to find and Rex was a good man. She didn't want to have to find another. They took so long to train. She pulled him into the living room and lay back on the leather sofa, spread her legs sufficiently that he could see into her, and dangling a finger over her clitoris, she teased. 'You sure you have to go to work right now? This second...?'

'Oh god,' he sighed. 'You make me so...'

She slid down the sofa a little. One finger became two.

'You little minx...'

She watched, smiling mischievously as, without taking his clothes off, he unzipped his trousers, releasing his at-the-ready erection, and slid it into her in one smooth, wet motion. She gasped at the hardness, and felt a moment's relief that he still fancied her so much.

'Oh Christ, you are so wet... ' With his long, slow motions, not the longest or slowest she'd ever known, but long and slow enough, her head bounced against the back of their beaten-up old Chesterfield. Ana loved fucking him; he was gentle and kind, not a wild animal, but the sex was good. Not the best, but good. Yes, good enough. Better than most. Better, certainly, than most of her happily settled friends, she suspected, but not the best, no. The best was gone. Long gone. And Rex was the right decision. He was. It was not a decision lightly made. It was not a decision made without robust analysis, protracted discussions with the girls. It was not a decision made without a spreadsheet.

Rex grabbed her by the hair as his pace quickened, pressing himself harder against her. He was quickening and she touched herself so they would come together. Perhaps this time she'd barely need it. Perhaps, she thought, the decision to use sex for procreation could improve the sex itself. Now that would be an interesting finding. There was no column on her spreadsheet for that life hack.

'Yes,' he groaned, 'now, come, baby, please,' and they both let out a cry of pleasure as he came, his body jerking on top of her. He rolled off her, panting, his dark hair damp, and his shirt crumpled. She looked at him, thinking to herself that for a 45-year-old guy, he really wasn't in bad shape – and the just-been-fucked look seemed to suit him. He was pretty scruffy anyway, with his unshaven face and unkempt hair, so this just seemed to complement his look. So far he'd avoided the middle-aged paunch and she hadn't found any grey hairs, yet.

'Now, anything else I need to do before I go to work,' he said roguishly, smiling at her. 'Just because I'm the boss, doesn't mean I can be hours late every day!' He jumped up, rearranged himself, leaned over to give her a kiss, and whispered in her ear, 'Now sleepy angel, don't you need to get that pert little ass to work as well?'

'Actually I have an appointment with the gynaecologist this morning.'

'Another?'

'I just want to check everything's in order. Nothing specific. Just a check-up. I'm nearly 40. I need to know the plumbing all works.'

'There's nothing I need to know?'

'Nothing. Nothing at all.'

'I'm sure everything is fine. How could it not be?' He leaned down and kissed the dark triangle of hair. 'A little extra kiss to send you on your way, and to make sure I don't forget to think about you all day...'

'You're gross, go on, away with you,' she shouted after him.

She lay there in the middle of their flat, still naked, as the first warm sun of spring moved across her. Rex was amazing, she knew that; she was lucky. He wasn't a rock star, or even a country star, no, but she knew he would be a great dad and he would always be there for her – he was kind, caring and steady. Twenty years ago those words would have filled her with dread, but she'd grown up. Now he was what she needed. The time for – what was it Dixie called them – the time for 'wild-cards' was over. Her life had been simply mapped onto the decades. Teen: discover sex, excel. Twenties: 'wild-card' sex, transcend. Thirties, baby daddy sex, effortless. Forties: parental/missionary sex, functional and recreational. Ana was never going to get married. That was a decision she'd made long ago. If you never got married, you could never regret getting married. OK, so her life with Rex wasn't the most exciting, but they had fun, they laughed, and as far as the happily-ever-after went, this wasn't the worst outcome. The spreadsheet didn't lie. And as long as they kept having sex, everything would be OK. Sex made everything OK.

CHAPTER THREE

Dixie

Dixie's Tinder life needed a spring-clean. She'd recently reset her age – again. She knew there was a limit to the number of times social media platforms permitted age changes, but she was going to be in Manhattan for a few days so, why not get some new selfies in the BA lounge then she could retouch them, add a bit here, lose a bit there... She could reinvent herself for a few days of fantasy fucking between the meetings and parties. Pouting into her phone as she primped her curly red hair, she congratulated herself on the Rimmel Radioactive Red lip gloss, and the mahogany tint she'd washed through her hair before last night's party. The floor-to-ceiling windows gave a magical light. She was, she thought, zooming in on an image, looking astounding, especially given the carnage of the night before. What was that guy's name? Something to do with cars? Lancia? Lance! 0–60 in 4.6 but he'll never get you to your destination. Dixie's ex-husband, Carlton, had driven a Lancia. Enough said. Aunt Pearl had told her the marriage would never work, but being Dixie she didn't listen. Being orphaned at a young age and brought up by your great aunt had its advantages, but Pearl had never managed to keep Dixie on the straight and narrow.

'Would you like me to take a picture for you?' came a low husky voice from behind her, shaking her out of her reverie.

'Sorry,' she said, 'are you talking to me?'

'Yes,' said the warm voice, resonating like a cello. Dixie turned and was taken aback to see a tall, slim, dark-haired man with lively blue eyes and half a smile. 'I wondered if you would like me to take a photo of you so you can maybe get a better angle. Did you want the Dreamliner in the background?'

Fuck, he's hot, thought Dixie. A wedding ring, yes, but still, he was hot. But that could be good, couldn't it? No crying when she didn't want to see him again.

'Dreamliner? So that's what they call it. Good plane knowledge,' she smirked, wondering if he was some kind of weird plane nerd. 'Yes, a photo would be great, thank you.'

To her surprise he knew exactly what he was doing – held the phone high to get the right angle (makes you look thinner) and took about five pictures in quick succession so she could choose the best one. He must have a demanding wife, she thought.

'Quite the expert,' said Dixie, holding her hand out and flashing her green eyes. 'I am Dixie, and you are?'

'Freddie, nice to meet you. And where might you be headed? Off to meet your boyfriend?'

She hadn't clocked him checking her ring finger. Player, she decided. Why not? she thought.

'Oh, New York, just a few meetings. Nothing special. And you?'

She allowed her gaze to linger on his wedding band, seeing how he'd react.

'Looks like I am heading east with you – we have offices in London so I regularly fly out. I love London, but I chose New York. London's all water, and Manhattan, electricity.'

'I totally know what you mean, there is something so energising about the place. Not to mention the awesome shopping!' she said, but then checked herself, worried she was sounding far too enthusiastic. Let him do the work, she thought. 'Anyway, it's been nice to meet you, Freddie, and I hope you have a successful trip... and thank you for the photo – maybe see you on the other side.' With that, she strode away, knowing damn well his eyes were following her decisive exit. Always quit while you are ahead, that was her motto. Leave them wanting more. Besides, her nose was running and tender, and elsewhere there was something leaking. She needed a restroom.

As the staff at the gate scanned her boarding pass, she heard the little beep and saw the red light that she longed for and, abracadabra, she was upgraded to business. So far, so good, she thought to herself – a hot man and an upgrade. Not bad for a glorified PA. She had worked for Peter Pomerov for nearly fifteen years. He had a Russian name, but a background as English as most Tory prime ministers: Eton, Oxford, The Bar. He trusted her like a wife – actually more. She did everything for him, arranging his travel, flying around the world managing his properties, and in return he had a way of orchestrating things like upgrades. They adored each other, and the truth was she would have done anything for him. He ran a family office, the complete history of which she remained unaware. He had his finger in multiple pies (but never hers!), and she was aware of how lucky she was to have landed such a great job with such a kind, tolerant and honest man. It was supposed to be a stopgap when she'd needed work while the divorce came through. She'd always dreamed of being an illustrator – she'd even started a children's book fifteen years before – of using her brain and her artistic skills, but she couldn't see an achievable career path, and with her messy divorce dragging on, she'd needed something simple and well paid. She'd been offered internships, but the money was virtually non-existent, and pretty soon the draw of mingling with men with money and power was something she took for granted, and she was unable to walk away. She needed money and men like she needed food and water. She was just increasingly happier with *more* money and *many* men. Like her ideal career path, the path to settled domesticity and monogamy was a road she couldn't imagine travelling.

Having settled into her seat, unfortunately one of the central, side-by-side seats, she nearly choked on her champagne when someone collapsed into the aisle seat beside her and she turned and found herself looking into Freddie's big blues. Next to her, but facing her, with a screen she could put up as soon as they were in the air; or, she thought, she could spend the next hours drinking and seeing how hard he'd try to seduce her, while she decided whether she wanted to fuck him. The latter was definitely more interesting, but she'd made herself a promise she would use the flight to work on illustrations for the long-unfinished book, and there were those selfies to photoshop. But they could wait… there was always tomorrow, and besides, she might not need Tinder, at least for a while.

She watched him unpack his pyjamas and organise his personal space.

When finished he sat back and smiled at her. 'Well, well, this has just made the flight a little bit more interesting. Cheers,' he said, holding aloft his champagne.

'I guess it has. Cheers,' she toasted back, then, theatrically, tied her flaming red hair messily on top of her head, intentionally letting a few bits escape around her face. She smiled, watching him watch her.

It always occurred to Dixie how awkward these seats were, that you found yourself basically in bed, for six hours, with a person you had never met before. She'd had shorter relationships. Turn the wrong way and your arse would touch their leg, or you could fall asleep and snore with your mouth wide open. It was all so invasive of personal space. A sweating, overweight businessman was settling in right next to her in the other central seat. Thank god for the serendipitous delivery of an ageing Rob Lowe.

'Can I offer you some champagne?' the stewardess asked Freddie.

'Yes please,' he replied, 'and I think my friend will need a refill before long. Keep it coming.'

Champagne in hand, Dixie decided things were looking up. This guy had all the moves, she thought, and I've got a few myself, checking the location of the nearest toilet.

'So what is it you do then Freddie, or shall I guess...? I think you look like you wish you were in a creative industry, but that somehow passed you by, and you ended up enjoying the financial rewards of a more stable career... and now you are a lawyer, yes, an M&A lawyer... Making the world a better place, one merger at a time... how right am I?'

Freddie was laughing, his eyes glistening. 'Well, well,' he said, 'quite the Mystic Meg, but no, I am sorry to tell you, I am a scientist, of sorts: gene therapy. We research degenerative conditions. I love what I do... although I appreciate it sounds very boring to someone like you.'

'You are so wrong,' spluttered Dixie. 'I'm just a humble PA. It is so refreshing to meet someone with a brain, someone who loves what they do. Believe me, I have met enough lawyers to last me a lifetime, so someone who is actually helping people is inspiring. Unless, of course, the whole thing is just made up to try and impress me...'

'Well, for now, that is for me to know, and you to find out,' he said.

Dixie was starting to like this Freddie's game. Maybe pulling on an aeroplane was a better way than Tinder to find her next hook-up.

When Dixie woke with a start, she was shocked to find them landing in JFK. She was sitting upright. She'd never even made the bed! She prayed to all the gods of personal hygiene that she hadn't dribbled. Her hair was still piled on top of her head, just. Had she been snoring? Her sinuses were stinging and congested. Her tongue dry and hard like a cat's. She'd had too much champagne.

Freddie was sitting there staring at her, grinning.

Must get my crap together, she thought.

She remembered laughing a lot. And the purser asking them

to keep it down. Then it all became a bit of a blur and she hoped she'd just dozed off.

'Morning, sleepyhead,' he said, a little too affectionately.

'Must have... d-dozed off,' she stammered. 'Sorry about that. Anyway, always good to power nap and, you know, err, hit the ground running!'

'Let's blame the bubbles... Mind you, I will share a bottle with you anytime if you make more promises like last night... Though passing out mid-sentence – my sentence at that – is a new one.'

She felt herself turn crimson. Her embarrassment made worse by the fear she looked like a red-haired beetroot daubed in Radioactive Red lip gloss and smeared in smudge-proof Maybelline mascara. She pulled down her hair and shook it out to hide her face, before quickly tidying around her eyes and lips while she wondered what the hell had gone on.

'Freddie, I assume you are teasing me. I am far too well behaved to make reckless promises while under the influence,' she said, anxiously scrabbling in her bag for a Polo to lubricate her tongue and mask her booze breath.

'Oh, I don't know about that,' he said. 'I was rather looking forward to tonight. It all sounds quite racy. I assume you are a woman of your word?'

'Absolutely,' she laughed, thinking that this was definitely getting out of hand. What was she capable of promising while drunk to the point of blackout on a transatlantic flight? The only consolation was that she'd been trading promises, not favours. She glanced anxiously at the toilets. It wouldn't have been the first time she'd found herself in there.

God, why did she always do this? What was wrong with her! Still, the girls would love the story. So Dixie! they'd hoot. A handsome, married man, a bottle of champagne and six hours in a bed. What did they expect!

By now the jetty was attached and they were preparing to deplane.

'It's been lovely to meet you, Freddie.'

'You too, Dixie Dressler.'

God, she'd told him her real name! What else had they discussed?

'I'll see you later then?'

'I wouldn't miss it for the world,' she smiled, styling it out, knowing she was on the point of escape. 'Don't be late!'

'Seven at your hotel bar should be fine. I'll text you if it changes,' he said, waggling his phone.

'Great. Listen, I *must* run.'

'You don't want to share my car service?'

'No need.'

They kissed. His hand on her lower back, pulling her against him.

'Laters, lover boy!'

As she strode into the terminal, she chastised herself. What was the point of having all these adventures if she couldn't remember the detail? There was a flash of regret that she hadn't had time to refresh her Tinder profile. Having botched face-to-face flirtation, she was going to have to rely on her well-used Tinder profile to keep her trip interesting.

CHAPTER FOUR

Stella

Rory was sitting upright in the Victorian bath, naked. She'd removed his clothes, showered and dried him and left him sitting there. It was literally the only safe space in the house. He could neither escape nor cause havoc. But he was not happy and he scowled as he watched her wet-wipe her face, arms and most of the brown graffiti from the front of her Pineapple sweatshirt. (Olivia was not the only victim of his chocolatey two-year-old wandering hands.) She tried to make her hair behave, primped, flatten, teased, but the humidity and infrequency of conditioning limited her ability to control it.

Her phone rang – *Number Withheld* – but she knew who it was.

'God damn you people, can't you leave a message?'

Leaning closer to the mirror, she plucked a single black hair that persistently re-appeared on her cheek. It was thicker than any hair she'd ever seen and reappeared overnight every two weeks. She was certain that each time it surfaced, it was a little stiffer, a little broader. Like her. It used to be funny, but Jake didn't laugh much any more. Neither of them did. A ping from her phone told her there was another voicemail. How could this Barclaycard problem be connected to Jake's extended absences, sullenness and quick temper? Or his unwillingness to discuss a vacation and his insistence that she didn't need a nanny anymore? He was a partner in a law firm, not a very big one, but a partner, and their mortgage was big, but not unmanageable. She wanted a nanny. A nanny like Coco, who could mesmerise her volatile little terror, who had hair that shone like a gemstone, and skin that smelled of the tropics. A nanny who could fold herself in half without slipping a disc. She deserved it, didn't she?

'Do I?' she asked the mirror. 'Am I worth it?'

She doubted herself.

The phone rang again.

'What?' she spat. It was Jake.

'Love you too, babe.'

'Sorry. I'm having an existential crisis. Listen, Barclaycard keep calling. Do you know—'

'Barclaycard. Oh that. Yes, of course. Don't worry, I'll sort it out.'

'Good, but I can—'

'Don't... I'll call them, OK? But, yes, the reason I called. New client. Late night. Etc etc. I'm sorry, babe. Not my call. Got it?'

'You utter shit. Again? Didn't we agree to have Jenny and Tim around for a drink? Actually, not we, didn't you? When you spent the whole of Sunday afternoon cleaning the useless motorbike you never ride?'

'I know. I'm sorry. There's how I wish things were and how

28

they are, and I have to be here. I'll make it up to you. We can watch *The X Factor* together on Friday night. The whole show. Without interruption, mockery or general disparagement.'

'Not possible. You hate *The X Factor*.'

'I promise. Not a bad word. Concentrated silence and focused attention.'

'You'll control the kids?'

'I'll even control the kids.'

'OK. But I might cancel Jenny and Tim. They're our neighbours not our friends. I've enough friends.' Stuck into the side of the mirror she had a framed photo of Dixie and Ana posing ridiculously as if applying make-up. Now that had been a fun night. 'I don't want any more, especially hangers-on. All that Jenny wants to do is social climb. She's convinced I'm some kind of conduit to celebrities. I was a fashion journalist, not a society hostess. I was—'

'I know. I'm sorry. I'll be home late. And I'll call Barclaycard. I'll deal with it.' And he was gone.

A spiralling conviction grew within her that something wasn't right. Jake hated *The X Factor*. He hated all reality TV. He called it a virus. Whatever she tried to watch, he wrecked with smart-arse comments and satirical impersonations. It was impossible to enjoy TV with him around. She regretted being bought off with the offer to share something Jake could only destroy. Marriage was a mystery, she thought. You fall in love with someone for all their differences and then you come to despise those same idiosyncrasies. It was a freaking paradox.

She was worried. The Barclaycard was the housekeeping

card, with which they collected points towards a holiday whose date still remained unfixed. The balance was paid off in full from the joint account. It must be a mistake, she thought. Jake's salary went into the joint account. The mortgage payments came out of the joint account. There was plenty of money in the joint account. Of course there was. Jake would deal with it. She deleted the voicemail without listening to it.

Rory was staring at her from the bottom of the empty bath, soundless, and wearing a worried frown.

'Oh baby, don't stress. The world is full of automated fools. Daddy will sort it out.'

There was a pop like something had burst and then Rory's mouth opened and she saw the trail of chocolate poo streaming between his chubby legs. He let out of howl of protest.

Half an hour later, she'd been forced to replace the irredeemably soiled Pineapple Studios sweatshirt with a totally inappropriate, but fortunately, clean blouse from Stella McCartney. It was a few years old and the pussy bow gave it a retro *Charlie's Angels* look. It had once been her go-to work/drinks blouse. It had witnessed many forgotten but unforgettable Friday nights in Soho House. Back then she'd been flexing the magazine's Gold Amex card and thought she ruled the world. The short-sighted arrogance of youth. She sighed. She missed the Nineties. She missed Friday nights.

She was determined not to be late to pick up Tom from school. The headmistress was losing her patience. That hideously judgemental look, the long nose, the glasses on a chain.

The truth was that since Jake had insisted she cut back on the nanny, Betty, a Belgian student built like a rugby player, whose mere physical presence induced in both Rory and Tom a kind of hypnotised lethargy that made them completely biddable, Stella had been struggling. It was not that she couldn't get through the thousand and one tediously repetitive tasks, it was that they bored her into a kind of imbecilic incompetence. Every single mind-destroying chore served only to remind Stella of the woman she used to be: feared and respected for her concise insight and forensic ability to deconstruct fashion and outline trends, she was now wearing fashion from ten years ago (high fashion, but still) while serving as a scullery-maid-cum-Uber-driver to two ungrateful savages and an absent husband.

Applying a fresh coat of gloss to her chapped lips and reassessing her decaying epidermis – just in case she was forced to confront Olivia or one of her army of clones, or, heaven forbid, one of those hot single dads who sometimes appeared awkwardly trying to pick out their progeny from the streaming mass of uniformed delinquents who attended the local pre-school – she was reminded of her rash statement to Olivia that she was considering a return to work. It had of course been on her mind for months. She tried to ignore it because Rory was still young enough that his mother should be around. It would be too easy for the sneering Olivia and her frenemies to blame his behavioural difficulties on an awol mother, but he was two now and there was a vague and uncomfortable thought at the back of her mind that they might be better off with Bulky Betty or the mesmerising Coco even. They'd be clean. They'd be on time to arrive at and leave school.

She was a good mother. She knew that because she loved her children, but maybe someone else could be a better waitress and Uber driver. These were not her skills. She was a professional, a journalist, an acerbic and admired judge and commentator in a fast-moving industry. When she thought of Coco, she couldn't help recall that smell, my god, it was angelic, and those arms. Perhaps, she thought, Coco might be at the school gates – one of the Van Nesses' smug little prigs was in Tom's class. Perhaps she could ask if she'd be able to help out? Rory was obviously smitten, which could only ease the transition. Everyone's lives would be improved, she thought, as she bundled Rory into his pyjamas for the school run, if she got back to what she was good at, and left parenting to those with the skill set. Jake could hardly object if that was how she chose to spend her money. She pinioned Rory into his car seat, and emerged to a spring afternoon lit up by the sun and felt happier than she had for weeks.

CHAPTER FIVE

Ana

When the morning sun broke through the curtains at her bedroom window, Ana pulled herself together, gave her fanny a quick rinse, ran a hairdryer through her long brown hair, and pulled on her skinny jeans. It was Tuesday – a blue day – so with her beloved baby blue sweatshirt and her electric blue Stan Smith trainers, she felt armoured for the day ahead. Tuesdays were tricky – she was never sure how well blue went with her South American skin tone. She grabbed her bashed-up old canvas bag (blue, obvs) and dashed out of the door, being careful not to scrape against the gorgeous new orange and yellow retro wallpaper she had just put in the hallway. The flat may be tiny, but it was theirs, and she was thrilled with all the little improvements they were making. They were building something. Her favourite bit was their little terrace that overlooked the park opposite – it gave her the illusion of space, and she loved to sit there alone and people-watch for hours.

Ana bundled herself onto the overcrowded bus, nipped past some people arguing over a payment issue and stole the last seat on the top deck. London was still magical to her. Every morning for fifteen years she'd done this commute, watching the hustle and bustle below, drinking in the energy of it all whilst sipping the coffee she picked up from the local barista who always greeted her with a smile and her order, the same every day: Skinny Mocha Latte, half the milk, add a sweetener. The routine was comforting and even though she had worked in the West End forever, it still gave her a happy buzz. Even amongst the swirling chaos she could keep a stable centre. The bus jerked to a stop, jolting her out of her reverie and, barging through everyone, apologising as she went, she leaped off. She grinned to herself thinking she wouldn't be able to do that when she was pregnant!

Ana entered the stark, minimalist surgery and looked around at all the women waiting patiently for their turn, hoping their dreams would come true, and she felt her heart sink. It was such a strange place, very modern with no personality and just a few copies of *Country Life* magazine lying around to distract them from the horror of the news they might receive. She twirled her turquoise pendant for reassurance. No one made eye contact, any conversation was hushed and the air was heavy with expectation. Everyone was here because they wanted a baby. It felt quite similar to going to an STD clinic where people either buried their faces in their phones or wore sunglasses trying not to be spotted. It smelled the same: stale air and disinfectant. Every woman had her own story. Ana had certainly had her fair share, though as a (mostly) serial monogamist, she'd had less call for their services than Dixie, who probably had a weekly appointment somewhere exclusive.

She looked around and felt sorry for them. She was different.

She wasn't desperate for a baby like these women were, she was just trying it as a punt. It wasn't a make or break scenario for her, it was more like an experiment. She didn't want to miss out, if she could help it. Everyone (mostly Stella, to be fair) told Ana how hard it was having a baby anyway, how exhausting it was, the sleepless nights, the loss of identity. Maybe they were right, thought Ana. Then on the flip side, maybe not having a baby was even harder. When you are one of the people without a child, you are judged, unintentionally left out, and scrutinised. As your friends move on with their lives and their children, you are left trying to forge a new life for yourself, not one ruled by mealtimes and kids' clubs, but one simply ruled by shaping your own future. Of course the freedom of this is so liberating, but it doesn't necessarily make it easy. But then no one is ever really content. Stella, with two children and a husband with a large income, was obviously miserable. So what does actually make people happy? she wondered, and then she felt herself start to panic with fear that she might never find the happy ever after. A cold sweat started to form on her brow as her pulse quickened.

Then she heard her name being called. She stood up, swallowed hard and strode into the doctor's office. There was no turning back. She was dreading the questions.

An hour or so later Ana finally arrived at the office. She looked up with a smile at the big old Georgian building that had become like a second home to her. The auction house had been there for over a hundred years. The beautiful dark walls, high ceilings and intricate woodwork – the whole place was steeped in history and Ana couldn't imagine ever leaving it. She found it utterly captivating, and she never tired of the art that surrounded her day after day. As Exhibition Manager, she was responsible for the optimal arrangement and co-ordination of all the London exhibits. It was basically interior design using works of art. Talk about a dream job.

As she walked into the foyer, she saw Jan at her old oak desk, gave her a smile, a coffee and a doughnut. She had decided to try to avoid telling anyone at work what she was up to. It would just be an added pressure that she didn't need right now. She knew how tricky she could be and how annoyed she would get with people's sympathetic stares and questions; she was a very private person, and she really didn't like people knowing her business. The only person she did confide in was Jan, who missed nothing and was a fount of insights. They would sit and gossip about the hot art dealers, their sexy young secretaries, and who might be the highest bidder at each auction. What no one knew was that Jan's knowledge of art after being at the auction house for over twenty-five years probably far exceeded some of the experts'. She knew every work of art that came in and out of the doors, and she could spot a fake a mile off.

'Hello, beautiful Ana,' said Jan without looking up, her bi-focals perched gently on her nose. 'Got some good gossip for me?'

'How did you know it was me?' replied Ana, smiling.

'Oh, I would recognise the squeak of those trainers a mile off. What's up with you, honey?' she asked as she looked up and gave her fond smile.

'That's what I love about you, Jan, you are practically a spy in your own right!'

'So what brings you in so late today? Anything interesting?'

'I wish!' said Ana. 'Although if I sit here long enough I am sure someone interesting will come through those revolving doors. You have the best seat in the house.'

'That's why I won't let them promote me – I know more secrets about this place than anyone. They'll have to prise me out one day... What's up? I can see it in your face. Come on, I'm all ears. You're not the kind of girl to buy me a doughnut and my favourite coffee without a damn good reason.'

'I'm trying to have a baby,' blurted Ana, mortified by the admission, and recalling that Jan was childless and that she'd never asked why.

'Oh, Ana, that's wonderful news,' said Jan, her eyes slightly welling up. 'What a relief! I thought those ovaries would dry up and you would miss your chance!'

'Um, thanks, Jan. I think. Anyway, long story short, it's not working. I thought we would have lots of great sex, I would just get pregnant, it would all work naturally, and I would be pushing a Bugaboo about within months. Now that's not happening, I am starting to question everything. The gynaecologist was... confusing. I don't know if this is how things are supposed to go. Is it me? Is Rex the right man? Do we deserve a baby?'

'Do you love Rex, honey?' asked Jan, staring at her over the top of her glasses.

'Yes, of course, I mean—' said Ana, slightly blushing. 'Yes, I love him. Well, I think I love him anyway, in a isn't-he-nice, aren't-I-lucky kind of way. Which is fine, right? I mean how do you know if you ever *really* love someone? I would need Brad Pitt to walk in and offer to marry me to know if I really loved him!'

'Oh honey, when you know, you know. *You* know, right? Listen, life is full of decisions and surprises. You want a baby, and let's face it you're no spring chicken, so maybe you just need to carry on with Rex. See what happens. Nature has a deciding vote. Try and have a baby, tick that off the list, and then see how you feel afterwards. Or if that sounds too dull, walk out of here and book yourself a ticket to Hollywood, knock on Brad's door and see what happens. Let me know if you do the second option as I have always fancied a bit of *Thelma and Louise* so I might just come with you!'

They both collapsed into giggles, and then Ana said, 'If only it were that simple, Jan!'

'It is,' said Jan. 'Believe me, life's only as complicated as you make it. I learned that a long time ago.'

There was a hint of sadness to Jan's voice. Maybe Jan was right, maybe she was just overthinking everything. It was hardly like her life was bad, it was just changing. It dawned on her that she really didn't like change all that much, and that was a fundamental problem.

'Thanks, Jan – I had better get upstairs. I'll get in trouble if I'm spotted here loitering with you again. They'll think I don't like my real job!'

'Keep me updated, Ana, I worry about you and I like to know what's going on.'

As Ana made her way down the long corridor to the elevator, she paused to stare at Rembrandt's *Danae* that was waiting to go up for auction. She thought briefly that if she was a superstar's wife, she might be able to start her own collection of incredible art. Imagining that, she felt much better about her life.

CHAPTER SIX

Dixie

Dixie's day passed quickly enough as she completed a tour of Peter's New York properties and made sure the building managers were happy. Peter left her an envelope of cash to deal with any incidentals or issues and she enjoyed distributing his largesse. Her mind kept returning to Freddie and with every recurrence she felt a lurch of anxiety or excitement; whichever, it disturbed her. She was relieved that he hadn't given her his number because she might have texted him and that was not her style. She was obliged to attend a cocktail party on Peter's behalf, somewhere up near Trump Tower. She checked her phone. It would be nice to go with someone interesting. Oligarchs often have quite insistent friends. Grabbing a quick snack at the counter in Sushi Samba, and admiring the easy elegance of the Latino hostess, her phone pinged. **'I'll be at your hotel at 7 p.m. Try not to be too fashionably late. Fx'** Fuck, she had given him her number, but the butterflies told her that she was delighted she had, but what else had she told him?

She waited in her room until well after 7 p.m., sitting on her bed in her favourite black jeans and a low-cut emerald green top with slashed back, which revealed just enough to make people stare, but not enough to look like a street walker. She topped her outfit off with a pair of killer leopard print heels. Checking her hair again in the mirror, she knew that she looked hot. She *was* hot, she told herself, if red was your thing, that is. Before leaving she made sure everything looked acceptable if anyone was to come back with her, and strutted down to the bar. As she walked in and saw Freddie standing at the crowded bar, staring at her, she felt like Julia Roberts in *Pretty Woman*, and wondered if she'd made too much effort. He was as handsome as she remembered him from her hazy aeroplane fog, and with his faded jeans and crisp white shirt, he looked the full package. His blue eyes danced kindly in the soft light, and his brown hair fell haphazardly around his face, helping to frame his razor-sharp jawline.

The bar was buzzing, and Freddie was on his first martini.

'Good evening,' he smiled as she approached. 'I wondered if I would be drinking alone tonight, whether you were too good to be true. But here you are, a vision in green, and what's more, awake, and fashionable, and late. There will be consequences.'

'Good things are worth waiting for, aren't they? Glad to see you made it yourself.'

'What are you drinking? More champagne or something harder now it's past seven?'

'Vodka tonic for me please,' she replied, as she perched on a bar stool. She loved America, loved the vibe of it, the friendliness, and was always excited to be back. It had such a different atmosphere to London, which she often found a little oppressive and unfriendly. London's bars couldn't compete with Manhattan's. She often thought if she could find a way to move to the States and make her life work there, she would.

'So here we are,' said Freddie smiling. 'Just you and me, and to think we only met about twenty-four hours ago on another continent. I think it's time to get to know you. Let's see, if you could be or do anything in the world, what would it be?'

She looked around. 'If I could do anything, I would move to America. If I could be anything, I would be an illustrator. I would live on the East Coast and draw illustrations for children's books.'

'Children's books? Now that surprises me,' remarked Freddie. 'Everything you do seems so 18 Cert. I really can't imagine you sketching a picture of a happy toad trying to cross a road to get to a lost duckling on the other side.'

'I like to be surprised, don't you? Is the ugly duckling a story you know well?' Dixie laughed.

'No, but doesn't every kids' story have a duckling in it?'

'Not all of them, Freddie, no, but maybe I should try adding a duckling to see if it helps. Isn't the point that the duckling isn't a duckling?'

'See, I have helped you already. It's the start of something beautiful,' he said as he reached across her to grab an olive, his arm stroking her breast. His wedding ring glinted and the contact brought home to Dixie what she was doing there. She didn't want to start messing with someone's marriage. A drunken one-night-stand with a married man was one thing, but a proper date with cross-examination was another thing.

She had no idea of Freddie's intentions, but he was flirting, rather effectively. Maybe he was just a player who was looking for something exotic.

'Is your wife at home?' Dixie asked, surprising herself. Her question was followed by an uncomfortable silence and she watched as Freddie's eyes closed. She could see them searching for something behind the closed lids. Without opening them he spoke.

'I, err, lost my wife three years ago.' He paused, swallowed. 'Illness. It's been a tough time, but it's beginning to get easier.'

'Oh god, Freddie, I am so sorry, I had no idea.'

'Why should you? It's OK. It's best just to get it out in the open anyway, otherwise I tend to find it can kind of ruin a night out. Anyway, that is all incredibly depressing. I thought you were taking me to a party!'

'Oh good god, I am! I'd almost forgotten about that. I think we'll need a couple of shots first to get us in the mood. Are you ready? Are you sure you want to? Russian emigrés live unusual lives. There will be Jeroboams of Krug champagne, vodka on ice and only just more prostitutes than plastic surgeons working the room.'

'What could possibly go wrong?'

Two Bison Grass vodka shots later and they were both more relaxed about what lay ahead. Dixie was concerned she might have bigged the night up a little too much (she couldn't of course recall what she'd actually told him), but after ambushing him like that, she wanted to make sure he had a damn good night out. The poor man – she couldn't even begin to understand what he had been through and how he was coping. His loss made a mockery of her first-world concerns about where the next debauched indulgence was coming from and how she looked on Instagram or how many hits she got on Tinder. His evident pain scared her, and excited her. All that and he still managed to be kind and thoughtful, and light up a room with his smile. But she wondered what lay beneath, where all the hurt and worry was buried. No one ever left a tragedy unscathed, and as charming and engaging as he was, Dixie told herself to be careful and keep her distance. He was damaged goods.

The party was, as she suspected, underwhelming with sides of kitsch and cliché, but it was in the most incredible penthouse with insane views over Central Park. But the fact the party was half empty and full of boring old men and slutty-looking hostesses (she fitted right in!) just made the evening funnier. They both laughed and giggled all night long, standing by the caterer's door stealing the best canapés as they came by and drinking as much booze as they could handle. Their hands met occasionally, a brush, a light touch, but enough for Dixie to feel the electricity between them. The only awkward moment was when she was obliged to introduce Freddie to Evgeny Mobachov and stumbled over the introduction, describing him as her 'consort'. Where had she even found the word!? Evgeny quickly left them alone with a confused look and encouragement to make the most of all the facilities (whatever that meant!). She was sure that their evening was not quite what Peter had intended for her, but she really didn't care. She just felt elated and free.

When they finally decided to call it a night, Freddie took

her hand and offered to escort her back to SoHo. He stopped the cab a few blocks short, suggesting they walk a while. As they were strolling down Third Avenue, Dixie dreaming about what it would be like if she actually lived there, he suddenly grabbed her and pulled her into a dark side street that looked like something out of a cop show: empty bins rolling on the ground, steam drifting out of vents, and car horns blaring in the background. He slammed her up against the wall and started to kiss her with urgency and longing, searching her, wanting her, and she could feel him hard against her. She let out a moan of pleasure as he stroked her through her jeans. She wanted more but she felt so vulnerable. Nothing good ever happens in a dark alley. It was exciting and terrifying all at once knowing that anyone could be watching. With one deft move he undid her trousers and slipped his hand inside the silk, pressing into her wetness with his fingers. She was moist and ready, and as she reached for him, he pushed her hand away and immobilised her against the wall. As he kissed her, his tongue flicking and exploring hers, as the pressure of his finger grew, she could feel herself about to come. She wanted to resist but knew it was hopeless. She was out of control. He quickened his pace with the heel of his hand on her clit and his fingers deep inside her; she let out an uncontrollable groan as her body jolted against him.

'So,' Freddie said, eyes bright with excitement.

'Where did that come from? I haven't been finger-banged in the street in over twenty years!'

'Expect the unexpected, young Dixie... I just wanted to

give you something to remember me by. Just in case you were thinking about trying to forget me.'

'Forget you? Now why would I want to do that,' she whispered breathlessly as she rearranged herself, tucking her green silk shirt back into her jeans, totally thrown by the whole episode. Freddie, the scientist. Hmm, it seemed there was more to him than she'd first thought. Perhaps she had finally met her match.

He put his arm around her and lit a cigarette as they continued the three-block walk back to SoHo House. It was a cold night, but the sky was clear and even in the hustle and bustle of the city that never sleeps, there was a calmness between them, a funny familiarity like they had known each other for years, like they were old souls. As they reached the dimly lit lobby of the hotel, Freddie turned to her and kissed her on the lips and whispered in her ear a quiet, seductive 'goodnight', nothing more, and then disappeared into the back of a waiting cab before she'd had time to react. Dixie was stunned. She couldn't believe he had just left, and yet it made her smile. Usually she was the boss, she was the one who pulled the stunts, but not this time. Expect the unexpected? What the hell? It left her wanting more and made her completely intrigued with him. In twenty-four hours her life had been turned upside down by a man with a dead wife. That was certainly not in the game plan. And when was she going to see him again? What was happening to her? Dixie Dressler never worried about the next date, unless it was how to elegantly avoid it!

She couldn't rest. Her stomach was in knots and she lay on her king-size hotel bed doodling, pondering whether she really did to want to see him again, or whether she just enjoyed being surprised. She ordered herself a big bowl of fries, turned on CNN so she didn't feel so isolated, and started to draw. Sketching was her escape, her personal form of expression. She often just drew without really even knowing she was doing it. She could draw anything that didn't require her thought and commitment, but the minute it was her book, she couldn't deliver. She was terrified of the judgement, of not being good enough. Coming around, she was surprised to see that she had drawn an illustration of Freddie. She had caught that wicked glint in his eye, that slightly foppish hair, the long searching fingers, and as she stared down at the picture and into his eyes, she knew she was feeling things that she really wasn't very used to. She felt a little nauseous, like vertigo. Eventually she dozed off to sleep, wondering as she did where Freddie was now, and if he was wishing he was in her bed as much as she was.

Dixie was woken early by the traffic in the street below. Brakes screeching and horns competing through the double glazing. It was 9 a.m. The night's exertions had overcome any jet lag. She jumped in the shower, chose a killer pencil skirt and clingy cashmere jumper, and headed downstairs to grab a cab. Heading down in the lift, she noted that she'd checked neither Instagram nor Tinder. She was irritated that there was nothing from Freddie, but then the receptionist handed her a piece of paper.

'A gentleman left this for you early this morning.'

'Thank you,' Dixie stuttered, taking it nonchalantly while bursting inside.

It was a leaflet for an exhibition by an artist that she must have mentioned, and it was on only a few blocks from her hotel. On it he had written, 'I thought you might enjoy this. Sorry I can't join you, but maybe see you on the other side of the pond. Fx'

Initially she was disappointed she wasn't going to be seeing him again in NY. But this was such a kind thought. Handsome and caring?! Too good to be true. That's just the way the world works. Waiting while the doorman hailed her a cab, she posted a photo of the hotel frontage with a comment: *Always expect the unexpected*. Out of habit, or perhaps to try to distract her mixed emotions, she flicked through Tinder, swiping right on a few possibilities. None, she was irritated to note, anywhere near as hot or mysterious as Freddie. But she knew a smart girl always keeps her options open. No good ever came of getting too attached, too soon. Never.

CHAPTER SEVEN

Stella

Friday was another grey rainy day in London as Stella bundled herself and Rory up to head out to the bleak concrete playground – again. Tom was at school meaning there were no arguments and no choices. She couldn't understand what Rory saw in the playground, but she was coming to believe his first word would be 'swing' and he was destined to be a pilot or maybe a paratrooper. He was absolutely fearless when it came to heights and seemed to have no attachment needs at all. He would just wobble off without looking back and if Stella didn't pay constant attention, he would disappear over the horizon. Sometimes she wondered what would happen if she just let him go. Would he return in sixteen years, all grown up, a veteran of several wars, a member of the French Foreign Legion, thankful to Stella for her trust in his abilities, or would he be taken in by social services and Stella charged with criminal negligence? Thank god Jake was a lawyer.

Stella was having a tough morning. After a couple of days indulging fantasies of all the roles she might return to, she'd begun to make the first tentative steps towards going back to employment. Still having to hide from Jenny and Tim – she'd cancelled drinks by text, citing a vicious viral infection which had cost her her voice – she'd crept out to the newsagent while Rory was taking his 5–10-second post-lunch nap. To extend her alibi, in case of meeting either one of the couple, she'd donned one of Jake's Crombie jackets, a thick striped scarf (Jake's again), sunglasses and a faux fur aviator hat with drooping earpieces. Careful to use her own credit card to avoid further embarrassment or delay, she'd purchased all the fashion and celebrity glossies on offer: *Grazia*, *Hello*, *Yes*, *Now!*, *So* and *Glamour*. For research and to see if the editorial listings included anyone she recognised, anyone who might be a useful lead.

Seven years is a long time in politics, in a marriage, but in fashion journalism, it was an epoch. Where once every name would have been someone familiar, now it was as alien as this year's *X Factor* entries.

Three names rang a bell with Stella, and not all of them were good. One she'd fired from *Grazia* for persistent lateness (industry code for a party girl with a narcotics problem). One she'd offended when she threw her out of her Christmas party, as she'd thrown up into Stella's vintage Chanel handbag. But I mean, wouldn't you!?

There was one name that stood out. Lucy 'Left Eye' Witherington-Smiley. 'Left Eye', obviously, because she'd lost an eye in an unlikely collision during a charity polo match at Cowdray Park. She had many faults, but she was a straight talker and was now editor in chief at *Now!* and features editor for the *Mail on Sunday*. She was a formidable woman whom Stella had given a significant leg-up, her first column in *Grazia*. They'd always got on as long as Stella could keep her gaze fixed on the moving and expressive right eye. The Left Eye was a no-go area.

Stella had fantasies that Left Eye would welcome her back with gratitude, reciprocating Stella's contribution to her career, that a position would be made available or perhaps offer something freelance until another position opened up. The first inkling of a problem came as she flicked through the pages wearing her editor's hat (figuratively, as she was still in the faux fur aviator). The nature of fashion had changed. The 18–24, and even the 25–35 age ranges were almost unrecognisable. There were references to brands she'd only vaguely heard of, certainly never worn. There were links and references to bloggers and vloggers and Pinterest and Instagram accounts she'd never encountered. She dismissed these first flutterings of doubt with the idea that once you can ride a bike, you never forget; it's merely a matter of adapting to new terrain. The second wrinkle appeared when Lucy's PA twice refused to put Stella through, and insisted, twice, that she spell her surname, in spite of Stella using her most casually presumptive tone to enunciate, 'Hammer–Son. As in Hammer and Son. No, one word. Hammerson. Yes. Stella. No, Stella. Not Estella. Where am I from? It's a personal call. She'll know who I am. No, she might not have my number. Yes, yes, well, actually I'm a former colleague.'

'From the last fucking decade,' she spat, flushing hot and sweating. She threw the fur hat ineffectively across the room. She wanted to break something, something glass. The way that girl had spoken to her!

And, no, in spite of the passing of three tedious hours, Lucy had still not returned her call.

As she neared the concrete oblong, the cries, screeches, wails and weeping grew in volume. She was not ready for the shiny mothers fresh from their weekly microdermabrasion, their judging eyes. Seven years ago, before two children, two caesareans, and at least 2,500 chocolate muffins, 5,000 full-fat mochaccinos, equivalent bottles of cheap Rioja and value packs of cheesey puffs, Stella had had a trim(ish) waist, a thigh gap (almost), and fantastic breasts that defied gravity and opened doors (literally and metaphorically). Now she was wrapped up in thick duck down that camouflaged any physical outline. She'd wanted to wear jeans today, but the button wouldn't close. She blamed the tumble dryer. She was certain there was an issue with the temperature gauge, too many of her clothes were shrinking.

She looked around at the grey rectangular space, chocka with kids, nannies and bug-eyed mothers side-stepping dog crap. She sighed and prepared herself. Stella found any kids that were not her own an irritant, and she loathed the cheery chumminess demanded as they buffeted and bullied her and her child. Snotty little vermin chasing around desperate for space. She remembered swearing that she would never be this woman, stood staring into the distance day after day pushing the swing, willing the hours away. But here she was. Her career vanishing behind her and a husband who was married to the law more than he was to her.

She remembered that she must ask Jake about the bank account. She'd tried to log in to the online joint account and her password had not been recognised.

Besides, she said to herself, did she really want to be a fashion journalist any more? It was so meaningless. What did she really want from her life? Rory was scowling at her until she pushed harder and sent him higher and they laughed together. She so wanted to be able to tell people she was more than a housewife, wanted to escape the side glances and sneers of the lycra–clad women at the school gates. She missed the respect she'd had when she'd been an editor. She'd set the agenda. It might only be in the realm of fashion and celebrity but she made the news, moved trends, mocked the unfortunate and celebrated the best. That was incredibly important to her, to her self–respect, and more than that, to her place in the world, her relationship to Jake. She shook her head, she knew she was whining, hoped it would pass. She pushed Rory hard, maybe too hard, and he flew high up, giggling. He didn't notice but she scared herself with the force of her action and she pulled a frowning Rory from the seat and deposited him on the ground with a shove towards the merry-go-round.

Dark clouds were blowing in from the west. She was going to get wet later, she thought.

She was snapped out of her melancholy by the distant screams of 'Mummy!' And then she found herself running towards Rory who had fallen and was throwing himself around on the ground like he'd been shot. A striking young woman with glossy brown hair and olive skin was comforting him. It was the girl from the supermarket, Coco.

'Ah, I thought I recognised this little hero. There, there, Rory.' She leaned down and kissed his grazed knee with her full cherry lips, before facing Stella. 'All better now.'

Good god, that smile! Stella felt her stomach lurch, like she'd just dropped six feet.

'Yes, thank you, I must have lost sight of him for a moment, thank you so much,' said Stella.

'It's no problem. He'll be fine. Perhaps some chocolate, and all will be forgotten.'

'Ah, the joys of being a toddler! Your tragedies are so easily corrected. Thank you again.'

Coco didn't leave. She stood there, her Mediterranean beauty out of place in that grey concrete jungle. She giggled and began to play with Rory and her two charges. Her full red lips set off her white teeth, and her bright green eyes glowed as she laughed. Stella just watched in admiration. Coco reminded her of a wild bird, of what it would be like to be free and young. A wave of sadness swept over her as she felt a pang of loss of her own sense of fun and identity.

She turned to Stella and chirped, 'I see you look as happy to be here today as you do most days. I think this must be your idea of hell.'

'What, no, no not at all,' spluttered Stella, oddly thrown by her directness. 'It's all a bit monotonous. I just need a pick-me-up, nothing a coffee couldn't fix. You probably don't have to come here every day!'

'You are only truly blessed when you can find the face of God in a square foot of concrete. I see you here nearly every day, but you are often in a dream world so you never see me. Live in the moment, Stella. Don't let life be something you wish away. But if it's a coffee that will fix it, let me buy you one,' Coco said, resting her hand enticingly on Stella's arm and smiling mischievously, which was fortunate as it almost made up for the sanctimony.

'Oh, you are very kind, but maybe not today. I haven't even showered. I look a mess, and I'm probably not very good company. Besides, I am sure it is me who owes you a coffee! Maybe another day.'

'OK, I understand, maybe tomorrow. We could probably cheer each other up. Come on, kids! Raymondo! Fleur!' Coco yelled across the playground. 'Let's go!' They ran to her without hesitation. She knelt down and kissed Rory on the top of his head, laid her hand again on Stella's arm and sashayed away, her pert bottom flicking from side to side as she gave one child a piggyback and chased the other.

Who the hell is that girl, thought Stella. She was certain she'd never seen her there before. She was happy, hot and opinionated, and quite frankly, invasive of personal space. It was so unusual, un-London. Stella liked it. Feeling like she'd missed out on something, she scooped up her now-sulking child and dragged him down to the high street to her favourite coffee shop for a full fat latte and a muffin. Nothing mattered but to fill the void with super-fast carbs. The consequences would come later and she would deal with them then. It wasn't like Jake was going to notice the increasing rolls of flab around her stomach. They hadn't had sex in so long she barely remembered what a penis felt like. She could of course go to the gym, she thought, like all those uptight Yummies who turn up every morning in their gym gear, on their way for a coffee (she often wondered if they actually went to the gym or just strutted around in trainers and leggings to make people like her feel crap about themselves), or for a run, which people promised would be a cure for body and soul, but why should she? This muffin made her feel better, right now, and that was all that mattered. Rory didn't agree. He threw his half-eaten croissant to the floor. His mischievous laugh was infectious and they giggled together.

CHAPTER EIGHT

Dixie

It had been five days since Dixie got back from New York. Not a word from Freddie. She was preoccupied with this thought as she fought off the jet lag. The time she generally spent on Tinder was now spent wondering why she'd heard nothing. Not even the courtesy of a text. Christ, he hadn't even shown enough initiative to find and follow her on Instagram. He was either not playing by the rules or he'd lost interest. At different levels she *knew* both to be true. Perhaps she should have been more demur about the finger-banging, but what the hell, she'd enjoyed it, and so had he. She reminded herself that she was not some passive doll, that she could write her own rules. Dixie Dressler waits on no man.

She texted, **'Thanks for the finger-guided tour of the back streets of NY. I know a few alleyways in London I could show you. How about Weds at 8 p.m., Dover Street Wine Bar? Dix x'**.

And then she sat and waited.

And waited.

She bit her nails and checked her phone to make sure her text had gone, had been delivered. It had.

And then when she couldn't bear it any longer, she threw on her trainers and went for a run along the river. She ran like a banshee. She was now furious with herself for sending the text. Her neediness shamed her. He was obviously still so messed up about the death of his wife, he was never going to be available for anything more than side-street shenanigans. She should have known it would never come to anything. Good men didn't want women like her. Breathing heavily as she climbed the stairs back to her flat, she resolved to put him out of her mind. She had plenty going on. They'd both got what they wanted. A New York dalliance.

★

Peter kept a small family office off Regent Street. She smiled at the girls on reception as she strode towards the lift. She was wearing her red Alexa Chung heels and they made the most satisfying clack on the marble flooring. She was late, she was busy, and she was feeling much more herself.

One of the girls called her over. She couldn't remember her name. 'Dixie, it looks like you have an admirer!'

On the desk was the most enormous bunch of red roses she had ever seen. An envelope contained a simple card, *'So glad you decided to text. I thought maybe it was game over. Thursday, south-west corner of Red Lion Square, 7.30? Fx'*

She actually felt giddy, a torrent of emotions flooded through her. She felt herself blush. She never blushed. She chose to ignore his assumption that Thursday was just as easy for her as

Wednesday, but she admired his confidence. Maybe there was something there. Maybe Freddie was someone a bit different. Maybe they could write their own rules.

'So who is it, Dixie?' demanded the receptionist. 'Who is "F"?'

'How do you know what the card says?!' asked Dixie.

She shrugged and held up her hands in innocence.

'You're outrageous, and it is none of your business,' she laughed.

As she manoeuvred the bouquet into the lift, she found herself smiling. Unfinished business, you're right there, she thought, and pinched her legs together. Only forty-eight hours to wait, she thought, and we'll really start to find out what that devious Freddie is all about.

On Thursday night Dixie left work earlier. She was excited. As she had sat at her desk, she had doodled every possible outfit combination. Sketching her clothing options, picturing things, helped her process her ideas. She had always used her sketching as a way to process her emotions. Her mother had died when she was young, and when her distant cousin, the great Aunt Pearl, had taken her in, her aunt had taught her to use it as a coping mechanism, and she had never looked back. Too slutty, too cool, too smart, too sexy, too Madonna-ish, too Elizabeth I, too Elizabeth II, too Amy Shumer, too fashionista, she'd thought as she ran through all the options. So in the end she settled on one of her favourite mini dresses, tights and some knee-high boots. Sexy, figure-tested combination.

She didn't want to be the one waiting on the street corner, so she made sure to arrive her standard six minutes late. She saw him there as she approached, not on his phone like most people, but leaning against the wall, arms folded, watching the world go by. He was dressed casually in a pair of low-slung jeans and a checked shirt, looking as hot as she had anticipated. Several passing girls gave him a second glance as they went by. Bitches, she thought. He's mine.

He caught her eye as she approached. 'Hey, hot stuff,' he said. 'You looking for a date?'

'Did you try that on all those girls?' she asked, indicating the girls now in the distance.

'No, just the filthy redheads,' he whispered in her ear, as he kissed her lightly in greeting. 'Drink, or food and drink? I've booked both.'

'Duh, food *and* drink,' she said.

'Perfect, a girl after my own heart.'

They set off and she was startled when he took her hand and pulled her into a doorway. He pushed her up against the door and started kissing her, first slowly, then with more passion. Oh god, she thought, not here, not again! Then he just pulled away.

'Just wanted to break the ice,' he said. 'Get us back to where we left off.'

And they set off again. She was left just a little bit behind. She was very flustered. The swelling excitement in her stomach didn't stop there. She was going to have to be on her game to keep up with this guy, and that wasn't something she was used to. She was used to having the upper hand, to calling the shots, and she knew that was why this was so interesting. As she walked behind him, she found herself admiring his posture.

He was tall and in charge. He also had a very tight ass, she just wanted to—

'Everything all right, you look... hungry?'

She laughed off her embarrassment.

The restaurant was down some steep little stairs – nothing fancy, very understated and quite dark. There were candles burning on little wooden tables, and for the middle of the city it was very rustic. Like a secret you would only find if someone told you about it.

'This is my favourite place in London for a steak – please tell me you eat steak. I love a woman who likes meat.'

'I do eat meat,' said Dixie. 'I would have thought that you would have gleaned that...'

'Well, you're in the right place then.'

Without another word, he ordered a bottle of house red, two steak frites, rare, and a green salad, if it was included.

'Quite the control freak,' said Dixie.

'Not really,' he replied. 'I just wanted to get the boring bit out of the way so I could focus on you.'

'Are you as in control as you appear?' asked Dixie.

In that moment, she saw a flicker of doubt flash across his face, and he thought for a moment, then spoke slowly. 'It's impossible to control everything, but I try to control what I can, yes.'

Dixie was certain this was a reference to his wife. She reached out and took his wrist. The contact thrilled her. She could feel his pulse thumping under the light touch of her fingers. Was it something that a person ever managed to move on from? Would there ever be room for someone else?

'Does it still hurt?' she asked.

He looked down, flustered or confused.

'Your wife?' she said, instantly regretting bringing her into the room. 'Sorry,' she said. 'It's not my business and I don't even know you. I shouldn't have said anything.'

'It's fine,' he said. 'Sometimes I forget for a moment and then...' He covered her hand with his, sandwiching hers. He looked her in the eye, sadness emanating from his bottomless pools of sexiness. His stare was magnetic. She felt like she had known him forever, like the attraction was stronger than she was, and it terrified her. 'I'm glad you did. Yes, her absence is always present, you know it's there, like the moon, even when you can't see it, but that doesn't mean that I can't live my life. What happened was bloody awful. No one's life should be cut so short, no one should suffer like that, but I was lucky we had the time we did. She wouldn't want me to become a monk. Even doing what I do, it's hard to get my head around what we lost. Life is not fair, which is why we've got to grab everything good that passes us.'

'Are you lonely?' She didn't know where the question came from.

'Aren't you?' he said.

'I don't think so,' she said. 'I always take things as they come, just go with whatever is thrown at me. I've never lost a man that mattered to me, not even my ex-husband!'

'Tell me more,' said Freddie.

'Well, I got married when I was 23 and divorced when I was 24 to a man I was never in love with. It was a great party though, and I have no regrets.'

He laughed. 'Well, that's very honest – and surprising! To be completely honest with you, I used to be scared of everything, terrified, and watching someone you love suffer is the most petrifying thing in the world. But I don't think I'm scared any more. I have nothing to be scared of. I've seen the worst that fate can deal, and I want to see where I end up.'

'Live every day like it's your last... but then I can never pay my bills at the end of the month! You know when that pair of D&G pumps are just begging me to buy them, and I think, well, what if this is my last day and I don't buy them... I would regret it forever! Who wants to die with regrets?'

'So how do you break that pattern? Will there be a handsome knight to come along and rescue young Dixie from her hedonism?'

'Sure, there have been a few self-described knights, some handsome, some not, most flattered to deceive, but none of them were riding quite the right horse. Besides, I am a free spirit, I ride my own horse. I make my own way, I may not have climbed every mountain, but I've not missed out on much.'

'Not many people can say that. So tell me, Dixie, what are the constants, what do you do when you are not getting fingered by strangers?'

She blushed again. He was so bloody direct. He held her stare. That was a look she wanted to capture on paper.

'You know what I do,' she answered, looking at him coyly. 'I am a PA, open book, nothing glam.'

'Oh yes, of course, what about that amazing doodle you did of that fat guy on the plane? Didn't you talk about a book?'

Shit, she couldn't recall mentioning her book. It was some-thing so personal, she often kept it to herself. Fuck, she had to cut back on the drinking, she thought, taking a slug of claret to erase her discomfort.

'I still have the doodle,' he said. 'It's brilliant. I figured if I ever saw you again, it might be a nice memento of our first meeting. So have you found a place for the duckling yet?'

She giggled. 'I am an illustrator, but an unpublished one, which makes me not an illustrator, just someone who doodles as a pastime.'

'And your dream,' he asked. 'What's the dream?'

'To be published, I guess. I've been working on a book for a while. I just need to finish the last illustrations and find a publisher. All sounds so simple!'

'What's it about?'

'Oh, you know, very highbrow, Freddie! It's about a young frog learning to cross the road with his family. He needs to get the height of his leap just right. He watches his friends and their families as they make their first attempts, and struggles to work out the difference between those who make it and those who end up... There are no ducklings in this one, yet!'

Freddie burst out laughing. 'I love it,' he said. 'Why a frog?!'

'Just because I love frogs and the colour green, that's why. I don't do complicated.'

'Is the frog a fallen prince? Will the frog turn out to be a prince or don't you do happy endings? No pun intended.'

When her eyes eventually left his, they were the last couple in the restaurant and it was well past 11 p.m. A waiter was sweeping between the tables. She was so caught up in the fascination of discovering a new person, gripped by sexual tension, that time had just flown by. Freddie insisted on paying, and as they walked out of the restaurant into the cold windy air, he put his arm around her and said, 'Yours, mine or a shop doorway?'

'You tell me,' she said.

And with that he hailed a cab. 'Your place. I want to see how you live.'

As they arrived at her little flat, she regretted leaving her sketches lying around the living room and the clothes crisis in her bedroom. She'd been certain that wherever they ended up, it wouldn't be back at hers. At least she had wine. She always had wine, houmous and pitta bread in the fridge (otherwise it was empty).

She loved her flat. It was a pokey affair in the less desirable part of Chelsea, the other side of World's End, but it was her safe place. Very few men had been so honoured, and only those acquired in that twilight after her memory had gone before she passed out. It was cozy and quiet and she'd taken years adding knick-knacks and bits-and-pieces from flea markets and boutiques. It was colourful and tiny, and it came with access to a small balcony where she would often go and sit day or night with a glass of wine and perhaps a consoling cigarette. She could sit unseen and watch the world go by.

'Nice pad,' said Freddie as he came up behind her, his hands idly wandering up her dress over her bottom.

'Nice? I don't do nice. IKEA is nice. This is not IKEA. If that's what you want, you're in the wrong place, fella.'

He kissed the back of her neck, while his hands continued their journey until they reached her breasts, where his fingers lingered over her nipples.

'No. Not nice. Nothing flat-packed here. Everything feels made-to-measure and fit-for-purpose.'

He bit her neck once and backed off suddenly. 'Some wine maybe?'

'Yes,' she answered, out of breath. 'Sorry, the fridge.' She was aching with excitement, she was wet, and her clitoris was swelling with anticipation. She worried what the hell would happen when he actually got her clothes off. She grabbed the white wine from the fridge and handed him a glass. He took a sip of the icy cold wine, pulled her towards him and kissed her, flooding her mouth with wine and his tongue, pushing his lean strong body against her. He lifted her onto the kitchen counter and pressed himself between her legs. They kissed and she lost awareness of everything else, enjoying him, nipping, nibbling, tasting; yes, she was hungry. But his hands didn't move to touch her again. Just his tongue, his lips, the light stubble. And just when she thought she was going to have to beg him to fuck her, he undid his jeans and lifted her up to pull off her tights and now very wet knickers. There was no more foreplay. He just slid easily into her wetness, grabbing her waist for support. He was thicker and longer than she'd expected and the relief of feeling him inside her made her gasp. He was gentle but forceful, starting slowly, then getting faster, taking her with him.

And then he stopped.

He bent down to lick her, gently teasing her now-thick

clitoris. She felt the climax coming and she wanted to share – she tried so hard to hold it back, she did, and just as she felt there was nothing more she could do, that she was helpless, he was back inside her, bigger than before, slamming her backwards as they came together. She heard herself cry out, and saw his head thrown back, his body bucking with pleasure. He collapsed with a laugh and kissed her as he retrieved his wine. They fell into a heap on the sofa, tangled up in one another, enjoying the moment of togetherness.

Dixie was surprised when Freddie stood up and straightened his clothes.

'Thank you for a lovely evening, Dixie. Till next time.' He turned to leave.

'Oh,' she said, trying hard to hide her disappointment. 'You're off? I can't tempt you to stay?' She let her legs fall apart.

'Not this time, but thank you – I have an early start tomorrow, and I'm sure we could both do with a few hours' sleep.'

'Will I see you again soon?' As she asked that, she hated herself, the neediness. She was not that sappy girl, who once fucked needed commitment and reassurance. She wasn't.

'I'm sure we can work something out,' he answered. 'Sleep well, my little redhead.' He leaned down and kissed her and he was gone.

Ditched on my own sofa, thought Dixie. His sperm still wet on her thigh. That's a new one! His glibness made her wonder how many women he'd slept with since his wife had died. Was this how he managed his grief? Using women for distraction? Or was she the first one?

She felt like they had shared so much in one evening. She'd loved every minute. He was different, but something about his need to wrong-foot her, to tease and withdraw, was dangerous, unpredictable. Being prepared for anything meant being prepared for disappointment, she counselled herself. But as she sat there, she found herself doodling a picture of the two of them at dinner, heads almost touching over the candle, like no one else in the world existed.

CHAPTER NINE

Stella

The bed was heaped with clothes. She'd really been so baffled about what to wear to a pub. She'd never been for a drink with a nanny who wanted she knew not what. In the end, she threw on her faithful Paige jeans. It was inevitable really, out of the twenty-eight pairs of jeans she owned, they were truly the only pair that actually fitted. But there was no way she was prepared to throw away the other twenty-seven pairs. As every girl knows: one day they will fit. They just sat in a big old pile in the corner of the room. She could even remember when she wore each pair. Somewhere under there were the jeans she'd worn the first time she'd invited Jake back to her room. There too were the pair she'd worn the last time they'd fucked in the living room. Jake had just received his bonus and was home smelling suspiciously of Scotch and cheap perfume. He was horny and happy. They'd been woken by Tom shouting, 'Mum, what are these jeans doing on the TV?' That would have been January, but Stella couldn't exactly recall if it was this year or last. The Paige jeans had been purchased when the trend was to wear a pair of jeans about five sizes too big for you, and then wear a belt to hold them up. She remembered the guy saying to her as he took her jeans off, 'Wow, you've lost a lot of weight since you bought these.' Did he think she'd once been obese or was he joking? These are not questions anyone needs answered on a one-night-stand.

As Stella approached the pub she regretted her decision to agree to a drink with Coco and wondered why she had. Why had she gone to all the trouble of getting a babysitter, of having a shower and washing her hair? At least, she thought, she'd opted for a local pub, one where they were certain not to meet anyone she knew. She had even put on some make-up, a bra that was capable of lifting and supporting her boobs, and her favourite flamingo silk shirt. But Coco did make her smile and laugh, and her attitudes challenged Stella. And she needed that, especially if she was going to return to work with this young, baffling generation. Also, it was so delightful to just watch her. Her smile was catching and her enthusiasm was a tonic to Stella's shrinking world. But now, on a cold spring evening with its hostile wind, it seemed like an odd decision.

The Builders was full of people at the bar laughing, regulars playing darts. Fairy lights flickered around the walls and the bar was garlanded in hops. Her hesitation melted and she felt quite at home. She made an immediate mental note to herself to get out more and try new things. There was a sign just above the bar: No carbs after 8 p.m. and why take the escalator when the stairs will work your glutes.

Coco was smiling at her from the bar. She looked taller and Stella noticed she was wearing some expensive-looking boots that gave her an extra three inches. In her Malanik pumps, Stella was a little intimidated.

'So glad you made it,' said Coco, her face alight and her eyes dancing. Her shiny hair was literally bouncing in the soft light. 'Would you like a drink?'

'Turn down an evening away from the children – are you insane? I'll have a gin and tonic – ooh, what's that?'

Coco held up her drink, a very grown-up drink in a round tumbler, adorned with a twist of orange.

'A Negroni. You don't know it? Try it.'

'Negroni – what's that?' She sipped, trying to avoid the lipstick prints. 'Mmm. Alcohol and there's something bitter. Is it Campari?'

'I'm not sure. It's Negroni. I don't need to know what's in it to know I like it! You like?' Before Stella could react, Coco had ordered her one. She heard the barman ask for £10.

'I'll get that.'

'No, Stella. It's OK. I've invited you.' And she pressed Stella away with a firm and strong grasp of her upper arm. 'Let's sit.' Coco propelled Stella towards a corner table and as she walked she felt Coco's eyes following her.

They sat at right angles with a view over the bar. As Stella settled back in her chair, she was aware of how wide and cumbersome she felt beside Coco's athleticism. She fidgeted, trying to find a position that obscured her rolls of fat, but also made her look comfortable. Note to self: fewer muffins (again), more gym (again), and now: sign up for a postural clinic. Being 40 was no excuse to give up. She'd spent her life dreaming of being thin (of course); if only she had appreciated the figure she'd bemoaned through her twenties. What she wouldn't give to be back in her 25-year-old body!

She smiled at Coco. 'Well, this is an improvement on standing in the playground. I mean, I have to do it. Rory is insistent. But what's your excuse?'

Coco laughed, throwing her head back. 'I love children and I enjoy it. Why would I do anything I don't want to in a city where anything is possible? This is not rural Spain. This is London.'

'Where is home?'

'Baiano, Galicia. But my family is South American. Most of my family are all still there. My father is from Brazil. Mi mama is from Colombia.'

'Don't you ever just want to run back to the sunshine? Piña coladas and volleyball on the beach?'

'Ha, I love that you think I play volleyball on the beach! I have done that once in my life. But life is not easy there, there is crime and drugs and many people are poor. I wanted change and London is amazing. I love that there are people from all over the world, every colour and voice, and they come here with their traditions and beliefs, their food and their styles. I swear you can see the whole world in this city. I love it. For me, the weather is a, how do you say it, a novelty, and I find the British so funny. They are funny, miserable and sarcastic all at the same time. I am here to prepare for the rest of my life and the whole world is here. I could end up anywhere.'

'I love that, miserable and sarcastic, it's so true, that's why

I would pack my bags and leave for the beach tomorrow. My god, I miss the feeling of sun on my skin, of the water. Tropical colours.'

'Would you really?' asked Coco. 'Is that why you always look so sad?'

Stella was aware of how often Coco wrong-footed her. The leaps from empty chit-chat to soul-baring and existential enquiry disturbed her. She picked up her drink, twisting the orange peel in her fingers, staring into its bottom.

'Do I? God, yes, standing in the playground, that makes me sad, but yes, I would absolutely go and live on the first island that I could afford.'

'Island life is much cheaper than you think. You can live for a whole day on many islands for the price of this drink. Think about that. How you say, bottoms up!'

They laughed.

'Ooh, we must get you excited about the city again! You need to see it through my eyes... through the eyes of a visitor, someone who's discovering the city, then you can be excited with me. And if I cannot get you excited about London again, I promise to help you find the island of your dreams. Bottoms up!'

Coco was in stitches at her joke. Young people are so random, thought Stella.

'Oh no, please tell me you aren't going to suggest something insufferable like a visit to the Tower of London?'

'Are you crazy?' shrieked Coco, grinning. 'I'm thinking maybe some parties, something a bit exciting. Something maybe a bit exotic. You need an escape, a fantasy. You need a rest from your everyday life and then you'll be much happier. One day, I promise, I'll come to the playground and I'll see you smiling, just because you need a rest from all the fun! I think you might like that.'

Anything to break the routine, Stella thought. Something new and fresh. New people doing new things in new places.

Then Coco touched her arm and reached for her cheek. Stella flinched, caught unawares, and was surprised by the tenderness of her touch.

'Here, make a wish. It's an eyelash.'

Make a wish, thought Stella… Wow, there is so much I could wish for right now, though I really wish for some freedom, for an escape from monotony. But she simply said, 'Wish made,' as she blew it away. 'I can't tell you what it is as then it won't come true.'

The incident disturbed her, perhaps because it was a long time since someone had asked her what she wanted, so long that other than the fantasy of desertion on a desert island, she could not make a wish.

As the night wore on, Stella lost track of time. She was having fun and felt relaxed. Perhaps she felt a little like she'd used to before the responsibilities of two children and the relative isolation of her domestic life. When last orders were called, Stella was shocked, and jumped up saying that she had to go – the poor babysitter would be desperate to get home. What she really feared was Jake being home and being forced to explain her whereabouts.

'Do not worry, Stella. Everything will be fine.'

Coco hugged her and placed a consoling kiss on each cheek. Her touch was so gentle and comforting that Stella wanted to hug her close and inhale that delicious shea butter scent. But she left hastily with an awkward wave and raced home. She was surprised by the spring in her step, the warmth that flooded through her. Perhaps talking to people outside her circle was what she needed: new relationships and a new outlook.

She quietly put her key in the door in case Jake was home and asleep, but to her surprise he was up and sitting on the sofa with a glass of red wine, watching TV. He never did that.

'Evening, party girl,' he said, rubbing his eyes. 'You been out secretly clubbing?'

'Hardly,' scoffed Stella. 'I actually just went out for a drink with someone I met in the playground, such is the glamour of my life!'

'Someone?! You went out drinking with "someone"? Should I be concerned?'

'Yes, why, what's wrong with that? She's a nanny. What do you think I do all day, stand around like an automaton, pushing swings and preparing alphabet shapes?'

'But what have you got in common with a nanny? Why would she want to hang out with some old bird with two kids?'

'Christ, Jake, really? We haven't seen each other in days and that is all you have to say to me? We don't all get to hang out at the Ivy drinking wine with our "clients". I just thought it would be good to get out.'

'OK, sorry, just sounded a bit odd, that's all. Was it fun... What did you talk about?'

'It was actually. She is a breath of fresh air. You might like her too, though perhaps in a different way. She's mid-twenties, Spanish, with some Colombian and some Brazilian. She's pretty hot, actually.' Feeling a little awkward, she made herself busy tidying around Jake.

'In that case, invite the poor girl for dinner.'

'So you can not turn up?'

'I've said I'm sorry about that. I've an enormous amount on at the moment. It's crucial I pull my weight. Listen, Stella, sit down a second. Here, have a glass of wine—'

'I don't want to mix—'

'Sit. Come here. Let me... Isn't that better?'

'What are you watching? Is that *X Factor*?'

He laughed. 'Just trying to catch up on everything so I'm ready for our big night in.'

It was nice to see him being a bit more relaxed, thought Stella. A bit more like the old Jake, the guy he used to be when she first met him. Perhaps she was being too hard on him. She felt good leaning against his warmth, his bulk. His hair was starting to grey a tiny bit around the temples, he looked tired, but he was still very handsome. She began to fiddle with a button on his shirt, sliding her fingers through the opening.

'So what's been happening your end? Any legal excitement for me? Life as a partner still turning you on?'

He was staring at her, not saying anything, not answering her question. Then he said, 'You look gorgeous tonight... What have you done, new hair?'

'Nope, no new hair, just me. Well, maybe it's clean, and a bit of make-up too... though I miss the chocolate fingerprints!'

His eyes shone as he leaned down to kiss her. This time it was her turn not to speak and she allowed her hand to wander down, passing each button until she reached his belt. She laid her hand on the bulge below.

'Really? It's that easy? Wow, if only I had known that when I used to prance around in my sexy underwear for you. Clean hair and a belly rub is all it takes.'

'Oh, no, those are some very happy memories indeed, but you are just as sexy to me now as you were then. And, by the way, we might be out of practice, but that's not my belly you're rubbing.'

Jake wasn't one for giving compliments, so when he did, it meant a lot. Maybe things weren't as bad as she had thought. Maybe if she tried a little harder they could find their way through this difficult period. She swigged another gulp of her Pinot Noir and slid down between his legs. Lowering his trousers and releasing him, she made eye contact with him and raised an eyebrow; he smiled encouragement as she took him in her mouth. He gasped. She knew blow jobs were once her special skill. She enjoyed them, she enjoyed the way men became completely submissive once you had them in your mouth. She gently sucked and licked him, in and out, letting him touch her breasts, glad she was wearing quality support. She was feeling sexy and horny, and his excitement fed hers. She slowed, and then froze, watching him, until his eyes begged and he pulled her head towards him. As she took his balls in one hand, gently stroking them, he whimpered, 'Yes, please, baby, yes.' She stopped. There was no way she was going to let him have all the fun. She pulled down her jeans and pristine underwear, the bottom of the lovely set, and climbed on top of him, letting him feel the full depth of her, feeling the satisfaction of owning him, of knowing he wanted her so badly. This was the one place she could still be the boss. She started to kiss him as he bucked. She was touching herself, teasing her clitoris, determined they would come together. She wanted the release, the bonding, the togetherness that it would create. He was wild and within seconds they both climaxed and fell about, panting and a bit giddy.

Sometimes, Stella thought, perhaps all you need is a good fuck to reset things. She reached out for Jake's cheek before kissing him lovingly and as she did she caught a whiff of shea butter on her hand. Thank you, Coco, she said to herself. Later that night, for the first time in a very long time, she allowed herself to fall asleep curled up in his arms. And she didn't even find it irritating.

CHAPTER TEN

Ana

Ana was usually on time, and that always meant first. This wasn't always the case. Before Stella had been constrained by motherhood, she would normally have been early, keen to get a head start. As for Dixie, she'd never been within six minutes of an agreed time in her life. The bar Dixie had chosen was under a theatre on Charing Cross Road. There was a TV blaring live music that Ana wanted to ask them to turn down.

Stella stumbled in first. My god, thought Ana, what is she wearing? Those same jeans and down jacket she always wore, now over a floral chemise that would have been more suited to a summer afternoon by a river than a basement bar in the West End. It was Wednesday, so Ana was wearing beige and brown, layered: a cashmere jumper, a Hermès scarf, and leather trousers.

'God, Ana, I am so sorry. Nothing clean. Literally nothing. I'm dressed like I passed a pile from a charity shop and just took the first thing that fitted. You look amazing, as always. Those colours go beautifully with your skin. Give me a hug. My god, you're so bony. How do you do it?'

'Breathe, Stella. Breathe. Are you OK?'

'Fine, just late. The nanny. Well, I say nanny. Jake's downgraded us and we now pay a neighbour's kid to babysit while she prepares for her GCSEs. She looks about 20, but apparently she's 15. Anyway, I'm here. Guess who had sex on Tuesday night?'

'I did.'

'So did I, that's news! Yours would only be news if you *didn't* have sex. How's Rex?'

'Tired. Obviously. The scheduling is quite demanding. The ovulation timing is crucial apparently. Yesterday we met and had sex in the toilets at the Soho Hotel at 6.15 p.m. We walked in at 6.10 and walked out at 6.20, job done. Wham bam, thank you, ma'am, and five minutes later Rex was back in a meeting.'

'It's supposed to be fun, you know? You're making a new life, not a robot.'

'Yes, it's supposed to be fun, until like most things, it isn't. There is a schedule. There is a time limit. We have to take this seriously to maximise the probability of success.'

'God, are you sure it's worth the effort? Kids destroy everything: body, clothes, minds. They're worse than puppies.'

'But more adorable. And obedient.'

'Honey, you are deluded.'

'Bitches!' The cry was Dixie. 'Don't hate the later. Bundles of excuses too boring to cite.'

Dixie was dressed in black. Black heels, black latex leggings, and a black sweatshirt with a scooping collar, which with her pale skin and red hair was stunning. Ana stared at the black bead necklace that hung over her cleavage.

'You like them, Ana? I thought you might, though they're not actually anal beads... but if you're in a fix.'

Dixie liked to try to embarrass Ana, but she failed.

Ana's attention had been caught by a profile on the TV and the first bars of a song. It was vaguely country and western, but more commercial, pop-country, was that a thing? What disturbed Ana was the face and the voice. She knew he'd released a new single, but—

'Holy shit,' exclaimed Stella, her eyes now following Ana's to the screen. 'Is that?'

Stella squinted. 'It is! It's what's his name. That Yank, the one you... Joel Abelard!'

'He. Is. Hot,' said Dixie.

Ana was gripped by a kind of terrified excitement. Her stomach churned and her legs were hollow. She wriggled along the bench, closer to the screen so she could get a better look.

'This is good,' said Dixie, throwing her arms around to emulate a hoedown, until Ana's glare told her to take a pew.

Ana had met Joel in Maine eight years ago. While working for Sotheby's in New York, Ana had been sent to meet a client whose old colonial-era house was crammed with Victorian British classics. She'd found herself in a two fishing-boat town for two nights. Her hotel had a garden with live music, and Friday night was country night.

She was perched on a high stool in the little bar trying to get phone reception, holding her phone as high up in the air as she could, reaching it up towards the satellites, hoping this would help. Stretching higher still, her stool toppled and she fell backwards, legs akimbo. Shocked and embarrassed, she stared up from the floor into a gorgeous smiling face with wicked deep brown eyes, and longish hair swept back behind his ears.

'Hello, angel,' he said, 'and what might you be doing down there?'

'Funny man. Here, help me up, for god's sake. Thanks,' she said, as he pulled her to her feet, flushed and flustered. It was a Friday so she'd brushed down her red Victoria Beckham skirt.

'Nothing damaged that can't be replaced,' he said, laughing. 'Did you get your phone working?'

'You do realise this is a new season VB?' she said, checking her behind for damage.

He positioned his Stetson on the back of his head with a mocking grin. 'And this is a timeless classic.'

Ana tried to laugh, but she was regretting that her Friday red was exaggerating her embarrassed blush. She couldn't remember what knickers she'd put on. She wasn't expecting any sex, she'd had sex the day before, she'd diarised the entry that morning, so it might have been the comfy M&S knickers or the new silky Victoria's Secret ones. The irony was that Joel now knew, but she didn't. She wriggled on her seat, but still couldn't tell which pair she'd chosen. She'd have to find a restroom and check: a smart girl does not go knickerblind into a one-night-stand.

Joel's smile said he was amused by her awkwardness. With a musical Southern twang, he drawled, 'It always makes me laugh how girls think if they hold their phone closer to the sky, it will work... I honestly don't think it makes any difference.

It's not an altitude problem or guys like me would always have better coverage than girls like you. What are you, 5'3" in heels?'

'In tights, actually, Mr Long Dog.'

'In my humble opinion, if your phone has no reception, it's for a reason: it's so I can buy you a drink and we can get to communicating in the good old-fashioned way.'

'I don't believe in fate, but I do believe in letting a man buy me a drink, so sure, I'll have what you're having. What exactly does "communicating in the old-fashioned way" mean?'

The PA system came alive with a hiss: 'Willy B. Goode to the stage, please.'

'That's my cue. Medium of song, honey. Hey, Nathan,' he called to the barman. 'Get the lady a Coors Light on my tab.'

'Sure thing, Joel.'

'Actually, I'll have an Old Fashioned.'

He gave her a surprised look.

'An Old Fashioned then. One, only, for the dark-haired beauty, Sue Ellen Ewing.'

Back then Joel had been a long-haired strip of a youth in battered Stetson with a passion for Van Morrison covers, especially 'Have I Told You Lately'. He was living hand to mouth on the coast. Willy B. Goode was his stage name, which was both ironic and puerile, Ana was to reflect when she knew him better.

'Look at her face!' laughed Dixie pointing. 'She's bright red. My god, are you about to come, Ana!?' Dixie was in pieces, pointing and laughing. 'My god, she's gotta be wetter than Marti Pellow. Do you need a towel, Ana?'

'Leave her alone, Dix. Poor Ana has never got over her Reverse Cowboy phase. She just can't put it behind her!'

Now they were both in hysterics.

'Hang on, wasn't he the one who wouldn't—'

'Exactly! Who'd have thought the way to Ana the Fox's heart was NOT with a cock!'

'I am going to the bar,' said Ana, dismissively. 'When you two have calmed down, I'll return. Same again?'

'What are you having?'

'Old Fashioned.'

'What the fuck, let's go hard and go home early,' laughed Stella, a glint in her eye.

When Ana returned, Joel's country pop chart-topper, 'Brown Eyed Girl', had finished, and the ever-excitable Dixie–Stella combo had moved on to the respective arts of the hard and fast blow job versus the long and languorous.

'Girls, can't we talk about something other than sex and men?'

'How,' said Dixie, 'can we talk about sex without talking about men?'

She looked at Stella for confirmation. For a split-second Stella looked a little vexed, then nodded. 'Sex and men, yes, like wine and cheese, tea and toast—'

'Tea and a muffin is a perfectly good option. You two are drunk. Can we not spend a bit of time on us? We haven't planned this year's trip yet? I've got to be honest, I need a little tour.'

'A tour,' shrieked Dixie. Now clearly drunk and perhaps high, thought Ana. 'A little Eiffel "tour".'

'No, Provence. I thought biking in Provence. There'll be wine and cheese for you two. And I might find a spicy local saucisson, you know, just for a little variety.'

And then they all guffawed. Ana knew the jokes were clichéd, and repeated every time they met, but this was the consolation of friends, this was the ritual of re-establishing the foundations of their relationship. The jokes might not be funny, but they were their jokes, and they were going to enjoy them.

'Biking... biking? Do you know who we are, Ana? There's only one thing I'm gonna be riding when we go away and it has balls, not wheels.'

'I'm serious. We all love Provence. We can spend a night in St Tropez and then get out into the countryside and really enjoy ourselves.'

'Listen, Ana, if I go away, it's to get away from the everyday. I want something wild and crazy. Provence is fine if you're married and middle-aged... oh!' Stella stopped herself in time to laugh before they did. 'OK, OK. What about something a little less extravagant, a little more debauched?'

'What about something like the Edinburgh Festival? We could—' Stella was cut off by her phone buzzing. Ana noticed that Stella seemed both shocked and preoccupied by the message. She was about to quiz her when Dixie barked, 'Scotland!'

'Don't be stupid,' snapped Stella.

Ana wondered at her vitriol. Something was up with her. While she'd known them both since they were in their early teens, Dixie and Stella had been fast friends since pre-school. This familiarity, and Stella's natural authority, meant Dixie tolerated her put-downs, but even for Stella this seemed out of character.

'I'm serious,' said Stella. 'I can't go spending thousands on a trip to St Tropez and Provence. It's literally the most expensive playground in Europe. I'm sure Peter has a place in Edinburgh. There'll be booze, parties, and loads of wildness. I want something new and fresh, something different. Let's go wild, not pedal around Provence like three middle-aged women.'

'Let's talk about this next time,' said Dixie hastily. 'I'm up for it, of course. But I've got a lot on. I'm having to spend much more time in New York than I'd expected. I'll have to check my calendar.'

Ana and Stella gave each other a look.

'Spill,' said Stella.

'What?'

'That voice. Those excuses. Come on...' said Ana. She could see Dixie redden. 'What's his name?'

Dixie snorted. 'This is *not* about a man. Peter's on my case. I'm serious.'

Ana and Stella smirked at each other.

'OK, look. Maybe Edinburgh will work. I'll—'

She was interrupted by Joel's 'Brown Eyed Girl' blaring again from the TV.

'Oh my god,' laughed Stella. 'He's hotter than I remember!'

'Ana's moment of purity.'

Stella and Dixie laughed, but Ana couldn't. Whilst beautiful and exciting, looking back, those weekends with Joel might have been the most frustrating of her life. Joel smoked, he drank, he swore and he was gorgeous. They'd drink tequila late into the night, get so stoned they would laugh until it hurt, and then stay up eating pizza in her tiny room until the early hours. He would serenade her through the night on his guitar (he even wrote a song about her). It was in many ways a fantasy. He lacked any realistic prospects. She'd never told him, but though she loved country and western, she didn't think much of his voice. He was going to be playing bars and living with his mates forever, waiting for the big break that would never come. There were so many really talented wannabe musicians around that Ana couldn't really see any hope for him, so she never took their relationship seriously, though she savoured every moment they spent together and fancied the pants off him (many times). He was like a walking erection. They'd spend hours naked together, messing, caressing, licking, poking and prodding; hot, sweaty, exhausted, drunk, stoned – pure heaven. She only had to look at him to feel herself pulsate with longing.

There was one major catch: Joel Abelard would not engage in penetrative sex. Absurd as it seemed to Ana for whom the penetrating penis was almost a religious artefact, Joel had taken a purity pledge: until he was engaged to be married, all inter-course was off limits. There were of course a thousand and one surrogates, but for Ana there was nothing like the completion she felt when filled with cock. But to be fair to Joel, he had skills that almost compensated: long fingers and a longer tongue.

'When we're engaged, Ana, we can open up a whole new

circle of heaven. Isn't it better always to have something to look forward to?'

'Anal?'

'Don't laugh at me, Ana. There're not many things that are sacred to me, but this is and you are. When we're married...'

She would giggle as she sat curled up in tangled sheets, candles burning, and whisper back through her smiles, 'Yes, and then we could fuck all day and run around naked all night...' Then the more serious side of her would say, 'But Joel, we couldn't even afford to buy a shack... this is just a love song, just a dream.' She hated that her head ruled her heart, but she was a risk-averse middle-class girl. What was wrong with that? This wasn't the movies, this was real life, and dreams of running away with a penniless musician were just that, dreams.

'It's only a dream if you ain't prepared to follow it,' he cooed lazily as he looked at her, playing with her hair, undressing her with his eyes. 'It's only us who can make our dreams a reality. Like one day fucking you is my dream reality.'

'And actually getting fucked by a *real* cowboy is mine,' said Ana, a little shrewishly.

She remembered one weekend when, on a whim, they jumped in his old pick-up and headed up the coast. They drank wine, slept under the stars on the beach, froze half to death, but none of it mattered. It was life at its most raw, them and nature, Joel and his guitar. It was moments like that which made Ana wonder whether her vision of normal was enough. Settling was not an option, but her heart, head and vagina all had a vote. The good stuff that might lie ahead was always just a dream, but the memories were real.

'Are you getting too cold, baby?' asked Joel. 'I know somewhere we could go to warm up.'

'My god, yes, I'm bloody freezing.'

'Follow me, m'lady,' he said, as they clambered out of his old orange truck, Bert, his pride and joy. He helped her down and they wandered down the beach hand in hand, stopping in front of an impressive seafront hotel called Shutters. 'Follow me,' he whispered.

'Isn't this trespassing?'

'Only if we get caught. Come on, live a little… it's the middle of the night, no one will see us.'

Not wanting to be too uptight, she agreed, and he led her to a hot tub overlooking the ocean.

He ripped off his clothes and jumped straight in as she watched in amazement. 'Your turn. Come on, English, wanna take a bath?'

Not one to side-step a challenge, she slipped off her little summer dress and sweatshirt, savouring his hungry gaze. She climbed in, slowly giving him ample time to take in her perfectly shaped breasts, neatly shaven pussy, and round little butt.

'Honey, that there is evolution at its very finest.'

She slipped in next to him, closing her hand around his penis. He started to sing 'Have I Told You Lately' softly into her ear. The soft water bubbled around them and they slid together, skin on skin like silk on silk. There was something so sexy about being in the water, about knowing they were not meant to be there, that they might be caught. His hand crept down and he extended a single thick finger into her and pressed her clitoris like a button. She gasped and her hand closed tighter around him.

As Ana began to wonder for the umpteenth time whether he'd drop his foolish pledge, they were interrupted by a brusque voice, 'Excuse me, but the sign states the hot tub is closed from 10 p.m. It is now 2 a.m.'

'I am so sorry,' said Joel, clearing his throat and trying to keep a straight face. 'We'll go straight back to our room – we didn't realise the time.'

The security guard, short and round like Danny DeVito, carried his torch like a baton and shone it onto the foaming water. 'You didn't realise what the time was? You didn't realise that it was the middle of the night? What room are you in?'

'110,' answered Joel, not missing a beat, his free hand shielding his eyes from the halogen light.

'We don't have a room 110.'

'Er, right,' said Joel. 'Must have got that wrong. Let me just check.' He leaned across Ana towards his trousers.

Ana laughed aloud when the spotlight lit his white buttocks.

Joel whispered in her ear, 'Get ready to run.'

'Well, thanks for the hot tub. It's been awesome,' he said, and at that they both leaped up, grabbed their clothes and ran panting and giggling naked towards the beach, expecting to be arrested at any moment. Ana looked backed to see the security guard's torch wobbling as he shuffled through the thick sand. He must have been furious but the roar of the Atlantic drowned him out.

As they lay back in the truck recounting the story to one another, it seemed like nothing in the world mattered at all if they had each other. But that was then.

Of course Joel was now a bloody star, and not just any kind of star, but a country star. She had often thought about picking up the phone to him, to say, 'Hey, sorry I ditched you when I thought you were going nowhere, but now you are famous can we try again?' but she was ashamed.

Both Stella and Dixie had heard the whole Joel saga, every permutation, many times over the months and years. They'd pestered her to get in touch with him, even all these years later. Dixie was always telling her that sexual attraction like that was hard to find, that Joel would be thrilled to hear from her. Stella had been more pragmatic — she insisted that Ana must fuck him before they could get engaged. What if, in spite of all evidence to the contrary, he just couldn't actually perform? What if the purity pledge was the perfect alibi for some more serious issue? What if it wasn't that he wouldn't, but rather that he couldn't?

If the press reports were to be believed, Joel was still single, despite no doubt thousands of women throwing themselves at him, which meant, if he was true to his word, which she suspected he was, that he was still a virgin. She couldn't help but wonder at how much she had to teach him given the chance. All her years of preparation, the diary of experiences. Everything prepared her for exactly this scenario. She could still feel his breath on her stomach as he traced his finger down her taut abdomen, and then soon the weight of his tongue pressing into her. Just the memory was nearly enough to make her come.

'Marti! Marti! Woo hoo!' Dixie was waving her hands in front of Ana's eyes. 'One for the road. Old Fashioned?'

Ana looked at her watch. 'No, I have to go to be home for the next fertility window. Rex will be waiting. My work has just begun.' She laughed half-heartedly and gathered her stuff. 'Provence – think about it at least.'

CHAPTER ELEVEN

Stella

Still hungover from the Old Fashioned Ana had introduced to their girls' night out, Stella was impatiently throwing another load of the kids' and Jake's washing in the machine, bemoaning her lack of a cleaner, and fantasising about the glamorous trips she'd get when she was back in work (maybe then she'd be able to afford long weekends in Provence), when Coco's follow-up text arrived: **'As promised, I now have a suitably wild party for you. You wanted variety and adventure: Shoreditch High Street Station, Tuesday, 8 p.m. Cx PS It's on the ginger line!'**

Stella had received Coco's text while sat with Dix and Ana, and she'd been shocked. **'Up for something different? Tuesday night? Cx'** The invite would have disconcerted her anyway, but to receive it while surrounded by her closest friends had compounded its power. What was she getting herself into? She wanted to talk to them about it, but knew she couldn't. They'd laugh at her. In her Uber home, she'd obsessed about what to say. She wanted to go. She ached to go. But it felt so out of character, so she wrote then deleted several texts, alternately agreeing with enthusiasm and declining with decorum. Eventually, as the car

pulled up outside 8 Cathcart Road, she'd sent: **'Absolutely. S'**
At the last minute, she'd deleted an x.

Shoreditch High Street, she thought with a smile. She'd
been there, of course she had, but only by car to the doors of
Shoreditch House. She'd never actually been out there, with
people from around there, with 25-year-old Spanish-Brazilian-
Colombian au pairs. What if this was an elaborate confidence
trick? What if— She stopped herself when she realised that these
were unhinged thoughts. Coco was the Van Nesses' nanny, not
Myra Hindley or Rose West. She was not going to end up dead
or restrained in a basement.

But what did 'different' mean? The word could cover anything. Literally, anything other than the circular reality of
Stella's everyday. Different was exactly what she wanted. Before
her paranoid and overactive imagination could retake control,
she sent a hasty and very casual: **'Sounds great. See you there.**
S' Again she had to delete an x. It just did not seem appropriate.

Soon she began to panic about what to wear. She knew she
needed to look cool, like she hadn't made an effort, and not
too fat. But of course looking like you haven't made an effort
takes a shitload of effort. And she didn't know when she'd last
looked cool. And by most common BMI standards she was
overweight. She was a size 12, OK, maybe 14, no more than
that, definitely. What she wanted and what she was seemed to
be continually in conflict these days, but she still had options.
She could either wash some of her clothes, but with this thought
she looked down at the backload of Jake's shirts and Tom's sports
gear and made an executive decision: she needed a new outfit

and she needed some tlc. At the very minimum she needed her hair done. An afternoon in the West End should resolve that. She still had some emergency slack on her credit card. This was an opportunity to use it on herself. Just herself.

She quickly called the stylist around the corner from her old office in Soho and fixed a Monday p.m. 'Roots'n'all'. She was relieved they were still in business; a purple rinse from Cool Cutz on Bellevue Road was not going to do the trick. If the GCSE kid could look after Rory, she'd have time to shop for clothes and be home before Tom needed picking up from school (he had chess club on a Monday).

Having made the commitment and begun her preparations, she felt a surge of energy, a kick of optimism like she could rule the world. Someone was interested in spending time with her, someone apart from her old friends found her interesting, and it made her feel good. There was a spring in her step she hadn't felt for a long time.

As Tuesday night approached, Stella started to feel oddly nervous. She had no idea why. She was a 40-year-old mother of two, who'd edited one of the UK's most popular fashion magazines for many years. She could run with the best of them. OK, maybe she was a little out of practice. Besides, she didn't know what Coco had planned; maybe it was just going to be a chilled evening. Perhaps it was the uncertainty that rattled her, or the feeling it might be wilder than she was ready for. Remember how off-the-wall she'd been at 25! Actually she couldn't, but that told a story of its own.

She poured herself into her new J Brand jeans. Jeans were

timeless and she'd resolved to expand her collection of wearable jeans to two... OK, these were so tight she could hardly breathe, but they held her arse in position and she was pretty pleased with the outcome. The downside was that all her fat was pushed upwards. A white muffin rode over the top of the jeans, but it had to go somewhere. She decided it was better to push her fat up to her stomach where with careful dress choice she could hide it. Hopefully her boobs would distract from this imperfection. She had the technology to strap them up and out. But as she stood there half naked scrutinising herself in the mirror, she laughed when she found herself making another promise to cut out carbs and sugar for a month.

She grabbed her new loose-fitting peasant top out of the Fenwick's bag and slipped it on. She admired her skills. She still had it. It was perfect, low at the top, but baggy around the middle. It hid the fatty tissue roll, drew the eye towards the boobs and then the face. She loved her new hair, blonde to the roots, light and bouncy, and all the ends intact. She ran her fingers through the unrecognisable silkiness. She could easily pass for her early thirties, easily – in candlelight.

Christ, she thought, get a grip, Stella, you are only going out with a young nanny from down the road. Why does it matter so much! She wasn't sure she knew, but she did know she was enjoying how she felt, like she was worth something. She tossed her hair in the mirror again and shook her head. 'Because I'm worth it,' she thought and as she looked at herself with a critical eye, she thought she wasn't too bad... not exactly Jennifer A, but there was some semblance of the old Stella in there somewhere.

She often wondered what would happen if Jake left her, fell for some bimbo, and she had to find someone else, could she bear it? Maybe with her new look there was a chance she'd survive, but often her only hope was that she could find a man with a fetish for fatty rolls (there must be a website). Right now he really seemed so preoccupied with work. He'd kept his commitment to make it home for *The X Factor* two weeks running, though he did spend most of the time on his phone. But at least he was trying. Other than that she'd barely seen him. She wondered how long his indifference would last. These things, she knew from experience, go in phases. Maybe when he saw how good she was looking, he'd make some time. But then again, would he be around to notice?

By the time her train limped into Shoreditch High St, Stella had, at every single lingering stop, seriously considered turning straight around and going home. She was a married 40-year-old mother of two children. What business had she gallivanting around East London with a stunning millennial in her mid-twenties?

Approaching the exit barriers, she'd almost decided once and for all to turn on her heel, when she heard a squeal (yes, an actual squeal of excitement) and her name echoing through the brightly lit hallway. Coco was skipping towards her, her shiny hair curled and bouncing, her eyes bright and wild.

'Stella!' she yelled, hugging her. 'SO glad you made it!'

My god, that smell: shea butter with a coconut tang. It made her mouth water. She pulled herself free. A little embarrassed that anyone watching might have got the wrong idea.

'Hi, Coco, yes, I'm here. I made it – just!'

'What do you mean "just"? You're SO funny. You're looking great... there is something different about you! What is it... I know, your hair... have you done something?'

Pleased, but determined to hide it, she replied, 'Just had some highlights put in, decided it was time to sort out my roots. I swear to god having dark roots makes any blonde depressed. Sometimes these things just creep up on you. Everything's fine and then the next day you wake up with four-inch roots. And to think some people call it a trend nowadays... to let your roots grow out, I mean. I might be a child of the Seventies but I always think the blonder the better.'

Coco giggled as she grabbed her arm, and teased, 'It's a little early to be showing your age, Stella. I think you will find balayage is all the rage nowadays... but you look phenomenal.'

Stella laughed freely. 'Anyway, sod the hair, what's the plan?'

'We're heading east. Bethnal Green.'

Stella look around, concerned. She didn't know there was anything east of Shoreditch, except Essex and the sea.

'There's a party going on. Very intimate. Very beautiful. Unlike anything in Wandsworth, I promise, but very lovely people with a great attitude to life. Artists and creatives. People who make their own way in the world. They are inspiring. I thought you'd enjoy that.'

Whilst this was exactly what Stella had decided she needed, she now found the whole suggestion quite pretentious. Besides, she was already miles from home, from the kids, but she feigned nonchalance and agreed. 'I can do East London, Coco. You are talking to a journalist who worked in Soho for ten years. I'm pretty sure there's nothing that can shock me out here...'

Coco's announcement that it was just a short bus ride was a minor setback. Stella didn't have the resilience to admit she'd not been on a bus since they got rid of conductors. But she jumped on and they settled in for the journey. Stella found herself surprised again at how easy it was to talk to Coco, and how much they had in common, even though their lives were so different. Coco was so interested in everything she had to say. She asked questions. It was so refreshing! For once she felt like more than a mother, and launched into reminiscences of her life as a journo. She wanted to show Coco that she was more than a depressed mother and wife, and she thought, quite frankly, who didn't love a chance to talk about themselves (... except Jake, a thought she quickly dismissed).

Coco pulled some mini bottles of vodka out of her bag. Stella's first thought was 'If I start drinking now I'll never make it through the night.' Her second was 'In for a penny, in for a pound, I've got to let go of all these shoulds and cants if I'm going to enjoy this adventure!' As the bus rattled to another halt, there was a rush of alien-looking millennials with facial hair and discordant fashion choices (yes, people were wearing dungarees and Doc Martens) getting on board. People were heading out for dates and fun. They both downed their first shot of the night and Stella relished the warmth as the vodka tumbled down her throat and warmed her insides. Her lips were burning. She licked them as Coco watched her smiling encouragingly.

'Tell me about your husband,' said Coco. 'You never talk

about him. What is there to know about this delicious husband of yours... Is he hot, like you?' she joked.

'Jake, hot?' she laughed. 'I never really think about him like that any more. When I first met him I thought he was the hottest thing I had ever seen. I laid eyes on him and just knew I had to have him. He was cool, indifferent, hot and at the centre of every party. We met at uni and once we got together we were like Sandy and Danny. At the time, it was love's young dream.'

Stella felt a surge of loss and regret.

'And what happened to all that magic?' pushed Coco. 'Are you going destroy my future? Tell me love never lasts?'

'No, but things obviously change. Life gets in the way. I look back at the all-night parties, the fun, the holidays – the Nineties was one long party. We had no responsibility. Once we'd left uni and had jobs, we travelled whenever we wanted, we stayed out until all hours, we screwed all night. That's the nature of our twenties – we don't know how lucky we are and then it's over before you notice. Responsibility creeps up on you. Jake has a demanding job, I have two children to bring up, and it's just not what it used to be. We're not who we used to be. I still love Jake, of course. I just want something different.'

Coco gave her an understanding look and stroked Stella's arm.

'That all sounds very serious, Stella... Does all the fun really need to go?'

'You know what, Coco, maybe you're right. Maybe I just need someone to show me how to have fun again!'

'Yes! And I am totally your girl! Do you think Jake feels like this too? Mr Van Ness is a lawyer too. I think he has a pretty good life. Everyday he is "entertaining clients", while his Mrs Van Ness is stuck at home. Well, actually she is out getting her nails done most days, but I don't think this makes her very happy. It is hard for women in marriage, no?'

The bus stuttered and stopped.

'Oops, this is our stop! Quick!'

They tumbled into the street, laughing breathlessly. Stella was already light-headed from the vodka, so she was relieved to be out in the fresh air, able to breathe. It was starting to rain, and there was traffic everywhere. Taxi drivers pounding on their horns; people fighting over cabs as the weather set in; umbrellas knocking into one another as people rushed about. They weren't dressed like anyone she knew. The men all had facial hair and heavy tweed coats. The women wore no make-up and she was probably the only woman within a mile who'd blow-dried her hair that afternoon. She followed Coco, a hand held aloft in a futile effort to protect her 'do' from the cold rain and wind, as she foraged for her umbrella in her handbag. They huddled together under the fragile umbrella and Stella quickly texted the babysitter to make sure everything was OK, then tucked her phone safely back into her bag. It was pouring. Stella could feel her feet getting wetter and knew her hair would be starting to frizz. They arrived at an unmarked door. It looked like a normal front door, so Stella assumed it was just a friend's flat. But once buzzed in, they were ushered down instead of up. The hairs on Stella's neck stood on end.

The walls were painted matt black and the lighting was minimal: small low-voltage bulbs hidden in red velvet shades.

'Where *are* we?' asked Stella. 'Is this a dungeon?'

Coco laughed and they burst through a pair of thick double doors into a room thronging with laughing people, inviting ambient music and a mass of colours and styles. The atmosphere was like nothing Stella had ever seen outside a film. There were people in masks wearing headdresses of fascinators and feathers. Others were wearing long leather coats. There were bright tropical colours of turquoise and verdigris. Ana would really struggle with the dress code, thought Stella, wishing Ana was with her, but also knowing she wouldn't be able to enjoy it in the same way if she was.

'Welcome,' said Coco. 'Time to relax, forget about your worries and your strife!'

The room was decked out in vibrant colours, rich purples and deep reds. There were giggling, happy and quite frankly gorgeous girls everywhere. In the middle of the room was a circular bar, crowded but not crammed. People were just sitting and chatting on sofas that lined the walls. These were clearly Coco's people, young, stylish, full of life – no wonder she was always so happy! There was such a relaxed vibe everywhere, no one seemed stressed. It was like being on a film set for the beautiful people. This was so different to the last drinks party Stella had attended: Jenny and Tim's joint birthday drinks down the street – Prosecco and canapés. She'd nearly lost her mind at the banality of the chat: house prices, school logistics and local parking restrictions. She'd drunk too much and Jake and her had fought on the short walk home and he'd slept on the couch. But here she felt she could be anyone she wanted to be.

Coco returned from the bar with a ravishing six-foot blonde in silver pumps, Helmut Lang jeans and a sequinned top.

'Enchantée,' she whispered in the most sultry French accent. 'I'm Renée.'

She must be a model, thought Stella. My god, those legs started at the floor and ended somewhere around Stella's shoulder.

'I was just telling Coco about my travel plans. I am thinking about Florence, it is such a romantic city. So much history and art and style. And the setting... the river, the bridges and cathedrals. The clothes and the food. It's a feast of the senses, you know? Or maybe Russia!'

'How amazing to have so many choices!' replied Stella, making an effort not to sound bitter. 'Russia and Tuscany though, two pretty big extremes. What are you looking for... in Russia?'

'Do you know the Trans-Siberian railway? We read about it recently. Do you know it starts in St Petersburg and ends in Beijing? Three weeks of living on a train. Crossing a continent like that would be unforgettable.'

'Crammed into a cupboard, sharing a sink to wash in, living so close together that you can't escape!'

'That doesn't sound too bad. Of course you need to be with the right people,' said Coco with a gleam in her eye.

They all laughed, and Stella wondered whether she'd missed some joke.

'Well, I might as well do it while I can,' exclaimed Renée. 'Who knows what tomorrow holds. I'd like to think I'd try anything once.'

'How do you travel?' asked Stella. 'Solo or in a group?'

'No, no, I travel with my partner, Stef.'

'Oh that's great. What do you guys do for work?'

'Oh, that is work. We're travel bloggers,' said Renée. 'We get to do what we love together and get paid while we do it! We started it together, and it's exceeded our wildest dreams. Now we just travel, take loads of photos and write up locations and issues. We are trying to persuade Coco to join us on our next adventure to spice things up!'

'Wouldn't three be a crowd?'

Renée laughed. 'With Coco, no way. We'd love to have her along.'

'Is your partner here?'

'Yes, that's Stef over there, the blonde under that tall Italian lamp.'

Stella's eyes followed Renée's gesture. Under the lamp was a petite silvery blonde, a waif with the body of a ballet dancer, dressed from foot to neck in shiny latex.

The penny dropped and Stella swallowed and quickly restored her interested and non-judgemental expression. So that was her girlfriend? Yes. They were lesbians. Yes.

They were such an unfeasibly hot couple. Like they'd been cut out of a Who's Who column in a fashion magazine and placed together by central casting.

Stella steadied herself, took a sip of her drink. She was pleased to note she recognised it as a Negroni. 'Cool, I see. Brilliant to have a partner who likes to travel as much as you!' What a life they must lead, thought Stella. They were like a man's wet dream, then realised that they must be first of all each other's wet dream. She was, she realised, really out of her depth. Stef walked towards them and she grew more beautiful as she approached. Like a silvery Scandinavian elf with her fine features, her ice-blue eyes.

'Hello, gorgeous,' she whispered as she and Renée kissed. Stella saw her hand rest lightly on Renée's arse. 'Are you talking about me?'

'Not exactly! Just discussing our plans.'

'Well, you know my vote – I say we go hardcore and head to Beijing via Russia. The photos from Florence would be beautiful, if a little clichéd, but our readers will be way more intrigued by our experiences in the wilderness. Don't you think?'

'What's your blog?' asked Stella.

'It's a travel blog for lesbians. It's called Two Girls, One Trip. We travel all over the world and try to find all the hotspots for the LGBT+ community. We try to find the best a city or country has to offer. We try to help our readers understand how they'll be accepted, what bigotry or intolerance they'll encounter, what laws they might be breaking. For example, we're trying to get some time with Pussy Riot while we're in Russia. Well, I am. Renée's a little more cautious than me.'

Stella was surprised to see her slap Renée's buttock.

'OMG, that is amazing. I have read about people making blogging a career, but I didn't know it really happened. Maybe I need to start one too! I need an angle.'

'We just solved a problem that we've had: where can a lesbian have a good time, and what might mess with that. We have a social as well as a travel mission.'

'Who wouldn't want to look at photos of you in exotic locations!' shrilled Stella.

Coco laughed, 'You are so bad!'

'It is about more than titillating photos of lesbians,' said Stef seriously, 'but it doesn't hurt,' she continued laughing and gave Renée's butt another slap.

'I'm not sure my body will have quite the same draw as you two! But then again maybe there is a market for the more rotund, life-experienced 40-year-old. I just need to find my mission.'

They all burst out laughing again.

'So how did you two meet?' asked Stella, feeling a bit more confident now. She drained her Negroni.

Her question hung in the air awkwardly, then Stef cleared her throat and spoke. 'Well, it was a little complicated at the time. I was married to a property developer, living in Hong Kong, when I met Renée. Renée was our lodger. We all became great friends, partied, even went on holiday together, and then, long story short, I found myself falling in love with Renée. She made me feel alive!'

'Oh!' exclaimed Stella. 'I see... I guess that is kind of complicated! I mean it's quite a leap.'

'Yes, it was, completely unexpected. I'd never had any interest in women, and then along comes this one, and I was smitten. I see now, it was inevitable.'

Stella watched Renée and Stef kiss with such tenderness and desire. How lucky they were to have each other, she thought.

'How did your husband take it?' asked Stella.

'Ha, not great to start with. His ego took quite a battering and as you can imagine he struggled to accept it. There was a lot of denial. He was convinced I was hiding something!'

'But I bet he wouldn't have minded if you had invited him to join in,' quipped Coco naughtily.

'We did think about it, but he wasn't really my type. What with the penis and everything!' laughed Renée.

'Anyway, it has all worked out,' said Stef. 'We're friends now. Rick even has a new fiancée... but probably won't have another lodger!'

Stella was having the best time she'd had in a long time – how juicy was this! Wait until she told the girls. She was loving it. This was better than standing in circles complaining about taxation and the struggle to book a holiday over half-term. This was Life. People following their dreams, breaking rules, crossing boundaries. She loved their wit and strength. Her journalistic nosiness had gone into overdrive, and she was frantic for details, but soon felt she had probably asked enough questions for one night. Could a woman really just discover she was a lesbian when she met the right woman? Surely it wasn't that simple? This was what she should be writing about. This was the kind of journalism she could be doing. But then Stella realised she didn't really know anyone who was gay.

At some point later, after another Negroni or two, Stella was really quite pissed and decided she should probably make her way home before she crossed some line. As she turned to Coco to tell her she was going to have to leave, she did a double-take.

The sofas that lined the walls were fully occupied with people kissing. And all of them were girls. In fact as she looked around, drunk and wide-eyed, she discovered that there were only girls. She was drunk at a lesbian night. Which meant... She gave Coco a look. Was Coco gay? Or just hanging out with her friends? And did it matter anyway? Her mind started to spin. She found herself facing Coco. She was suddenly speechless, thrown as to what to say. She stared at her wide-eyed and vulnerable. Coco leaned over and kissed her gently on the lips. She didn't move. She didn't respond, but she didn't pull away. Coco did it again. Gently, sweetly, softly. A little part of Stella didn't want to run, another part wanted to see what would happen next. As their lips touched for the third time, Stella felt herself returning the kiss. Coco's lips began to part and she felt a flickering tongue part hers. She recoiled. She had to leave. She had to leave immediately, but she had to be cool. But how does a 40-year-old escape a basement club full of hot lesbians? She stared at Coco, hastily thanked her for a great night, gave her a quick peck on the side of the mouth, grabbed her coat and strode towards the door without a look back.

She threw herself in the first taxi she found, heart pounding and mind racing. She crossed her legs and arms and wondered what the hell had just happened.

As soon as Stella got home, she ran upstairs and scrubbed all the make-up off her face, had a shower and put on her PJs. She lay on the bed beside Jake, who smelled strongly of whisky and was snoring. It was unbearable. She couldn't get the images and feeling from the evening out of her mind.

She went downstairs, put on the kettle and made herself toast and Marmite. Since she was 18, she had found this the only way to settle herself when she was excited or drunk, or both. Jake hadn't even heard her come in. She checked her phone and curled up on the sofa under a blanket. She looked around her living room like it was the first time she'd seen it. The array of photos. Her wedding. Tom crawling around at a photo shoot. A portrait of the family. The bridesmaid's photos from Dixie's wedding to Carlton about twenty years ago when they were all so young and innocent. How could memories so familiar look so distant and alien?

Her phone buzzed. She jumped. It was Coco. **'Thanks for a fun night, my friends all loved you. Hope we can do it again soon. Cx'**

Do it again soon?! Do what again soon? The thing? The end thing? No, she can't mean that, she must just mean go and have drinks again. Be calm, thought Stella. It was nothing. I just had too much to drink. The evening *had* been brilliant and hilarious. She'd felt more herself than she had in at least two years. Recklessly, she knew, and knowing she might regret it in the morning, she embraced her new give-everything-a-go mantra and she decided to text back. But should she wait, she thought, do it tomorrow, or just do it now? Now, she thought; after all, she is just a mate. It's not like there is anything else to it. Stella knew she was not a lesbian. She was too fond of cock for that. So she tapped out: **'Loved it, thanks for taking me. Sx'**

Then panicked and deleted it. I can't say 'loved it', she thought. What will she think 'it' is? She might think 'it' was 'it' rather than the evening. Argh. So she simply put **'Great fun, you have great friends, speak soon Sx'.** Better she thought, less misleading. Nothing in there to misinterpret. And she pressed send.

And noticed that she'd added an x. It was just a kiss. What did that matter?

Within seconds she simply got back a **'Sleep well. X'** That's fine, she thought, just a friend telling another friend to sleep well. She put her phone down and lay her head back on the sofa.

The next thing she knew Tom was pulling her hair and screaming, 'I'm hungry, Mummy!'

It was like last night was just a dream, a wild dream. Nothing to regret.

CHAPTER TWELVE

Stella

Stella replayed the kiss over and over in her head in the days that followed. Had she misinterpreted it? Had Coco just been kissing her goodbye? She'd been very drunk, she had a wild imagination, so it was possible that she had fabricated the extent of the kiss. It had been a while, but it wouldn't be the first time she'd misremembered something. She knew she was spending too much time exploring her memory, but when she thought about the night, the people, the style, glamour and freedom, she swelled with excitement.

While Rory was occupied, she perched at the counter in the kitchen, trying to get access to the joint account. Jake had told her that the password hadn't changed, that she must have mistyped it. It was still their postcode and house number; the same one she'd been trying. Of course it was. She might not be at the top of her game, but she wasn't so broken that she couldn't recall and enter eight figures.

But when it failed again, exasperated, she followed the 'Forgotten your password?' link. Two security questions, Jake's mum's maiden name and his first car, a Hillman Imp (she'd always found that hilarious) and she was permitted to reset the password. She shrugged and entered their postcode and house number again.

'Idiots!' What a waste of time, she thought, and clicked through to their balance.

'What the...?'

The account was overdrawn. Seriously overdrawn. There must be some mistake. Had they been hacked?

Clicking on the statement and the news was worse. There had been a number of transfers out of the account to a company called IG. Stella didn't know an IG. She'd never done business with an IG. Over the previous two months there had been six transfers, all of them solid four-figure sums. There was no pattern.

She called Jake. Voicemail. 'Jake, have you seen our fucking account! We've been hacked. There's thousands gone. Everything in the account has gone! We need to contact the bank. Listen, call me back.'

Putting her phone aside, she stared at the statement trying to make sense of it. How do these people get away with this? Why hadn't the bank informed them? These massive transfers must have alerted someone? No wonder their Barclaycard hadn't been paid. Jesus. She considered moving some money from their savings account, but thought better of it. Only a fool would transfer more cash into an account that was being regularly pillaged.

The phone buzzed. Thank god, she thought, Jake.

But it wasn't, it was a text from Coco inviting her to lunch.

Why? Why did Coco want to have lunch with her? Was it simply a friend asking her over for a baguette and some mozzarella balls, or was it more than that? The whole thing was baffling. She really enjoyed Coco's company and the other night had been one of the best nights out in ages. She wanted more of that. What's more, her freed spirit (that or her guilt at the kiss), had improved things with Jake. She had made more of an effort. They had actually had sex twice in the last week, which would pretty much be a five-year record. Not wild and depraved fuck-me-till-I-scream sex, but good old, satisfying missionary. Neither of them really had the energy to do anything other than roll over, slip it in, gyrate a bit and push for the finish.

She needed to get a grip. Of course Coco just wanted to be her friend. Even if she was a bit lesbian, why on earth would she want some old bird whose vagina had been a portal for two 10 lb boys, when there were all those hard bodies like Renée and Stef? They were beautiful, liberated and enchanting women. So she texted back that she would love to have lunch. (She avoided a kiss, this time.)

Coco responded in a moment. **'Today? Come to the Van Nesses' at 1. The baby will be asleep and we can get some peace! 45 Willow Rd. Cx'**

Today? Why not? The Van Nesses were clearly away or there would be no 'peace'.

'See you then, Sx,' she texted.

It was only a 15-minute walk. The double-fronted Victorian house was immaculate. No broken tiles or mildewed paintwork on this house. She rang the doorbell and Coco was at the door, bounding down the steps, all teeth and flashing eyes. She was so energetic, like a puppy, as she helped get the pram into the house. Rory had fallen asleep on the way over so she just left him to sleep while they chatted.

'See? I promised. Peace!' said Coco. 'What a treat! Can I get you something to drink?'

'Just some water, thanks,' replied Stella, surprised that she was nervous. 'So how are you? Sorry I ran off the other night, I just suddenly realised how late it was, and to be honest, I was pissed!'

'Don't worry at all, I totally get it. I don't think I left until about two in the morning by the time we had all finished putting the world to rights! Did you enjoy yourself? Not too many girls for you?'

'I did! Your friends seem lovely, such a different bunch. I was intrigued – where were all the boys?'

Coco giggled. 'You're so funny! No boys allowed, Stella, that's the deal. We are all just women enjoying ourselves, chatting, relaxing, that is why it's so fun. It's a safe place. Everyone's safe to explore.'

'So, um, are you all, you know...'

'Gay?' responded Coco. 'No, everyone there is pretty fluid, we all enjoy being with other women, not always sexually. It's just about living a full life and making the most of everything that's, you know, on offer.' Coco gave her an encouraging smile, which terrified her. 'We don't need to label everything, do we? This is gay. This is straight. We know what we want to do and if it feels good, we do it again. Isn't that a pretty good rule for life? Why complicate it with labels, don't you think?'

Coco put some delicious-looking cheese on a plate and brought a salad to the table. It was medley of colours, deli-good.

Christ, does she cook like a goddess as well?

'I have had relationships with men, and with women. I just tend to prefer the relationships with women as they're less territorial, less controlling, and the chat's better, isn't it? Men can be so... uptight.'

'This food looks delicious, Coco,' Stella said, distracted 'Did you make this salad from scratch? I am impressed!'

'Ah, not just a pretty face,' teased Coco.

'Yes, anyway, sorry, I interrupted you, but it sounds like you have it pretty sorted, both men and women – that definitely gives you a lot more to choose from!'

'Well, it's not something I go out and boast about, it's just something that happens, that's all. I feel it's about the connection with someone special, about seeing what happens.'

After they had finished eating, Coco made them both a cup of tea and they moved to the sofa. As she sat down, Coco stopped behind her and started to rub Stella's shoulders.

'Soooo stressed, Stella,' said Coco.

Stella felt herself tense up at Coco's touch.

'Relax,' she soothed. 'I am pretty good at this. I have magic hands.'

Stella just tried to breathe, close her eyes, and enjoy the release. She was panicking.

Coco's fingers dug deeper now, really kneading her shoulders.

'Aaaah,' moaned Stella. 'You really do have magic hands, that feels great. I have been so stressed – the kids, my career, money, Jake.' The remembrance of the issue with the bank made her tense up again.

'You just need some time to yourself,' Coco remarked. 'Time to relax. Time to enjoy yourself without worrying about everyone else.'

And as she was talking, her hands started to move lower, towards Stella's breasts. Gently caressing them, sliding over the bra, roving over her nipples. Stella didn't move; it was thrilling. A heat swelled through her. Her heart thumped, and not only her heart.

I know I shouldn't be doing this, she thought, but I really don't want this to stop. A voice in her head was screaming: this is wrong – your youngest is asleep in his pram beside you. You are married! Her body was saying: but it's so nice, and what harm can it do, really... She let out another moan of pleasure, which Coco seemed to take as her cue to move things along. She slowly moved round to the sofa so that she was sitting astride Stella and without saying anything she gently pulled her face towards her and started kissing her. She really was kissing her. This was not her imagination. There was no ambiguity. It was so light and caring, nothing forceful about it, and it was in a weird way so different to kissing a man. The same urgency wasn't there. It was as if she knew how intimate it was, how special Stella was. Coco continued to caress her, and as if sensing Stella's hesitation, she took Stella's hand and guided it under her shirt. She wore no bra. Her breasts filled Stella's hand. The nipple was hard beneath her finger.

I don't know what do with a boob! Relax, she thought, I've touched my own breasts while masturbating, what do I like?

But it was so small, so firm, and the nipple was so erect. She just gently stroked it, and, as she did, felt Coco responding to her touch, and her confidence grew.

Stella was aware that she was now seriously aroused and thoughts began to churn, pulling her out of the moment. She knew she wasn't gay; she had never had any interest in women in her life, or ever felt that way about anyone female, so she was confused by how easy it was, and how her body was reacting. She found herself lying back on the sofa. Coco on top of her, kissing her, stroking her face, touching her breasts, reaching for her nipples and she was again lost for a moment.

Then without warning or thought, she was bolt upright, pushing Coco away. 'God, I'm sorry, Coco, I don't know what I'm doing. I am married. I'm straight. I really don't know what I am doing!'

'Hey now, calm down, it's fine. Although I have to say it seemed like you were enjoying yourself there, just for a minute,' giggled Coco. 'Maybe you are not as straight as you think!'

Stella was relieved that Coco seemed to be making light of the situation, but she wanted to run. This was more than she could deal with. It was a lunchtime and she was making out with the Van Nesses' nanny on their sofa in broad daylight.

'I had no idea what I was doing. I've never touched another boob in my life!' said Stella, hoping to sound light and jokey.

Coco laughed, and that was what Stella liked about her: she was so relaxed and happy. There was no judgement.

'I was enjoying it,' said Coco. 'Maybe you have a flair for this kind of thing after all!'

Their eyes met and Stella felt herself blush.

Rory was stirring, and Stella was grateful for the excuse to depart before things got any more... complicated.

'I'd better take him home, get ready for the school run – it's like groundhog day, isn't it, this merry-go-round of life!' she said, trying to sound natural, carefree, but aware it sounded inadequate after what had just happened.

'Thank you for lunch – a delicious salad. I might steal the recipe! Anyway, see you soon, I think, I hope, I don't know.'

As she opened the front door to leave, Coco followed and pushed it shut again. She kissed her on the lips and gently said, 'Live a little. There are no labels here. If we like it, we do it, no? No regrets, right?'

Then she opened the door for her, helped her down the steps, giving Rory another kiss on the lips (eeuw, thought Stella again) and waved her off.

There was something oddly familiar about disappearing from the scene of something illicit in broad daylight. Stella realised with a laugh that it was her first lesbian walk of shame.

Stella collected Tom from school and took them both for ice cream at McDonald's. It was an awful place, but Tom loved the swirly ice cream and Stella wanted to avoid the park. Tom was such a bright and observant kid that she didn't wish to encounter Coco again. He might pick up on something.

She called Jake again and was almost surprised when he picked up.

'Thank god, Jake. We've been hacked. There's literally tens of thousands gone from the account over the last month. Did you know?'

'Darling, would you relax. It's nothing, just a technical thing. I'll get it ironed out.'

'What do you mean a technical thing?'

'It's connected to the partner's contribution for the last six months. We've had some liquidity issues, short-term cash-flow inconsistencies. It's temporary. It'll all be back in the account in no time.'

'Jake, I have no idea what all that means. Who is IG? The payments are to a company called IG.'

'IG, oh that's nothing. It's... it's standard, the money is held in escrow for security. So it's safe. No one can touch it. Then it comes straight back to us as soon as the situation is resolved.'

'I don't understand. What situation?'

'As I said, it's a temporary cash-flow situation. Nothing to worry about. It's my fault really. Listen, Stella, I've got to go. I'm on a call in literally thirty seconds. I'll see you at home. I'll explain everything then.'

'What time will you be—'

But he'd gone and Stella was left standing in the middle of McDonald's with a giant vanilla shake in her hand. She didn't know what exactly or why, but she had a stomach-churning sense of impending doom. She buried herself in the whip, slurping at the sugary, stress-dissolving sweetness.

'Oh my god...'

'Mum!' screamed Tom. 'That's mine!'

Her mouth full with creamy goodness, she nodded, and tried to speak. 'I know. I know,' she mumbled. 'I'll get you another one. This. Is. Just. So. Good.'

CHAPTER THIRTEEN

Ana

Monday was now Ana's favourite day of the week: less sex with Rex and she got to wear yellow. Yellow was her colour. It highlighted her year-round tan (thank god for her Chilean ancestry). When her grandfather and father fled the Pinochet regime in 1974 (her grandmother was a journalist, but she never made the journey), they brought no legacy from their abandoned homeland, just a desire to live in peace and prosperity, with that resourceful entrepreneurialism that defines migrants – and a genetic bronzer. Yellow made her eyes shine bright 'like a lioness,' her grandfather used to say. Her father believed he'd died from the thought of never being able to return to Chile, but he'd survived long enough in the UK to become a defining influence on Ana. He loved art and his childcare consisted of hours spent in the museums and galleries. He would spend hours explaining the background to the tragedies; Goya was always his favourite. When he died, he left all his paintings to his 8-year-old granddaughter. Yellow made her skin glow. Yellow made her happy.

So she bounced into work with relief, confident in the

mustard yellow jacket she'd chosen to wear over a simple, sleeveless, sunflower yellow Karen Millen with yellow Adidas pumps.

'Someone's looking ready for the week,' said Jan, her smile welcoming. 'Wait a minute... you're not... are you? Is it—'

With that, Ana's face collapsed in tears. She scuttled behind the reception desk and into Jan's maternal embrace. Jan consoled her, stroked her hair. 'There, there. I'm sorry. You just looked so happy...'

'It's just I was so happy not to have to see Rex for a few hours. I'm so tired of this. We both are. We can't stand the sight of each other.'

'There, there.'

'Oh Jan, the hours I've spent trying to coax that flaccid little prick into life. I'm sick of the sight of it. I'm sick of him. The whole thing is just dreadful.' She looked up at Jan. 'They're so pathetic when they're soft. Honestly, it's like an... an oyster. It can't do anything. It just hangs there.'

And she mimed with her hand hanging and her face unhappy and they both laughed.

'Poor Rex,' said Jan with compassion, then struggled not to laugh, and failed, so resorted to clamping her hand over her mouth.

'I know, I know,' said Ana. 'For years we had sex, good sex, pretty good sex, but now. Honestly the last six weeks... OK, we started well. It was fun having organised, diarised sex. We really got to experience some new places. We did it on a Virgin train one weekend. In those big cubicles, it was terrifying. Lots of hotel restrooms. A pub. A Starbucks. We did it on a night bus. At first it was fun. We were experimenting. We were trying to create a new life, our own little baby. After the cat left, I was so excited about a new life. But then it became, I don't know, a chore. In the end it was formulaic. I haven't had an orgasm in weeks. It's not normal. I'm losing my mind. I just want to go upstairs and stay at work for the rest of my life. Last night we did it in a public toilet in Sloane Square. We were at the theatre. It was the only place we could find. It was disgusting.'

They collapsed giggling again.

'Maybe you need to go back to the gynaecologist? You know... get things checked again. Get some advice. There are options.'

Ana pulled herself together.

'Yes, it's the options that terrify me.' She realised then that she hadn't thought about Joel since she'd seen his photo on the side of the 19 bus to Piccadilly on her way to work.

Ana was late home from the office. Worse than that, she'd 'forgotten' they were scheduled for a 7.15 p.m. fornication. This was the day of her peak fertility. Now she was rolling her tired and bored tongue around the lifeless remnants of Rex's penis. Basically it was little more than an extended foreskin. Anything resembling a vertebra, a muscle, had wasted or withdrawn into his body. Cupping him encouragingly, Ana even surmised that his balls had diminished significantly. Were they drained dry? Had she been to the well too often and the well had run dry?

'Stop! Stop! Ana, please. This is... I don't know. This is humiliating. I just can't do it any more. Really.'

She stood, wiping her mouth dry with the back of her arm. She felt like she towered over him and she didn't like it. His blue eyes were rimmed with tears and he scrabbled to cover himself. Her heart burst with regret and sympathy. She threw her arms around him, held him close.

'I'm so sorry, Rex. It's not supposed to be this hard.' She regretted her word choice immediately. 'I mean there are options. We can't go on like this. We're getting nowhere.' She was aware that Rex was struggling and it seemed that whatever she said was open to an uncharitable interpretation.

'Not now, Ana. Maybe later.'

He wouldn't meet her eyes. She shook him. 'Rex, please. Let's forget this. We've tried this. We need to explore other options.'

Jan had been such a solace throughout the day. She and her husband had struggled with fertility and ultimately failed, so Jan had a first-hand and informed perspective. Male pride is a fragile edifice. Traditional social expectations about manhood and providing an heir pervaded TV and film. Henry VIII towered over them all as a cultural role model for all those who succeeded him.

'How many women had to die,' laughed Jan, 'just because he'd been short-seeded?'

'But Rex is a kind man,' retorted Ana.

'Then if he really cares about you, he'll see a specialist. You've been assuming you're the problem, but he's 45 years old. He owes it to you.'

Beyond assessing Rex's fertility, there were options (not Joel,

Ana had to remind herself): IVF, surrogacy, adoption, fostering. If someone really wants a child to love unconditionally, then modern science and social supports were all there.

Later, Rex agreed reluctantly to arrange a sperm assessment at a private clinic. Perhaps Ana shouldn't have pulled out the leaflet she'd downloaded from Mumsnet. Rex's look as he took it told her that he knew she'd had this in her bag while she'd been blowing his burst balloon. He was hurt. He looked cowed by the whole process. Cowed when what he needed was a bit more bull, thought Ana, successfully, this time thinking without speaking. Some progress, she thought.

The leaflet provided information on the process, extolled the hygienic and comfortable environment. A private space where time is not an issue, with relevant, quality materials to support the production of a sample.

Rex's eyes rolled as he scanned down the featureless blue cartoon of a nondescript male in a jacket with a sample pot, disappearing into a cubicle with an array of magazines on a low table, a TV and a comfortable chair.

'I have to go into one of these rooms and jizz in a cup. How does that even work? My penis when it's ready... well, it fires upwards, not down into a cup? What do I do, try to catch it before it lands in my hair?'

Because he was trying to smile, Ana tried a joke, 'That's hardly likely, now, is it?'

Rex didn't laugh.

'Can you come and help?'

No! was her first thought, and now, after this flaccid fiasco?

'You'll be fine. They're all so nice. Dr du Toit is very gentle.'

'I am not discussing this with some testosterone-fuelled South African, however soft his hands are.'

'I'm sure the nurse will be able to sort you out.'

She couldn't help laughing. Rex smiled for the first time that evening.

'Is she beautiful? Is she as beautiful as you?'

Ana nearly cried at his earnestness, and felt terribly guilty about Joel's frequent intrusions into her thoughts.

In the end she'd agreed to go with him. For moral support and to try to provide some romantic decorations for what amounted, as Rex put it, as she stroked his inner thigh in the taxi en route, to 'wanking in a cup to prove your virility'.

'What if I can't?'

'Does this help?' she said, as her fingernails scratched over his crotch. He fidgeted, looked out of the window into some middle distance. He was flushed, beads of sweat had formed on his cleanly shaven lip. He smelled strongly of a citrusy aftershave. It was not, she thought, her favourite.

As she waved him off down the corridor, led by a pear-shaped nurse with an elaborate bun, it flashed through her mind that this was how it might feel to wave a child off on their first day at school. She was relieved when he disappeared and the nurse returned, giving her an understanding and reassuring half smile. Relaxing, she pulled a magazine from the table and sat back. It was *GQ* and she only realised why she'd picked it up when she found herself scanning the table of contents: Country Star Steams The Charts. It was a double fold. It was a feature. It was Joel. Topless on a beach somewhere on the Atlantic coast. Jeans with a fat silver buckle, the guitar with the same shoulder strap he'd had back then. His hair was shorter, still touching his shoulders and he hadn't shaved in a couple of days. She could almost smell the salt and minerals and feel that coarse strip of hair that ran from his—

'Excuse me, madam.' It was the nurse with the bun. 'There seems to be a problem. Could you help?'

She felt a little weak. 'Yes, of course.'

'Mr Johnson has been in the donation room for fifteen minutes. I've tapped on the door, but there's no reply.'

Just then her phone pinged in her yellow imitation Chanel bag (purchased in Manhattan from a street vendor in Soho. Stella still thought it was genuine).

'OK, I'll come.'

Ana tapped gently on the door, her ear close as if she strained to hear.

'Yes! Yes! Yes!' It was louder than she'd expected.

She rapped twice.

Nothing.

She rapped again and called, 'Rex!'

Her phone sounded again. Impatiently she checked the message. It was from Rex. There were three. They were increasingly excited.

'I can't. It's not... x'

'Can you help me, please? I can't get a pulse. X'

'Get me out of here! NOW! X'

She knocked again. 'Rex, it's me! I have to go. We have to go. There's somewhere I need to be.'

The noises from within ceased. There was a shuffling and Rex's flushed face appeared in a crack. The door opened and Ana could see that the tail of his shirt was poking from his fly. Ironically it looked like a long blue penis. If only.

On the TV screen was the frozen face of a Japanese school-girl being ridden from behind by a long-haired muscleman in a lumberjack shirt.

She pulled him out of the room by the hand.

'Let's get out of here. This can all be sorted another time!'

Rex handed the empty cup to the nurse who looked at it sceptically and they left.

They didn't speak or touch in the taxi on the way home. It was only then that Ana discovered that in the rush, she'd slipped the GQ into her bag. Guiltily, she placed her hand on Rex's knee, patted him.

'Apparently we can do it at home if we go private. It'll cost a bit more, but we can't let this little setback derail us. Can we?'

Rex nodded. Ana didn't think she'd ever seen him look so sad. She leaned over and rested her head on his shoulder and caressed his stomach reassuringly.

'We'll get through this, Rex, and when we do we'll have our own little baby and this will all be very funny.'

Rex kissed the top of her head. She didn't believe he was convinced.

The private sperm count option was expensive, but with a team effort, Rex had safely deposited a reasonably healthy 30 ml of semen into a sample jar. Ana had, as they'd negotiated, delivered the labelled jar and its congealing contents to the nurse herself. Ana was also amused, she'd worn a nurse outfit, and they'd role-played to support the extraction.

'We'll have the results in forty-eight hours. You might want to make an appointment if you want the news together; otherwise we'll call Mr Johnson and inform him. We recommend a joint appointment if you wish to take things forward.'

'You sound like you know what we should expect,' said Ana, nodding at the jar.

The nurse smiled again, shook her head.

'No, dear, but you wouldn't be here if everything was going to be easy, would you?'

Ana made the appointment for them. A Friday evening appointment to be sure that Rex would be available. She opted not to mention the nurse's comments. There was no need to stress Rex further.

On Friday, they met in a wine bar opposite the clinic. Ana was early. She sat at a table in the window, twizzling a small glass of red wine. She was wearing red and was conscious of the stares of a group of rowdy estate agent types at the bar. She blanked out their comments, hoping that by ignoring them, she'd be left in peace.

She watched Rex approach. He'd taken off his jacket, draped it over one shoulder. He'd lost weight, she thought. He looked down. Poor Rex, she thought. He didn't deserve this. And she suspected it wasn't going to get any easier.

He spotted her and smiled, bravely.

'Another one?' he said.

'I better not. You have one.'

Rex had to push between the estate agents to find space at the bar.

'Steady on, old chap. Mind your elbows.'

Rex mumbled something and disappeared amongst them. Ana drifted off, staring into the glass.

'Sorry, pal. Did I spill your Babycham? Bloody sorry. Let me get you another one. Barkeep, another Babycham for the old boy here.'

Rex mumbled something and made his way back to her. Ana could see that he'd spilled some of his half pint of cider down his shirt.

'What idiots,' said Ana.

'They're just kids.'

'We should say something.' Ana looked over towards the bar. One of them caught her eye.

'Bloody hell, the old man's with the hottie in red.'

'Must be his PA.'

A rage grew in Ana like a forest fire. She was on the point of combustion, when Rex's hand on her forearm brought her back from the edge.

'It's OK, Ana. We don't need to react. We mustn't stoop to their level.'

'The... the... arrogance. How *dare* they?'

Rex smiled ruefully. 'They don't matter. We've more important things to deal with, no? Anyway, cheers. Here's to good news.'

Ana tried to hide the sadness in her eyes, for his sake. Poor kind, generous Rex, she thought.

They didn't have to wait long in the minimalist surgery. Ana had brought back the *GQ* she'd unwittingly stolen. She returned it to the pile on the table.

'What's that?' asked Rex.

'I picked it up by mistake. I felt bad about it.'

'You are so sweet,' said Rex, and kissed her on the temple as he reached for the magazine. As Ana feared, it flipped open to the Joel Abelard feature. She froze her features, not wanting to give anything away.

'Who's this little prima donna?' scoffed Rex. 'This country singer looks like a stripper. It's funny really. It's a long drop from Johnny Cash to this Joel-thing. The man in black vs this long-haired, topless human.'

Ana stared at Rex in disbelief. Is this what he thought? Or did he know something? How could he? Only Dixie and Stella knew the truth and they'd never say anything. Nevertheless she was relieved when they were then called into the gynaecologist's office.

It was worse than she'd imagined and when they left they were in a daze. They were silent until the car was halfway back to Battersea, gridlocked in Friday night traffic at Sloane Square.

'I'm sorry, Ana. Life's funny, isn't it? We have all these dreams and plans and then reality gives you a kick in the— Well, let's just say, I didn't expect to be having to deal with all this. I really didn't. Are you OK?'

Ana couldn't speak. Rex's decency just made it all the worse.

She patted his knee awkwardly. 'I'm fine, Rex. I'm fine. Just sad. Let's talk about this later.'

The cab had a TV between the flip-down seats. A advert for a subtle caffeine-derived hair-loss treatment ended and a music video began.

'Oh god, it's that Joel thing.'

Before Ana knew what was happening she was sobbing aloud.

'Bloody hell, Ana. It's not that bad,' laughed Rex, and Ana couldn't help joining in. 'I'll get him to turn it down, shall I?'

Ana nodded, laughing and crying and threw her arms around Rex's neck.

'I'm so sorry, Rex.'

'I know. I know. It's all going to work out. Somehow.'

'You promise?' she asked his neck, burying herself in his citrusy decency.

'I do.'

CHAPTER FOURTEEN

Dixie

Six minutes late, and Freddie was waiting.

'How long have you been there?'

He didn't look at his watch. 'Six minutes.'

'You're a saint. You know I'm never going to be on time, don't you?'

'And I will never be late.'

'Why here? You know that preppy chinos and washed-out pastels don't go with any of this.' She indicated the electric green bustier that pressed her breasts up at him.

'You look fantastic. Your hair is so red. It's on fire. And those eyes. Blue as a glacier... everything. You're like a Kandinsky.'

Freddie had asked her to meet him on the corner of Fifth Ave and West 54th. It was a GAP.

'I wanted to surprise you.'

It was a warm summer evening and New York was starting to get hot. Freddie was wearing just a pale blue shirt and, his sleeves rolled up, he pulled her to him as they walked, his bare forearm sliding against her breast.

For the last month and a half, Dixie had been in New York

for at least two or three days every couple of weeks. Peter had only made brief comments, asking if this had anything to do with the young man she was 'consorting' with at Evgeny Mobachov's party. Dixie had laughed it off, telling him that if he wanted to ground her in London and see what carnage was unleashed, he was more than welcome. 'No, no,' he'd laughed. 'As long as you do your job and keep your promises, there'll always be a place for you here. I trust you. We are family. We look after each other.'

Of course she'd had to lie to the girls or she'd never hear the end of it. Ana had a nose for romance, and Stella never let a juicy story stay hidden for long. Besides, she didn't want to jinx it by talking about it and couldn't talk about it because it involved 'feelings', and 'feelings' were not something that Dixie generally dealt with, unless 'fun' was a feeling or 'fucking' was a feeling. Everything was new and it was a surprise to Dixie to note that since that fortuitous flight to JFK, she'd not touched a class A.

Halfway down the block, the space opened up and Dixie saw they were outside MOMA. The exhibition was Kandinsky's *Window On The Abstract*.

Dixie groaned.

'So why have you brought me to see this ridiculous rubbish when you must know how much I hate modern art, Freddie?'

'Because I think it's good for you. It's far too easy for us all to get stuck in our ways, and maybe this will inspire your illustrations.'

Lovely Freddie, always so caring, she thought, even though daubing a wall with a few colour and lines and labelling it *The*

Impossible Entrance to The Non-Existent, or *Two Cats and A Dog*, and calling it art was far from inspirational. What he didn't know was that since meeting him, when they weren't together, she was at home drawing her heart out. It was as if she wanted to be her best self to justify having a man as lovely as him.

'Thanks, Fred,' and she leaned over and gave him a kiss. 'Let's give it a go!'

Standing before *The Cow*, Freddie asked, 'So what does that say to you?'

'Three Fried Eggs sunny side up.'

'That's good and also true.'

Dixie got increasingly agitated and Freddie laughed at her discomfort.

'Why, Dix, does everything have to be taken literally? Why can't we deconstruct things to represent a new way of seeing them. If all art had to be literal and realist, how barren the imagination would be. There's a place for realism and there's a place for symbolism and imagination. Neither owns the truth. There is no truth.'

'Freddie, if you want to date a philosopher, I suggest you don't pick up girls on planes. I'm a PA/illustrator, not an artist. There is room for all of us, but I don't have time for them. Maybe when I'm old and infirm, but right now I'm hot and young-ish and this, all this abstract just feels like a waste of time. I like things to look like what they are. I like things I can hold in my hand.' She grabbed him. 'And say, this is a penis. Do I have your attention now? I have never understood the likes of Tracey Emin. To me, it's just not art. I could find a loo, put it in the middle of the room with some books around it, make up some bullshit story and call it Capitalism, but that's not what I do. I try to tell a story with pictures. I know anything can be art, but it's not my art, and I really don't want to waste my time looking at it. Can we go now? PLEASE? It just fucks me off. Sorry,' she laughed. 'I have no idea why I'm so angry.'

'You are tempestuous,' he laughed. 'That fiery red hair doesn't lie! Lucky Tracey's not here to hear your thoughts! Maybe it'll grow on you. It amuses me to challenge you. Look how upset you get. It's very sexy.'

'You brought me here knowing it would fire my temper because you find it sexy? What kind of sick bastard are you?'

He pulled her closer. 'You know how fucking sexy I think you are, and if it wouldn't get me arrested I would throw you up against that wall, in front of all these people, and screw your brains out.'

'Hmm, call it performance art and you might get away with it,' she snorted. 'But that's the kind of art I might be able to tolerate.'

'Come on, let's get out of here.'

'Where are we going?' she asked.

'How about we go to mine and sit on the terrace and have a glass of wine – fancy that?'

'You have a terrace?'

'Overlooking Central Park.'

'Sounds divine, yes, please,' and she left it at that, not wanting to comment on why he had finally decided to let her see his home. She was fascinated. She had wondered many times what kind of pad he had, what he might be hiding, and if she would be able to feel the presence of his dead wife. Had they lived together there? Had he brought other women back since? Because he'd never even suggested his place (they'd always returned to her hotel), she'd just assumed his home was sacred, maybe a shrine, or perhaps he was just a filthy bachelor who lived in squalor.

Just past Columbus Circle, the doorman welcomed them into The Tower. They took the lift to the penultimate floor.

'Not the top floor? You disappoint me, Mr Eastman.'

'The top floor is still owned by the developer. He's a former slum landlord from Queen's. Ivan Kashlow. He was convicted of incest. Get this, with his daughter, Donna. That's why they had to change the name. It was formerly Donna's Tower. New York, the best of the best and the worst of the worst. They say she's still in there, a recluse, spends all her time buying online tat. Everything is gold, they say. Quiet neighbour though, so that's the important thing.'

He opened the door to a spacious, open-plan apartment with views over the park.

'Here we are,' he said. 'This is what I call home.'

'O-M-Gee,' exclaimed Dixie, her hands over her mouth. 'This is... The views are amazing.'

'That's why we bought it,' he said. 'I knew I wanted a view, and I didn't want a house with a garden. I don't have kids, and a garden seems to me like it's just a waste of time. Besides this is Manhattan, not Battersea. This was the perfect compromise.'

Dixie looked around. Enormous glass windows with

far-reaching views across the greenery to brownstones doubled as sliding doors. It was more masculine in feel than she'd
expected, which made her think that a lot of his wife's stuff had
been removed. There were a few girly touches around, loads of
cushions on the sofas, and everyone knows the only people who
buy mountains of cushions are girls! But the style was sterile,
quite corporate. There were no photos and that both pleased
and intrigued her.

'So,' he said as he handed her a glass of chilled white wine
and led her through the doors onto a terrace with a large rattan
sofa and two armchairs, an electric barbecue and a large parasol.

'This is the perfect place to entertain. Oh my god, Stells and
Ana would go mad for this. Chardonnay on the terrace over
Central Park. Can we?' She waved the phone.

'Sure. Here, let me.'

'No, I mean the two of us, with this once-in-a-lifetime
backdrop.'

'No, just let me take one of you.'

There was a little wrestle over her phone, but Dixie could
feel he was not going to concede and let it go.

'That is a great photo,' she said examining his work. 'Seriously
the only thing that could improve it is you.'

'I'm not really at the couple-y social media selfie stage.
Perhaps it's my advanced age.'

'Just for the girls?' she tried, convinced that some firm charm
would bring him around.

'Another time,' he said dismissively, surprising her. 'So how
are the girls? What's the latest gossip?'

'I don't think we're really at the sharing secrets stage yet,' said Dixie coquettishly, as she curled up on one of the outdoor sofas.

'Touché!' He toasted her. 'Everyone knows the true measure of a woman is her friends. No man is a woman's soul mate, that's her closest friends.'

Dixie smiled and nodded.

'Wow, Fred, that might be the smartest thing any man has said to me. I've never thought about it that way. You might be right... so far.'

'I know I am right – men come and go, but women are always there. I mean you might be a complicated species, but you are loyal and when push comes to shove, you are always there for each other. Women need one another; men can often take it or leave it.'

'So who are your best friends then?' asked Dixie. 'Is there anyone I should meet?'

'Not really. I have a brother, Charlie. He is a legend and has been there for me through everything. He is married with two kids so leads a pretty different life to me. We only get time for the occasional pint. Weddings. Funerals... We both love to motorbike, so when we have the time, that's what we always do.'

'You're a biker?' asked Dixie, although to be honest she really wasn't that surprised. It suited his personality, or what she knew thus far.

'Yup, my only vice. I even buy the magazines and pile them up. It's therapeutic, and I think the thing I love about it the most is that it completely clears your head. You are so caught up in staying alive that you don't have time to think about anything else!' Yes, issues of independence and control, she thought ruefully.

Freddie refilled their glasses and brought out a light blanket for her.

'So come on, there must be some gossip from home on the girls?'

'Ana's on a back-breaking sex marathon with a man firing blanks, while obsessing over some ex. Stella is angry and mean and she'll be absolutely fine. She's the strongest of us all.'

'Stronger than you?'

'Nothing shakes Stella. She wants something. She goes for it. She gets it. No prisoners. No procrastination. If she wasn't my best friend, I'd be terrified of her.'

'So, is Ana gonna cheat?'

'Huh?'

'With the ex?'

'God knows! Ana's a kind of weird sex nun. Well, mostly. A sex-mad nun. She has sex more often than nuns pray, but she's a rule-based monogamist. Stella's more likely to go wild than Ana. She used to be a high-flying fashion editor and now she spends her days making dinner for an absent husband, and single-handedly raising two kids. Besides, Ana's ex is Joel Abelard.'

Freddie looked blank.

She tried to sing a few lines from 'Brown eyed girl'.

'Sorry, nothing.'

'Check him out. It's better than it sounds, I promise.'

'And what's happened to Stella's husband?'

'Oh god, nothing like that, no, he's a partner in a law firm. They've been together for nearly twenty years. Things just, you know, lose their magic.'

'It's not magic, it's oxytocin. It's a hormone. The love hormone. A temporary chemical bond. It gets us together and then we have to find a why or how to stay together.'

She laughed. 'Yes, Professor Scientist.'

'Have you ever wanted kids?' he asked.

She was taken aback, so her first answer was, as always, 'No. Never,' but now she found herself smiling into Freddie's eyes and continuing, 'I don't think I have ever met the right person.' Seeing a shadow cross his eyes, she stumbled on, 'But right now I have made peace with the fact I will probably never be a mother.'

The shadow was gone. 'Well, never say never, Dixie, you never know what the future holds.'

'No, I do know I am nearly 40 and my eggs are nearly all fried! How about you? Ever seen yourself as a dad? Someone to pass those cynical professor genes on to?'

'I don't know. I mean I guess I thought I would have kids, but since... I haven't really thought about it. It's been more about survival than anything else, but now I have seen how fragile life is, I suppose it scares me even more.'

'Wow, we seem to be getting very serious,' said Dixie as she curled her legs up under her.

'You're right, enough talking.'

He undressed her on the sofa. They battled for control, for the right to give pleasure. She held him down and took him in her mouth, determined to have the last word. He fought back, whipped her beneath him and they came together.

'Now that was a fair fight with a joyous ending,' laughed Dixie, lifting her glass to him.

'This is one of my favourite things, lying under the stars, fully satisfied.'

Dixie chose to ignore the implication, she was too sated. She curled up under his arm, allowing herself to feel his warmth, and wondering what happened now. Was he going to ask her to leave? Or was he going to let her sleep there? Hopefully not outside on the freezing sofa – but in her desire to be near him, she refused to tell him she was feeling the cold, so she just snuggled in, trying to stop her body from shaking. Of course, she was also thinking what an amazing Instagram moment this would be... Them, the sofa, wine in hand, the brightly lit interior, the location. But that wasn't an option.

'There was, of course, no window,' she mumbled.

'What?'

'The exhibition. *Window On The Abstract.* Not a single window.'

He kissed the top of her head. 'Really, are you sure? Wasn't MOMA one big window? Aren't we all windows opening onto our own worlds?'

CHAPTER FIFTEEN

Stella

Stella had decided that an Uber was the appropriate transport to her first interview in over ten years. Sweating was an issue. She had to avoid sweating, but, sitting in the car, the foremost issue was old-fashioned panic. Her phone told her she was four minutes from Redchurch St. Her last trip to Shoreditch had ended in her first lesbian kiss. She was trying to block that from her mind, but in her heightened condition, this stimulated a sweat. She flapped her elbows like a chicken to try to cool herself. Breathe, she said to herself, breathe, and realised that she was holding her breath. Again.

The interview was for editor of a web portal in the health and wellbeing 'space'. They were looking for a 'thought leader', 'innovative editor', 'connected style creator' for a health–lifestyle–fashion web base for the modern professional, metro woman. Stella read 'modern' as 'young'. She knew this was a leap from her former roles in paper-based media, but her conversations with Coco, Stef and Renée told her that this was the future and knowing that she was presently the past, any success in this area would bring her right to the centre of the market. There was no doubt this was a major step down from Editor at *Candy* mag, Contributing Editor at *Spring*, and Features Editor of a major weekend supplement. The pay was a fraction of her 2008 salary, but this was about building a future, not reliving the past. Fully aware of the gaps in her knowledge, she'd found a copy of *Dummies Guide To Social Media* in WHSmiths, she'd done a search of #health #wellbeing on Twitter and Instagram and spent more than her usual quantity of time scanning dailymail. com for stories and personalities in 'the space'. The idea of an entirely digital, continuously changing online lifestyle magazine terrified her, but she knew that a good publication comes from gathering the right people and delegating effectively. She might be a bit behind on the dietary ins-and-outs of Lena Dunham and Taylor Swift, but she knew how to pull together a focused publication. At least, that was what she told herself between hot flushes.

The Prius whispered to a halt outside 9 Redchurch, one of those glass-fronted, converted warehouse buildings.

She sat and stared, waiting for the driver to tell her the fare and then panicked as she remembered that all that was taken care of by the credit card. (At least she hoped so. Jake had promised there'd be no more issues!)

She strode towards the doors and when they failed to open, she froze. The interior was how Stella imagined a modern youth club in the style of Cliff Richard's *Summer Holiday*. Long wooden tables, an indoor coffee cart, swathes and blobs of primary colours resembling a nursery. Her clothing choice for the day was off, she now realised, way off. She'd had the usual clothing crisis, whipping through and discarding piles of clothes dismissing them with exasperation: too Nineties, too small, too floral, too many wine stains, not mine, too Eighties, too matronly, too mutton, too long, too short. She was left with a silk dress that covered her knees, which was a relief as on a bad day they looked like two little faces. It was a little too tight around the chest, but with a pair of heels she felt a little less round and a little more 'sexy, fearless dominatrix'.

Someone pushed past her impatiently and she noted that the doors were opened by a big red button on a pillar. She looked at it wistfully, wishing that it fired an ejector seat. Movement was still impossible.

She'd been shocked when they'd invited her in for an interview. The application had been 99 per cent speculative, but their brand name had made her smile: Slop! If anything, it told her they had a sense of humour. Frozen in front of the sealed doors, she now seriously doubted her decision. She'd been specifically conscious that there would be many nerdy millennials, drinking cat-shit coffee and raving about colon cleanses and gender issues, but she still wasn't ready for the freak show that confronted her. Kids, beardy weird kids with top knots and dungarees, wearing Doc Martens and Oxfam rejects. Teenagers playing pool and darts, lounging on electric pink sofas (want one, thought Stella). This was an alien environment. Stella had never seen anything like this. Her first job had been as an assistant on a tabloid fashion section. Her interview had been in the Coach & Horses on Brewer St and she couldn't remember how it ended. Feeling the panic rising and knowing that if she didn't go in now, she might never, she smacked her hand down on the red ejector button and strode directly to the reception desk.

'Excuse me. Loos?'

'Loos?'

'Yes. I'm here for an interview, but I need to use the loo.'

'Ah; OK. The restrooms are behind you. Can I take a name?'

'Stella Hammerson. Here for Slop!'

Locked in the cubicle, she began an emergency restyling drill. Generally this would have taken place in front of the flattering 10' x 8' mirror with soft lighting, but she could not risk anyone witnessing this fashion triage. The heels were gone, replaced by the battered silver Adidas she'd carried in preparation for the dispirited journey home. She did up the buttons at the front of her dress to obscure her cleavage (WTF!) and she found an old muslin scarf in purples and pinks at the bottom of her bag and used this to hold back the hair that she back-combed and fluffed for curated casualness. She even found a pair of old 45 denier tights to cover her legs. They seemed intact, just a few lacerations in the crotch area. Best not to linger on that, she thought. She exited the cubicle with a guilty and pointless flush. She knew that millennials were triggered by environmental issues, but needs-must when you found yourself in a youth club in Shoreditch, and you were dressed for an awards ceremony at The Savoy.

Shabby chic, she thought, as she messed her hair a little more. Like a Border Collie. Good. And wiped away the lustrous watermelon lipstick she'd chosen to go with the fruity dress. Antique chic, the annoyed face in the mirror mouthed at her.

The receptionist pointed her to one of the low pink sofas and announced, 'Someone will be right down.'

She settled to pick some of the shellac from her nails. She doubted very much that girls in dungarees with red striped socks and Doc Martens, hair hidden by a hairnet, spent their monthly salary on a good shellac-ing.

'Stella? Is that how you say it? Stella?'

A tall blade of a boy with curly blond hair piled on top of his head, like Big Bird, and a mini-Björk in double denim, a neon crop top and sand-brown brogues, were both holding out their hands at the end of ruler-straight arms.

'I'm Gabriel. I'm Project Impressario.'

'I'm Pippi. I'm Thought Leader and Inclusion Enabler.'

'We're both Sloppy!' they chorused.

Stella was surprised to find herself giggling with them.

She followed them past the pool table ('this is the recreation zone', indicated Pippi), and through a kind of playpen of young-looking people all lounging around the place looking at phones and laptops, wearing headphones, one was singing 'A Total Eclipse of The Heart'. ('This is the creative "non-area". There are no boundaries to creativity so we didn't want to call it an area. Areas are so limiting.')

'Great tune,' said Stella. 'Can't go wrong with a bit of Bonnie.'

'Bonnie?' asked Pippi.

'Bonnie Tyler.'

'I don't know her. Is she a designer?'

'No. Yes. Kind of.' Oh dear, thought Stella. Beware cultural references from the Eighties.

As she was taken through to the pod at the end of the big long room, they collapsed into a circle of blue and green bean bags. Stella stood there, wondering what the hell to do.

'Where, er, do you want me?'

'Take the weight off. We're all cool.'

Sit? On one of those? How will I ever get up again? She had an awful flashback to her last Pilates class when she was carried out on a stretcher, her back in spasm.

'Cool,' she smiled, and as casually as she could, lowered herself onto the edge of the nearest beanbag. The beads started to shift gradually beneath her like a landslide and she found her dress was caught at a bad angle and the silk fabric was stretching. Extreme forces were building across her chest and buttocks and the fabric was riding up as her legs fell open. She was relieved to be wearing the 45 deniers, but was now concerned, as she collapsed, that the gusset was under an unexpectedly heavy load. Those lacerations could easily give way and the flood gates would open. She was sweating again, and she could think about nothing apart from the sweat, and, should she slide another inch, her imminent wardrobe failure.

'Soooooo,' was the first word from the languid Gabriel, 'we loved your CV. Interesting background. Unlike any of the other applicants. Tell us a bit about what you have been up to recently... we see you haven't done anything for a few years.'

'Oh hi, OK. Yes, well, great to meet you,' said Stella, with a big grin, trying to conceal her absolute certainty that this was a total fail and wondering how quickly she could escape. 'So I have actually taken a few years out to have children and...'

'Respect,' interrupted Gabriel.

'Yes. Respect. Where would we be without mothers,' added Pippi.

'Indeed. Yes, I guess you could say that,' smiled Stella, 'but now I am keen to get back into the workplace.'

'Your experience is primarily in print. Commercial, mass-market print journalism. Do you have a lot of experience in social media?'

'Everything we do now is digital. Is that an area where you excel?' followed Pippi, the elfin, miniature human.

'Oh god, yes, totally,' exclaimed Stella a little overenthusiastically. 'Like I am massive fan of veeeeee-logging. I've been working on a pro bono basis with a couple of travel veeee-loggers.'

'Veeeeee-logging?' asked Gabriel.

'Yes, you know, when you blog on video rather than just writing it? Am I saying it right? Do you call it something different?'

'Ah ha, vlogging... but yes, it is certainly an important channel now. Who are your favourite vloggers? Who were you working with?'

'Renée and Stef. They're...' No, Stella. Don't say lesbians. Don't. 'Exploring the travel sphere from a uniquely feminine perspective.'

The sweat patches under her arms were so big she hardly dared move. She was claustrophobic and could barely breathe. Her chest was palpitating.

'What's their insta handle?' asked Pippi, taking notes on an iPad with a pencil.

'Oh, two girls, one cup— Oh god! Sorry, that just came out. I didn't...' Gabriel and Pippi (what an apt name, thought Stella, before pulling herself together) were stone-faced. 'Two Girls, One Trip. That's what it's called. I helped them with reader segmentation, content development and reader lock-in. I think you call it stickiness now. Euw. It's one of those words, isn't it? Like moist.'

They were stone-faced.

'They have 83,000 followers on Instagram.'

Oh god, thought Stella, seeing Pee-Pee – (No!) Pippi – jotting down details. I hope they don't look at it and think I'm a lesbian. Actually, maybe that would be suitably metrosexual, now: hip, modern, fluid. Maybe that would earn her some kudos.

'Also, I've worked a lot with Trinny Woodall. She's hilarious. People like that are SO easy for me to get in touch with. She's very close to the healthy eating space, isn't she?'

'Well,' said Gabriel. 'Our main focus is health and wellbeing. Fashion is relevant, but we see diet and exercise as part of fashion. Take your dress. That's a vintage Westwood, isn't it? It looks fabulous on you. You're the perfect frame for that cut.'

'Keep talking,' said Stella, fighting back the urge to wink.

'The body within the dress is part of the look. They can't be separated. We're selling and servicing the whole look. Inside and outside. Is that a concept that fires your imagination?'

'Yes. You can a sculpt a look around a thin blade like you or a rubber ball like me. But you've got to get the styling right. AmIrite?'

'But this Tiny Wood,' said Pippi. 'I don't know her. Is she an omnivore? We need an omnivore. We're looking at a special on omnivores.'

'I will literally eat anything.'

'We need a face of omnivorism. How would you sell omnivorism? Or try this: a client's looking to sell a new lentil-based crisp to omnivores. What would you suggest for something like that?'

Shit, thought Stella. I have only bought one packet of lentils. They were French for a stew. Poo lentils. Think, she thought, think – who would possibly be interesting and interested in launching some rarely edible legumes?

They were waiting. She had nothing. She could say she needed the loo, but that would mean trying to get out of the bean bag, and that was something she really didn't need to do twice.

Then it came like a gift from the gods of journalism.

'There's this guy from a boy band. Although I think he spends most of his time on his organic fish farm now.'

Stella knew him. At least she thought she did, she just couldn't remember his name. She'd taken Dixie to the Brit Awards one year as her plus one and she'd blown him in the disabled toilets. At least she thought it was him. It might have been an actual fisherman. Actually, it might have been anyone.

Pippi spoke first. 'There is something kind of retro and interesting about that, Stella. I like the way you are thinking. It's got a bit of edge bringing a member of a boy band back into the public eye... most people wouldn't take the risk. I like the kind of retro Nineties Brit Pop edge. The reinvented "Cool Dad". It could work. It's very retro edgy.'

'Yes!' said Stella, not really understanding what she was saying. 'The farming angle works. He's hot. He appeals across generations and segments. He makes his own gravlax.'

'Oh, gravlax,' said Gabriel, holding his pencil up like an exclamation mark. He shook his head. 'No, no. No gravlax. Too old-fashioned. It's all about gin and tonic-cured salmon or beetroot staining, now.'

Stella looked from Big Bird to The Elf and had to smile just to hold her jaw up. The smile was more of a grimace.

'Gin and tonic salmon?'

'Yes,' said The Elf, who was almost bouncing with excitement. 'It's fantabulous. I can't tell you. Tastes exactly as you'd imagine.'

'Anyway,' Gabriel cut in. 'No gravlax, not cool any more. Agreed?'

'Back to the lentil project. Lentils to omnivores. Any other ideas?' asked Pippi.

Lentils. Lentils. Flatulent lentils. Michael Flatley? No. Not cool. Healthy and cool, metro... Nothing.

Stella could see the disappointment creeping across their faces. Brows were furrowing. Pencils had ceased to squeak across iPad screens. All the life hissed out of her. This wasn't going to work. What was she doing here with these clowns? She was pinioned to the bean bags in a flop sweat trying to generate culturally relevant campaigns for Mork and Mindy. She wriggled herself into a more upright position and fixed each of them with a stare.

'Listen. Thank you for the chance to interview. It's been an absolute pleasure. It was always a bit of a punt. I'll try anything once. Well, pretty much anything. Well, not anything. The point is that I'm 40 years old. I've been raising my kids for five years. I was... I am a serious journalist and I have the track record to prove it. I might be new to all this online stuff, but I know what I know and I can create content, systematically. You give me the right team and I'll give you a portal that will exceed every one of your expectations. But I can't sit here like I'm interviewing for a graduate placement scheme. I like you both. I've got good ideas. I've got skills and experience. You'd be getting me cheap. Believe me. But don't let's pretend I'm like you or the other candidates for this job. I'm not.'

She wanted to stand, but was terrified her ungainly staggering and groaning would undermine the impact of her monologue. She waited.

They looked at each other. Pippi was nodding, but Gabriel was stony-faced.

'You mentioned inclusion. Well, try this. I'm a 40-year-old mother of two. You need a bit of diversity. Take another look at my CV. Take a look at my track record.'

This time she risked her dignity and went for the side-roll, all fours, onto knees and eventually upright. She couldn't help laughing. Pippi catapulted to her feet and tried to help her. They were both laughing as Gabriel opened the door for her.

'Thank you for your time, Stella. We'll be in touch.'

'Thank you. Thank you both of you.'

She took the long walk through the Non-Area and The

Recreation Zone with her head held high. She nodded to the receptionist, noting that she wore double braces. The doors opened and Stella escaped.

She didn't look back as she waited for her Uber. She had to fight the desire to giggle. Her first thought was that the girls were going to prolapse when they heard this story. Her second was: I wonder what Coco is up to?

CHAPTER SIXTEEN

Ana

Ana and Stella arrived at the rowdy West London Italian restaurant in sync and from opposite directions. Ana from work and Stella from Wandsworth. Dixie would of course be late. They found a table outside. It was a warm evening so they quickly ordered a bottle of rosé and settled down in silence.

'Are you all right, Ana?' asked Stella.

Ana was preoccupied, but she wasn't sure she wanted to share her news with Stella... or Dixie. They'd never been fans of Rex as they had always felt she was settling for second best, and she wasn't sure she was robust enough to bear their critical commentary. She still needed time to process.

'Fine. Just some work stuff.'

'What's up?'

'It's nothing.'

'How's the sexual olympics? Still on the clock?'

Ana did not feel well. Her stomach was tied in knots.

'Ana? Come on... There's no faking it. It's written all over you in bold. Spill...'

'Oh, Stella, it's just—'

'Bitches! Take a look at that. It's a record. It's five past eight. I'm only five minutes late.'

'Your watch is wrong, Dix.'

'Oh.' She checked her phone. 'Yeah. Oops.'

'*Where* have you been? Every time I call you I get an overseas ring tone and you NEVER pick up.'

'You look so... vibrant, Dix. Is that a new foundation?' asked Ana.

'New York. It's the jet-lag tan. The first couple of trips seemed to really throw me and now I'm thriving on it. My sleep need is down to four hours. Seriously, I am a machine. I am literally living out of a handbag. Look!'

She hefted an enormous Prada shoulder bag onto the table.

'It's got everything I need. Toiletries. Change of clothes. Underwear, obvs. Painkillers. Condoms. Wet wipes. This is capsule packing at its best.'

'Why all the New York trips?' asked Stella suspiciously. 'London Tinder dried up? Are you dating a dealer?'

'No. Just work. You know...'

'You *are* dating someone?'

'No! I am not. Excuse me, waiter! Another glass, please. Forza pronto. Necessito. Immediamente. Is that even Italian?' Dixie laughed raucously at her joke.

Ana was relieved the focus was now off her, but Stella caught her eye.

'Ana was just about to tell me something.'

'You're pregnant! I knew it!' said Dixie.

Ana just lifted the wine glass. 'Guess again, genius.'

'Oh, sorry. I didn't... I'll shut up. Are you OK?'

'I'm fine. I mean there's nothing actually wrong with me. It's...' Ana wanted to tell them, but then again, she didn't want to tell them everything. They could be so insistent. They might influence her. She chose her words carefully. 'Rex and I have been advised that if we want to have a child we're going to need to consider IVF.'

Just saying it aloud, even the partial truth, was upsetting. Ana drained her wine and reached for the bottle.

The looks of compassion and understanding on her two friends' faces shamed her in her half truth. They really did care and this almost made it all worse. She bit back the tears.

'It's going to cost a fortune. It's awful. It's so, I don't know, clinical. They harvest an egg from me. They take Rex's bottled sperm and they inject my harvested egg. It all happens in a test tube. A scientist in a white coat combines our DNA in a lab and the fertilising egg is stored in an incubator until it's okayed and can be returned to my womb. My god, it's obscene. All those years of sex, all that sex, and this is the only way to successfully breed. It's like the universe is playing a joke on me. Where's the love? Where's the magic? I know I shouldn't be so romantic. I know that we're lucky to have the option, but still. A test tube. The actual sexual act will be a medical procedure. Yes, more wine. Thanks.'

'Ah, Ana. It seems bad now, but it will all be worth it when you have a little Rex or a little Ana running around. You have great genes, look at you. You're a Chilean princess.' Dixie seemed to be acting genuine, so Ana was relieved when she continued, 'Rex, well, Rex, I'm sure he's partly inbred, but he's a decent man, I suppose.'

'Honestly, Ana, the more you can streamline the process, the better. If I could go back I'd have the whole pregnancy carried out in an incubator. It would be so much less stress. And as for the wear and tear, don't get me started. Remember this: You. Never. Recover. Believe it.'

'Can you afford it?'

'Aaah, I love you, Dixie. Straight in with the financials.'

'Well, doesn't it cost a fortune? Do they do Hire Purchase?' teased Dixie.

'We get one free go on the NHS, so we're going to take it – nothing to lose I guess! But then that's it, I don't think he will do it again as we would have to pay, and that would be 8k! If it doesn't work, I'm... well, not stuffed, obviously. If it doesn't work, I don't know what I'm going to do. We have a good life, me and Rex, and all we need to make it perfect is a baby.'

'Yeah, shit-a-brick. That's some mind-bending existential shit, right there,' said Dixie, being unusually reflective.

'Fucking men, honestly. Where the do they get off? One strike. What is this, a stupid game!?' Stella said.

Ana could see Stella was angry. Very angry. Not just wine in the sun indignant, she was genuinely mad as hell and someone was going to pay. 'He owes you. Shit, he's lucky to have you. He's lucky you put up with him. It's not like he's the best car on the lot. Look at you! You're smart, stable, sex-mad. I mean. What the actual fuck! One strike. Puh!'

Ana couldn't control her laughter.

'Stella, I love you, but I'm sure if we can afford it, Rex will come round.'

'Fuck him, even if you can't afford it. This isn't some holiday in Mauritius he's blowing off. This is your goddamn right as a woman. The gift of fertility and he thinks he can deprive you of that cos he's got cash-flow concerns. Off with his balls. He does not deserve you!'

'Jake still not putting out, hey, Stells?'

'Fuck you, Dix!'

And then they were all laughing.

'Stella's right. Go and do what you need to do. If Rex is prepared to pay, and you feel it is the right thing, then go and do it. You know in your gut. It isn't for anybody else to tell you whether or not you should have a child, and how you should do it.'

Dixie gave her a reassuring pat on the arm.

'Dixie, are you high?' asked Ana, confused by the out-of-character gentle solicitude.

'God, can't I just be nice? I care about you.'

'I know you do, but you don't, like, pat people. Anyway, while you are in a nice frame of mind, where are we with plans? Anyone coming round to Provence yet?'

'Noooo!'

'Absolutely not!'

'Then what? Any progress on Edinburgh, Dix?'

'I have had way too much to do to talk to Peter about that. I'm sorry but I don't think it's going to happen.'

There was an awkward silence. Ana was crushed. She needed a break. She needed some time away from London, work, Rex. She needed some time with her friends.

'Dixie?'

'Yes, Stella.'

'What's going on with you? You're up to something...'

'I am not.'

'What is in NY? Who is in NY?'

'Listen. It's nothing. I have a lot on.' Dixie was on her feet. 'I'm just going for a wizz. Get another bottle. Watch that.' She placed her bag on her seat and was gone.

'She's hiding something.'

'I know.'

'Stella... don't!'

Stella was opening Dixie's bag. She pulled out an A4 sketch pad and flipped it open.

'As I thought,' said Stella and turned the page to Ana.

The sketch was a highly stylised, almost anime conjuring of a New York skyline as backdrop to a sexualised image of Dixie at her most erotic, a post-coital sex-kittenish look of satisfaction on her face, a glass held aloft in a toast and in the glass a reflection of a tall athletic man taking a photo of her with an iPhone.

'So that's the New York drug.'

'Put it back, Stella.'

'No. We don't have secrets.' Stella closed the pad and placed it on the table. 'Waiter, can we get another bottle?'

'You utter bitch,' were the first words Dixie said when she saw her notepad on the table.

'It was too easy.'

'I tried to stop her.'

'You did? I can see the bruises...'

'Who is he?' asked Ana.

Dixie sat back with a sigh, twiddling her glass. 'Freddie Eastman. Millionaire Biotech entrepreneur. British. Forty-seven years old. Looks 42. Lives on Central Park. Healthy seven-inch penis with appropriate girth. Likes hot pussy and redheads. The game is on.'

'Look at her!' laughed Stella. 'Literally the cat that got the cream. How long's this been going on?'

'Seven weeks.'

Ana and Stella's jaws dropped. They gawped at each other and Ana mouthed SEVEN again. Dixie hadn't had a seven-week relationship since her divorce. Ana picked up the artist's pad and leafed back through the pages. Each page revealed Freddie from another angle. Freddie eating sushi. Freddie in a towel. A close-up of Freddie. Freddie kissing Dixie. The top of Freddie's head buried between Dixie's thighs. She turned the page to Stella.

'Ah ha!'

'When do we get to meet him?'

'Oh my god,' said Ana. 'Yes. When?'

'I don't know. He's not here much at the moment.'

'Then,' said Ana, 'we will come to New York. Forget Provence. Forget Edinburgh. It's Manhattan, ladies. The sexy in the city.'

'Yes. When?' said Stella.

'I don't know. I hadn't planned.'

'Do not play coy, Dixie Dressler. We are coming to New York to meet Mr Fred just as soon as humanly possible.'

'Really? Oh god. Then I suppose... I wasn't going to say anything. It felt too early. I didn't want to jinx it. In three weeks, Saturday 28th. It's Freddie's birthday. He's having a massive bash on Long Island. One of his investors has a pad there, so they are celebrating Freddie's birthday and the tenth anniversary of the business. There's a band. Dancing in the gardens. Do you want to come? Will you? It would be fantastic.'

'Will I? It's a Saturday. I've already picked my outfit! I'll wear the vintage Chanel two-piece. It's black and white. Chevrons. I knew I'd find a home for it. This is kismet.'

Stella was silent.

'Stella?' asked Dixie.

'I don't know. I didn't want to say anything. Jake's having a bit of a cash-flow issue. He's asked me to rein things in for a while.'

'For fuck's sake,' said Dixie. 'He's a partner in a law firm.'

'Look, I'm not happy about it. They've cancelled our Barclaycard. I'm living on fumes.'

Ana looked at Dixie. 'Surely we can do something?'

'Air miles? I've a companion voucher. If you have enough miles, Ana, you can get another free. But you'll need to fly economy.'

Ana squealed. 'If we get to go to Long Island via Manhattan to meet Dixie's seven-inch love interest, I'll ride in the hold.'

'Say yes, Stella. Please.'

'It's very kind of you, Dixie. Really. I'll have to see. I've a few things on the horizon that I can't afford to miss.'

'Like what? Lunches with yummy mummies? Coffee with the nanny? Mid-morning Pilates? I'm offering to fly you to JFK and you're playing hard to get?'

Stella gave them both a long stare. 'Three weeks, you say? Listen I'll get back to you. I'll have to talk to Jake.'

Stella looked at her watch. Ana could see that Stella was hurt by Dixie's comments about Jake's cash-flow issues, but knew her well enough not to patronise her. Stella would work it out. Stella made her excuses: nanny, late, Jake, etc, and left.

'Awks,' said Dixie as soon as Stella was in her Uber.

'Yup, what is up with her!?'

'Whoa, she is angry!? Poor old Jake must come home and cower in the corner. She's a fucking warrior when she's cornered.'

'But she'll come?' asked Ana.

'Never doubt Stella. If there's a way, she'll be there. If she doesn't come, we should be seriously concerned.'

'Is he really so lovely?'

Dixie paused. 'He might be the best thing that's ever happened to me.'

'How come he's single? Is there an ex-wife?'

'No ex. He's all mine.'

'Forty-seven and single. There must be a story. No significant other? You sure? He's not, you know?'

'Gay?'

'Religious?'

'No. Freddie's not religious and there's no significant other.'

'Good for you, Dixie. You deserve a bit of something decent after all the pond life you've indulged!'

They both laughed, but Ana had the strong suspicion that Dixie was hiding something. She desperately hoped Freddie wasn't another coke head. Dixie had a trick for attracting complicated men with convoluted lifestyles. Walking home she was glad to be heading back to the stability and reliability of Rex, until she found in her jacket pocket the sprig of heather from the gypsy woman and recalled her reading. Seed in fantasy. Take a journey. She shivered as she considered that the first step of the journey may already be on the off. Rex would not be happy she was disappearing to the States so soon after the IVF, but that would be Rex's problem. This was her fate and she was going to follow it.

CHAPTER SEVENTEEN

Ana

Ana was lying on their small two-seater sofa. It was ideally small, so small that she could lie with her head on one arm and legs propped up at a thirty-degree angle on the other. This was not on account of any specific medical advice. It just made sense. As did the hot water bottle on her stomach. She couldn't tell whether the cramps were stress or 'pregnancy related'. In fewer than three weeks she would know whether the embryo had taken. The consultant had explained how a small hole had been drilled to maximise the probabilities of success. 'Assisted hatching,' they had called it. The hole assisted with the 'implantation'. The language, Ana often thought, could be improved. She felt somewhere between a gardener and a poultry farmer. She sighed deeply as she considered the success of her spider plants in the window. She chose to ignore the empty pots where once geraniums had endured, at the vacant sun spot where the recently eloped cat had lain and considered its options. The sedation from the implantation was wearing off and Ana heard Rex curse again from the kitchen. He'd insisted, sweetly enough, in 'taking care of her', which meant reproducing, for the fifty-somethingth time, his dead mother's sausage casserole. If only she'd insisted on a takeaway. She wasn't sure she had the strength to fake enthusiasm for undercooked sausage in a watery tomato sauce. She really hoped he hadn't added sweetcorn, 'for colour,' as he often said, but also, 'to bulk it up so you can live off it for a couple of days'.

In maybe two weeks they'd know whether they were having a baby. So much can happen in two weeks, a fact highlighted by the speed with which all this had happened. This felt like the first time in a month that Ana had had any time to reflect. The results of Rex's sperm test had been a disruptive shock to them both. They'd both assumed that it was Ana's 40-year-old eggs that were the issue, so when the specialist, in roundabout language, had talked of viability and vitality and morphology (shape issues), the quantity of technical data had made their cause appear hopeless. It seemed that only in terms of volume did Rex reach reference limits. His 4 ml of hard-won ejaculate was in the second quartile. In terms of sperm count, concentration, motility and morphology, well, the less said the better, but the consultant's face told them this was going to be difficult, and it wasn't long before they'd signed up for an £8,000 targeted insertion of a single viable sperm into a lucky egg, rather than wait for the NHS. Yuck, Ana had thought.

Her disappointment was aggravated by the requirement to regulate her menstrual cycle and prepare her ovaries with two weeks of birth control. Ana despised the pill. It affected her physically and emotionally. She'd not taken it since her late teens, insisting it caused liver problems, mood swings and catastrophic, ankle-swelling water retention. She endured the side-effects for two weeks; and this two weeks had to be endured in more than one way. Rex had reacted badly to the news about his sperm's low vitality and despite Ana being on the pill, and the expressed aim of the process the eventual birth of a child, Rex had become unappeasably horny. He wanted sex in the morning on waking and sex in the evening when back from work, and sex before sleep. Just, he said, to help him sleep. When he wasn't pestering her for sex, he was briefing against the girls' trip to New York and Long Island.

'Fuck!' shouted Rex. He'd clearly burned his finger again trying to slide the casserole dish out of the oven.

Now, she reflected with relief, that her egg was in her oven, he couldn't demand sex, and she'd no longer have to accept to appease his broken ego. And she'd made clear that she was going to New York no matter what happened. Being pregnant wasn't a disability and she wasn't going to let it rule every part of her life. Everybody needs a break from their everyday. If it was the right thing for her, then, in this case, it had to be the right thing for them. She would not be emotionally blackmailed into missing out on the trip of a lifetime. She needed time with her friends to balance the sacrifices she was making. She wouldn't let money and childbirth be the only ruling factors in her life.

As she'd indicated to the girls at their last meeting two weeks earlier, the money issue made a second bout of IVF an indulgence they couldn't really afford, but the past weeks had been so testing that Ana wasn't sure whether she'd even want to make a second attempt. This insight caused her considerable anguish. Several times she'd had to fight off the overwhelming cloud of terror that she was doing the wrong thing, that it wasn't her fate to have a child with Rex. But then she'd acknowledge that her hormonal rollercoaster undermined the extent to which she could trust her feelings. She had to remind herself that she was a 39-year-old woman in a stable and settled relationship with a man she loved, that together they'd started down this road as willing, informed adults and that the decision had been made on the basis of facts and experience. She reminded herself that Rex himself had been selected after detailed analysis from a handful of eligible possibles. She wondered whether now might be the time to revisit the spreadsheet for a reminder of why Rex was the right man for her.

'You want peas? We've got some frozen peas? I can throw them in.'

Peas! Frozen peas in a casserole!? Was he trying to break her?

'They're frozen straight from the field. Rich in proteins and vitamin C.'

'It's your recipe, Rex. Just don't do that thing when you keep adding ingredients until it's reheated leftovers...'

'It's not MY recipe. I just want to make sure you're getting all your greens. You know. To make you strong and...'

'... and a viable incubator for your progeny.'

'Err, yes, I guess, if you want to put it like that.'

Rex appeared in the kitchen doorway. His face was flushed and his reading glasses on top of his head were still steamed from the heat of the oven. His face beamed with pride at his nurturing efforts. He was still in his work shirt. Baby blue. He wore the same colour (more or less) every day, she realised as if for the first time. Her pinny was too small for him. A present to her from her father. A 'joke' apron: The Turkey Will Be Ready for Xmas... Next Year! Hilarious.

'Food'll be ready in two minutes. Just trying to boil the rice dry.'

He came and sat beside her, perched on the edge of the sofa. He stroked her head, as if, she thought, he was trying to calm her – she used to love it when he did that. He stared at the blank TV screen. She let her gaze return to the window ledge where the last of the sun had disappeared. A cat miaowed outside and she wondered if it was Boris come to beg forgiveness.

'What's on TV?' he asked after a pause, and reached for the remote.

'Oh, please, Rex. I can't.'

'Sorry. Right. Absolutely. Can I get you anything? A cold towel.'

He was trying, she knew that. He was trying so hard, but the harder he tried, the more trying he was.

Ana and Rex were just carrying on with life as normal. They had spent the previous weeks going through a range of emotions: Ana's mind trying to come to terms with the fact that she might or might not be a mum, and that she had possibly left it too late. She kept tearing up, and having to walk out of the room so that Rex couldn't see. She didn't want him to see her suffering, her doubts, to know how hard it was hitting her. It was probably just her hormones settling down, she told herself. It also wasn't just something that you could think about and be fine with, like the decision had been made, and you just needed to accept it, because life wasn't that simple, and the prognosis was not that black and white. The fact was that she could in reality just say: never mind, that didn't work, and they could return to normal life, sex, and hoping that a little miracle might happen. But she wasn't quite there yet, they had to try this route, and it was making her question everything. Had she put enough time into finding the right man? Was this the right time to be having a baby? If she'd really wanted one, wouldn't she have done it earlier? Even if she was lucky enough to have a child, she thought, she would be lucky to see them grow up – she would most likely be dead by then! These sad thoughts led her back to the loss of her own mother. Was post-IVF depression a thing?

And then with all this swilling around her head, she started to find Rex incredibly annoying, and not just his insistence on frequent and for Ana, pointless pill-safe-sex. The way he slurped his tea was disgusting, and she loathed the way he casually played with his balls all the time while he was watching TV – she wanted to shout at him to leave them alone! His failings taunted her... and as for his brown hoodie, his weekend, dress-down style, that bore the name of his favourite teen rock band, well, she just wanted to burn it. He was 45, for god's sake, and was probably oblivious to all of this. If she mentioned it he would be mortified. Why was she suddenly so irritated by him? What did it mean? Was it normal?

'Dinner is served,' announced Rex. Thankfully, he'd taken off the pinafore. The casserole was served in large bowls. Ana took hers and wriggled upright.

'Sausage casserole with a rainbow of vegetables.'

Indeed, thought Ana. The onion and tomato base had been 'improved' with tinned sweetcorn, overcooked peas (now brown) and some slices of pickled beetroot. The dark blue glaze on the bowl highlighted the mess of colours.

'Latest nutritional advice recommends a rainbow of vegetables. Not bad, huh? No more pizza for you. No more curry. Instead, proper wholesome, home-cooked food.'

'Thank you, Rex. It looks… exciting.'

'TV? Isn't that baking programme on tonight?'

'No TV. Please… I'm a little fragile.'

'Radio? I could—'

'Just quiet, please.' She didn't mean to snap. But she'd had to stop listening to the radio. Joel's track was relentlessly climbing the charts and seemed to be the tune of choice for every pub, café, taxi, cab, shop. Every music channel and music show seemed to have prioritised playing 'Brown Eyed Girl' whenever Ana was in the area. It was starting to feel like a conspiracy to further destroy her equanimity.

She lifted a spoonful of the casserole. The fine grain of the pink sausage flesh did not bode well. The tomato sauce was separating into tomato essence and water. A mouthful confirmed her fears. Nothing had been properly fried and browned before simmering the tomatoes. Nothing had been reduced sufficiently to intensify any flavour there might have been and the additional peas, sweetcorn and beetroot added an unwelcome sweetness.

'Mmm. Taste the goodness. You like?'

'I like,' said Ana with what smile she could summon. She couldn't bear to hurt his feelings. She couldn't bring herself to tell him that she'd rather swallow one of Boris's unwelcome live sacrifices than endure a fragile pregnancy being catered for by Rex. He was a good, funny and kind man, but he was not a cook. If she tried to last until term on his cooking, their offspring would be born underweight and malnourished.

'Eat up! Oh god, poor you, Ana – you are feeling really shit, aren't you. Are you going to miss the sex? I think I'm going to miss the sex. Did you know that other than for forty-eight long hours every month, we have had sex nearly every day since we first "committed"? That's like two and a half years. Amazing, huh?'

It was three years, she thought, but didn't say anything. The doctor hadn't prohibited penetration so technically they could, but Ana was so relieved to have an excuse, and so physically averse to any kind of sexual interaction, that she'd suggested that they abstain until they'd had some good news.

She pushed the bowl away and fell back. 'It's lovely, Rex, but I'm just feeling a bit queasy at the moment.'

'Oh, darling, I'm so sorry. I'll put it in the fridge and we can microwave it later.'

'Is there any fruit? I think there's a banana in the bowl.'

Rex reappeared with the banana and began to peel it slowly and seductively, in jest.

'Just give it here, please,' said Ana, refusing to make eye contact with Rex. Her ability to eat a banana erotically had long been a shared joke. Ana ate as innocently as she was able while her insides bucked and roiled in panic. What if she got pregnant with this man's child and could no longer stand the sight of him? Was that fate, or was that some strange karma she'd earned somehow?

Rex was watching her, mulling over saying something. She could read his intent.

'There is no reason I can't fly. The doctor was explicit,' she said, pre-empting him.

Rex's head dropped.

'I know. I just worry. If this doesn't work, don't you want to know you did everything you could?'

She nodded slowly, brushing her dark hair off her face. She was very tired.

'I'm going to bed. Don't wake me.'

CHAPTER EIGHTEEN

Stella

After Stella had fed the kids and they were safely watching *PAW Patrol* for the fifteen-millionth time, she perched in front of her laptop. She had questions that needed answers.

'Am I gay?' was the first she googled, and then felt stupid. Of course she wasn't gay! What had Coco called it? 'Sexually fluid'? So she deleted gay and tried 'sexually fluid'. Rather too much about fluids, but scrolling down she found features and articles from around the world. OMG, maybe I am back in fashion! But was she actually 'sexually fluid'? Coco obviously was. But wasn't Stella merely a bored housewife overexcited by some sexual attention? There were many articles, some exploratory and encouraging diversity (mostly on Mumsnet, which covered everything nowadays). The deeper she trawled, the more she found. The consensus seemed to be that women were increasingly looking to explore their sexuality in their late thirties/early forties. Something was missing in their lives: a lack looking for an answer. But if, two months earlier, you had asked her what she was missing, she would have said it was a ripped toyboy with an enormous cock, not a perky, size eight, green-eyed Latin girl with firm breasts and a... Even thinking about the other bit made Stella blush. What if Coco tried to make her touch her fanny? She gasped, horrified. But perhaps this was less horrifying than the perfectly formed Coco seeing her less than well-kept bush and two-baby-fanny. Something fizzed between her thighs. OMG! What was she doing?

She slammed the computer shut and poured herself a glass of wine.

Her two innocent boys were sitting on the sofa, oblivious to everything but the talking TV dogs. They were her life, her everything, she told herself. She would do anything for them. But, if that were so, why was she happy to risk their family security to just have a little fun? She couldn't answer the question, but one thing was sure, it unsettled her.

Beside the laptop was the day's mail. A red border poked out from the middle of the pile and Stella wondered if it might be a card or an invite. It wasn't. The letter was 'Not A Circular' and was marked 'Private and Personal' for Jake Hammerson, Esq. She would have thrown it aside, but the logo caught her attention. IG. She knew an IG. That was where all the bloody money had been going.

She ripped it open. Look what it's come to, thought Stella, Jake's home so little that I am reduced to the role of PA. Actually, not PA, as Dixie clearly had a better relationship with Peter than Stella currently did with Jake.

Inside she found a detailed final demand. Flicking through the many pages of the statement, Stella's heart thumped, sweat erupted. Blood rushed to her extremities and she wanted to smash something. Jake had been lying to her, systematically and deliberately for... the statement covered a full quarter. Every transaction was listed. The scale of his betrayal, the size of each loss, the failed spread bets, and the escalating cumulative loss sent a chill through her.

'Jake, you lying, two-faced, shit-filled, scumbag, fuck-wit of a man!'

She was angry at him, but she was furious with herself, as she now saw that she'd known something was off. Now she knew that everything was off.

She grabbed her phone and dialled Jake's number. It rang and rang, as she felt her temper start to boil over. As it went to voicemail yet again, she started shouting down the phone to him. 'You don't even have the balls to answer my call, you lying little shit! Working at the office late, my arse!! Well, guess what, Jake, I am DONE! The kids are going to their grandparents for a few days and I am going to New York. You are a DICK!' And she hung up.

She dashed off a text to Dixie and Ana. **'Mind made up. NY here I come. Never have I needed to escape more. See you in 48 hours. Xxx'**

Her mind quickly turned to her own financial situation. Her savings would come in very handy. She wasn't going to let Jake's problems stop her living her life, stop her doing what she wanted for herself. The boys were mesmerised on the sofa, and about to rouse them and hustle them off to bed, she felt a spasm of love and fear. What if Jake's problem went further than the IG account? What if there was more bad news in other accounts?

With other bookmakers? Could Jake have risked their entire financial security? Their home? For what? Why? Why would he do that? The oft-quoted explanation that gambling was an addiction didn't appease Stella. Not one iota.

Stella's phone buzzed. She was expecting Jake to return her call, although she didn't know if he even had the balls to do it, or maybe it was more excited planning from the manic Ana and the love-lost Dixie, but it was from Coco saying, '**Time for a quick drink?**'

'**Not really, Jake's out and I really need to speak to him when he comes home! Sx**'

'**I could come to you? Cx**'

Fuck, thought Stella, I do want to see her, and it's not like it's weird to have another girl here if Jake comes home. A quick glass of wine can't hurt.

'**OK, a quick one. But if Jake appears, which I hope will be soon, you need to be gone.**'

'**On my way! 10 mins. X**'

She quickly rushed the boys up to bed, and then had a quick check of her reflection in her mirror. Hmm... leisurewear was a good look with the under-thirties. She smelt her armpits. Eugh. She had very little time to sort herself out, especially if she wished to look effortlessly sexy. She ripped off her clothes, jumped in the shower and scrubbed herself from top to toe. She didn't mess with her hair, grabbed some clean lacy knickers (she didn't give herself time to ask why), a clean bra and threw her sweats back on so it looked like she didn't care. It wasn't like her knickers and bra actually matched, in fact she didn't even know if she had any underwear sets in her possession. The only person she could think of who might wear a matching set was Dixie – she probably just had various degrees of 'fuck me' sets. Perhaps their trip to New York demanded an underwear upgrade.

The doorbell buzzed twice.

She ran down to the door, boobs bouncing and her blonde hair tied on top of her head.

'That was quick!' said Stella.

'Well, I was excited,' smiled Coco.

'Of course, great to see you,' said Stella, standing in her doorway. A curtain twitched at Jenny and Tim's window. What do I do next? she wondered. Do I kiss her hello? And if so where? On the lips!? No, for god's sake. She pulled her quickly into the hallway and closed the door behind her. Her heart was racing.

'I've got some cold white wine in the fridge, that work?'

'Perfect, thanks. I won't stay long. What's going on?'

Stella told her briefly that there were some issues with Jake, money issues, and that she was off to New York in the next forty-eight hours if she could get everything organised at the last minute.

Coco nodded with understanding, but Stella was certain that Coco had never been in as much jeopardy as presently hung over her marriage. 'That sounds shattering.'

'Oh yes, mentally and physically! But I can't tell you how nice it is to be heading off for a few days with NO MEN in tow, just to totally switch off and forget all the stresses of real life. I cannot wait!'

'Lucky you! I have to admit to feeling a little envious, but you deserve it. Nothing better than a few days hanging with the girls.'

As she said that, Stella couldn't help but think that Coco's idea of a few days hanging with girls was probably very different to hers. Stella looked at Coco as she took a sip of wine and munched a Pringle, not a care in the world. She seemed so grounded and at peace with herself, and Stella couldn't remember ever feeling like that, even at her age. She wondered whether it was because she had been brought up in such a different environment, and her priorities were different. Stella's England was all about class and hierarchy, where you were educated and who you knew. She had always found England a challenging place to live. How did an outsider like Coco make her way in such a cruel and judgemental country? She just seemed too nice to thrive in such a hostile environment.

'So are you working or playing this weekend?' Stella asked.

'I have the weekend off, so I am just going to relax, go walking, and I am going to meet some of my friends tomorrow night for a silent disco... Have you ever tried that?'

Stella laughed, 'Just can't imagine how ridiculous I would look rocking out to some Eighties rock while someone else is crumping to some hiphop.'

'That's hilarious!' screeched Coco. 'You don't listen to your own music, Stella! It's a shared experience. Communal. And no one cares what anybody else is doing. Everyone is in the same boat. I'll take you to one when you're back, you'll love it, it's very liberating!'

They continued chatting and giggling for over an hour, with Stella increasingly surprised by how easy it was spending time with Coco, and, weirdly, how she became more and more beautiful as she got to know her. She knew that she must have flaws, nobody was perfect, but she hadn't found them yet. In general Stella found something to resent about new acquaintances: a scent, a perfume, taste in colours or fabrics, poor application of make-up, tattoos, sound of laugh, absence of laugh. If only Jake wasn't coming home and she could chill with Coco.

Stella stood up and firmly told Coco that she had things to do, especially as she was hoping Jake would be home any minute. She had no idea if he was coming home as he hadn't even returned her call, but she was getting more and more stressed about the impending situation, and she knew they had to talk. Surely he had to come home at some point – he was her sodding husband! Also, they had finished off the entire bottle of wine. This was no time to be opening another.

'Right, Coco, I am now slightly pissed and have no idea where I last saw my passport.'

Giggling, Coco offered, 'Can I help you find it?'

'Nope, you need to go home,' and as Stella brushed past her, Coco caught her hand.

'Are you sure you want me to go home?' she asked flirtatiously. 'Absolutely definitely?' She pulled herself closer to Stella. 'I mean I can go,' she said, as she planted a soft kiss on Stella's lips. 'I could go right now,' she continued as she tantalisingly teased her with her tongue, 'or I could just stay for a few more minutes.'

Stella felt herself responding to Coco's touch. She allowed Coco to kiss her, to explore between her lips, to gently pull her closer. It was such a tender embrace, and such a sweet kiss. There was no urgency, just understanding, openness and desire.

'I really, really want you,' whispered Coco into her ear. 'You are so damn sexy and you don't even know it. All those curves, your breasts, your need to be loved. I want to take you and make love to you. I want to enjoy you. Let me.'

Stella was speechless. What if Jake came home, or what if one of the children woke up, what would she say? And yet she didn't want it to stop. Coco was right, she wanted to be touched by her and loved by her. She wanted to be hers. But now wasn't the right time. And yet she didn't stop it. Maybe the jeopardy was part of the fun. After all, he had been lying to her.

'You are an amazing kisser, Stella. Kissing you could become my favourite pastime.'

'Don't get too used to it, Coco, I am married, and I really have no idea what I am doing, in any sense!'

'Well, you seem to be doing pretty well to me,' said Coco.

Stella was aware that if this was going to go any further there was going to be vagina contact of some kind. She really had no idea how to deal with that. And as that thought was passing through her head, Coco pushed her up against the kitchen counter and was slowly undoing Stella's trousers, pulling them down.

'Oh god, I don't know, Coco. This is all moving really fast, honestly, maybe... and Jake could walk in at any minute.'

'Shh,' said Coco. 'Just wait.' And with that she swiftly pulled down her knickers and pressed her tongue onto Stella's clitoris. The warm softness, the shock, was unlike anything Stella had experienced. She let out a cry, and she felt like her legs weaken beneath her.

'Holy...' whispered Stella. 'Oh my god, oh yes, yes,' and she held Coco's head as she continued to lick and suck and tease Stella's clit until she thought she would explode. Just as she thought she couldn't take any more, Coco plunged a hot finger into her, finding her G spot in one deft move. Stella couldn't hold back any longer. She felt a wave of the most incredible orgasm come over her, her body convulse, with Coco hungrily lapping up her juices as she came. Time seemed to stop.

Coco slowly pulled Stella's clothes back up, and then kissed her on the lips, which was slightly *eeuw.*

'Just a little hint of what's to come. I think you might enjoy the journey,' said Coco wickedly.

'Wow,' said Stella, slightly breathlessly, 'that was unexpected, and incredible, and now slightly embarrassing!'

'Embarrassing? No, it's amazing. And I feel honoured to have been the first woman to share that with you. Not so bad, huh?'

'Well, er, that's very kind of you to say. OK, listen I really have to sort myself out, while wondering about my sexuality, so I guess it's a good time for you to go!'

Coco laughed, 'OK, I'm off. But Stella, this isn't about your sexuality, it's about what makes you happy, so don't overthink it, OK? I'll see you soon, have a great trip... if I don't see you before.'

When Stella had closed the door behind her, she leaned

against it, closed her eyes and stood, baffled, confused and elated. She recoiled a little at the memory of the taste of her own pussy in her mouth. Thank god she had washed, but still!

Her phone buzzed and she checked it excitedly, expecting something filthy and flirtatious from Coco.

Instead it was from Jake. He was going to have to pull an all-nighter. Deepest regret etc, etc. These clients won't bankrupt themselves. Don't do anything I wouldn't do!

She sent him a text back saying, **'Did you even listen to my voicemail?! FUCK YOU. I am going to New York. The kids will be with my parents.'**

Knowing what she now knew, she cursed IG, cursed Jake, and cursed the bitter irony of him joking about bankruptcy and fidelity. She was afraid of the possible ramifications, but she was nevertheless elated at the warm glow that lingered in her loins, so she went upstairs to try and find some outfits for three nights in the States.

CHAPTER NINETEEN

Dixie

Talk about work–life balance, Dixie thought, as she strode through the cavernous expanse of Grand Central Station searching for the understated entrance. Peter kept an office in the MetLife Building and visiting him there was one of her favourite day trips. An escalator that might have led to a mezzanine of Payless shoe stores and Kinko print shops instead led to lifts that whisked occupants high up to an office that could have doubled as a viewing platform for Manhattan. The family office, shared with a number of high–net–worths, had vistas north and south from the forty-ninth floor. The MetLife Building, in what seemed to Dixie a miracle of engineering, straddled Park Avenue, the vanishing point views were north towards Central Park and south to the empty shadows of the World Trade Center.

Dixie exited the lift and looked north towards Central Park and her new 'home' and wondered at the good fortune that had led her to seat 10D on Flight BA05 LHR–JFK and seated her next to the love bomb that was Freddie Eastman. Less than four months and she'd been lifted from transatlantic Tinder legend and part-time good-time girl to a lovestruck, marginally obsessed and always excited 39-year-old teenager living with the man of her dreams in a condo with views of Central Park. She loved London and she missed her friends, but this... this... She turned south, looking down over the serried rows of yellow cabs. It was 3 p.m., they were all heading back to base for change of shift. They made movies about things like this and she was Meg Ryan: a hotter, ginger Meg Ryan who had orgasms whenever she wanted and always found the man of her dreams.

'Ah, there you are, Dixie! Come in, come in. Tatjana, bring us some tea. Fresh tea.'

Peter's voice boomed, tinged with a hint of his Ukrainian origins. He was a bear of a man; well over six feet. A beard framed his face forming a single mass with his hair, which was mildly receding. Thick bushy eyebrows and hands the size of baseball mitts completed his look. He waddled (or swaggered depending on how you viewed him) to his desk. 'Seat. Seat.'

Peter dropped into a swivel chair that rocked and he fell backwards jovially, his hands on his widely spread thighs. Against her will, Dixie could see his swollen bollocks neatly separated by the gusset of his suit trousers. As for the slab of meat slung to the left, Dixie steadfastly held his stare as he adjusted himself.

'What can we talk about today? Are all my properties still standing? What is with your face? You look different... Have you had more of that microdermabrasion!? Or is there more to the story? Is my favourite independent woman falling into the trap of love? Is she no longer independent? Is she "in love"? Ah,

I see, I am right. She is in love with Freddie Eastman. I see the flush of love in her face. Or did Dixie run up forty-nine floors!? No, I did not think so. Love is dangerous. It makes fools of us all and no one trusts a fool.'

Dixie knew better than to rise to his provocations. Eventually he would grow tired of entertaining himself. He would settle and they could get down to business. Besides, she needed a favour and for that she needed to make him feel like he ruled the world. It was the only condition in which he found himself incapable of saying no.

Tatjana appeared and placed a tray with a samovar and ornate, gold-rimmed porcelain cups on a trolley beside the desk.

'Shall I pour?' she asked.

'Tomorrow is a very special day for us all, no? Tomorrow we meet the man who has stolen your heart. I am so happy for you. Is he very handsome in a kind of English movie-star way? Who is that man? Tom Fiddlestick. Tall and pale, like all the English since Henry the eight.' He boomed a laugh at his humour and Dixie smiled indulgently. 'I want to thank you for the invitation. I do want to see this wonderful estate. The Hamptons are always splendid, but The Chateau? Super mega-splendour. Mr Eastman must know some very special people. I will get to know Mr Frederick, I think, and we will be firm friends. Am I right?'

Dixie waited to be sure he'd finished.

'It's going to be amazing. The owner is an investor in Freddie's business, so it's to celebrate the tenth anniversary of the business and Freddie's birthday.'

He rearranged the slab of meat in his pants and grinned at her. He was sweating from the exertion of his monologue.

'You will come to the party, Peter, won't you?'

'Of course, Dixie, how could I say no to you. I am intrigued?'

'You'll be taking the big chopper?'

He smiled and cocked his head, waiting for what she knew he must be following: a request.

'Would you mind awfully if I joined you?'

He laughed and slapped his thigh. 'Of course not, my sweet thing. But won't you be travelling with Prince Charming?'

'Freddie's already there with his family, preparing.'

'Then of course. To arrive with a beautiful woman. This will make the journey worthwhile.'

'How about three beautiful women?'

'Three beautiful women! Three is my lucky number! Who are these beautiful women?'

'You remember Ana and Stella?'

'Ana is the tiny brunette and Stella the fierce blonde!'

'Ana and Stella are my best friends. You'll have us all to yourself.'

'Until I have to hand you over to Freddie Eastman.'

'You know you'll love the attention, Peter.'

He laughed. 'You know me so well. What would I do without you? I would be lost. We'll meet at the helipad at 5 p.m., this is OK? We will arrive as the party starts. Like movie stars, proper ones. Am I right? I am right.'

CHAPTER TWENTY

Ana

Indian Airlines Flight 977 from Bombay via London to Newark lacked a little of the glamour that a Premium Economy flight to New York conjured. The champagne wasn't champagne, it was warm Prosecco in a plastic egg cup. Ana's had a dark hair in it, but she didn't tell Stella, wanting to hold onto the glamour of their journey.

'To us. To all of us. To what goes on tour stays on tour. And to Dixie's love interest, the gorgeous and fabulous Freddie.'

'And to the utter bitch who, in spite of twenty-five years of sleeping her way around the globe on a cocktail of Class A drugs and top-shelf liquor is now in love with a handsome millionaire. It's Cinderella on drugs.'

'Bottoms up!'

Ana nearly gagged on the hot and acidic concoction. They were trying to maintain their spirits but it was tough. Travelling on Dixie's air miles, they'd had to check in together and Stella had arrived late with an enormous bag, way too big for carry-on. They'd had to join a queue of Indian families. It was forty-five minutes before they'd reached the counter.

Stella's bag, the size of a Smart car, had failed to meet the weight restriction and the check-in staff had insisted she remove something. Ana had stood aside with an impatient grimace as a flustered Stella had fussed and faffed and eventually removed a pair of knee-high leather boots and an overflowing make-up bag. She found room for the make-up in her shoulder bag and swapped her Converse for the boots.

At security they had been held up again when Stella had failed to remove all liquids over 100 ml and not followed instructions to use a clear plastic bag. In the end Stella had thrown the entire make-up bag into the rubbish bin and informed security that she was heading to New York for a fresh start and was delighted to be free of the dated cosmetics she'd garnered as a leading light in the London beauty industry. The gaggle of families watched her performance as if she were a reality star on day release.

They'd made it to the gate in time to join another queue to board. Their delayed progress through the airport meant that they'd missed Premium Economy boarding and were at the back of the economy queue. Ana had bitten back her annoyance at Stella's chaotic cock-ups because she could tell there was something terribly wrong. Stella always did things her own way, but she was never a mess nor a liability. Whatever had happened since her panicked decision to join them in New York, it was clearly massive, so massive that Ana was dreading the big reveal. Besides, Ana had her own preoccupations.

Ana could see that Stella's red eyes were lipped with tears. Her heart fizzed in sympathy and she dropped her head onto Stella's shoulder. Stella's hand comforted her.

'Is it all going to be all right?' whispered Ana.

'Fuck, yes!' shouted Stella, trying to wave her arm for another drink, which was packaged in a heavy faux-fur. Looking down at Stella's legs, which were uncomfortably crossed in the knee-high boots, Ana couldn't stop laughing.

'Don't laugh,' said Stella. 'I'm not wearing a bra. The jiggling is starting to hurt.'

Ana laughed more.

The flight passed in a disconnected nightmare of hydration and extended queueing for the toilets. Mostly water for the maybe pregnant Ana; gin for the volatile Stella. The food was superb though a chicken curry wouldn't have been Ana's first choice, nor would the sweet kulfi dessert. Fortunately they were on their way to see their best friend so they laughed and cried their way across the Atlantic.

They staggered off the plane in Newark and weaved and wobbled their way down dour, gruesomely carpeted corridors under strip lights that honestly made them look like they'd clawed their way out of their graves, not spent seven hours in Premium Economy. Despite the sign 'Welcome To The United States', the reception from the border protection was hostile. When Stella was asked the purpose of her visit and replied, 'Self-annihilation,' the moustachioed officer, who resembled the postman off *Cheers*, stared at her as if she'd roasted his mother.

'Sorry... Pleasure.'

When Stella couldn't remember the full address of Dixie's apartment, Ana stepped forward to help.

'Behind the line, please, ma'am.'

They were eventually admitted and having successfully declared with straight faces that they'd had no contact with farm animals in the previous six weeks, they'd marched arm in arm through the sliding doors.

'Do you think that Dixie will be here to collect us?'

'Not a freaking chance.'

'Will you call her?'

'You call her.'

A wall of expectant faces met them. Ana hopefully scanned the line of chauffeurs and limo drivers with white boards and branded signs. One brought her to a stop. A neat white board with a single underlined word.

'She wouldn't,' said Ana, laughing.

Stella guffawed.

Green pen on a white board read: BITCHES.

Dixie appeared from behind the small chauffeur, who looked terrified of them and her. They fell into each others' arms laughing.

'Bitches! How could you!'

'It was too easy.'

'I fucking love you, Dix,' said Ana.

Less than three hours later, they were seated at a table by the safe in the Campbell Apartment, one of their favourite bars in Grand Central Terminal. Three Thyme Collinses and three empty dishes that had once held lobster sliders. Stella had insisted on sticking with the gin theme.

'Sad people need sad drinks.'

Dixie was looking fabulous. Ana had never seen her look so

self-contained, so powerful. Something about her confidence and the protective shield of skin-tight leather gave the impression of a Marvel superhero or Trinity from the Matrix series. All black leather, high quality and clinging, topped off by a knee-length leather coat over which her long shiny locks tumbled a riot of red that glowed whenever she flicked her head. Dixie was making faces over Stella's head; she was mouthing something that seemed to be: Is she OK?

Ana shrugged. She knew Stella would need a trip to the loos eventually. No one's bladder could endure that much gin without a reaction.

'Do you think these people know who I am?' Stella asked, her voice gradually growing louder. 'Do you know who I am? Stella Hammerson. But you can call me The Boss. The boss of all of you. For why? For why because I have endured. I am the mistress of reinvention. Did I tell you girls that I am going to be the editor of a digital Slop. No, Sloppy! Don't forget the exclamation mark. It's evidence of the cutting edge on which I exist. And you know the old saying: If you're not on the edge, you're taking up too much room. Anyway, I got the job! I found out last night… I am now a working woman again! So screw Jake, I can do this on my own.'

'Congrats, Stella,' screeched Dixie, 'that is amazing!!'

The hostess appeared, and with that solicitous authority of a seasoned Manhattan professional, she asked if anyone needed anything, distracting from the Slop! chat.

Stella beckoned her closer.

'Do you know that – oh my god. Your eyes. They are so

green. They're incredible. Like shiny green beacons to guide one home. Can you tell that I am fluid? You know *fluid*? Ya hear me?'

Dixie intervened. 'I'm so sorry. She just had some good news. She is a little overexcited to say the least...'

'Fuck off Dixie, if I think...'

Ana and Dixie kicked her simultaneously.

'Just the check, please,' Dixie said with an apologetic smile.

'You're so boring. You're so straight. You look badass, but you're actually a bit stuck-up. Did you know that, Trixie Dixie? Isn't she, Ana?'

'We have plans tomorrow, Stells. You're clearly tired. I'm tired. According to our body clocks it's almost 2 a.m.'

'We want you at your best tomorrow morning. I have such a treat for you guys – the perfect cure for jet lag. Trust me. You're going to love this. It was Freddie's idea. He's such a doll. You're going to bust a gut.'

'I. Will. Not. Be busting anything. Least of all my gut.'

'The driver is picking us up at 10 a.m. I hope you have some comfortable, loose-fitting clothes.'

'For schizzle,' said Stella, sitting unnaturally upright and bouncing her breasts one at a time. Ana was mortified to see that she still wasn't wearing a bra.

They steered her towards Vanderbilt Avenue and folded her into a cab, taking a door each. She fell asleep on Ana's arm, mumbling something about the delicious scent of cocoa butter, or some such gibberish.

'At last,' sighed Dixie. 'What the fuck, Ana? You had one job.'

'God, she just won't stop.'

Ana proceeded to tell Dixie everything she'd gleaned from Stella between drinks and naps on the flight. Jake had betrayed her. The details were murky but he'd been gambling. It was the final straw. Ana knew there was more to the story, but Stella had dissolved into incoherent rants about throwing her life away on a man with the integrity of a Cheeto. How she hoped her children had her genes, cos Jake's genes would be a poor fit for anyone.

They were soon at Columbus Circle and escorting Stella safely past the anxious-looking porter and up to Freddie's flat. Stella came round and Dixie smothered her in the folds of her leather overcoat and they bustled her into the flat.

Having safely undressed Stella and parked her in the spare room in the recovery position, Ana opted to sleep on the sofa rather than share the bed with Stella. Dixie wished her a hasty goodnight and Ana lay there wishing there was someone to talk to about all her doubts and fears. She checked her phone. Nothing from Rex. He must, she thought, still be mad at her decision to disappear – in her condition – across the Atlantic for the weekend. Again, and still bitterly, she reminded herself that pregnancy was not an illness. Life must go on. But the guilt was creeping and spreading, filling her. She covered her belly with both hands and comforted herself, wondering whether the embryo was still there, whether it had taken. But she knew she'd made the right decision. Stella needed her and they had to share this moment with Dixie. All their lives were at crossroads and these were the moments when friends were worth more than their weight in gold.

CHAPTER TWENTY-ONE

Dixie

Dixie was surprised to find Ana up and about. The little pocket rocket was cleaning surfaces in the kitchen, running around in a sports bra and leggings, a dark ponytail hanging down her back like Lara Croft. She was humming a song Dixie recognised but couldn't name.

'Any sign of Stells?'

'I checked on her earlier and she was flat out on her back, naked, snoring with one hand over her eye, the other cupping her pussy. I covered her up. She needs the sleep.'

'We'd better wake her. We've got to leave soon.'

'Shotgun I don't do it!'

'Bitch!'

'It's better you do it. You're the host and, besides, she's still scared of you.'

Dixie made some tea in a large blue mug and took it in.

'Come on, Cinderella. We shall go to the ball. I need you up and dressed, casual sportswear, in twenty minutes.'

Stella groaned.

'Come on!'

'I don't do sports and I am *never* casual.'

'It will be worth it. Think hard bodies and an afterglow that will last all day. After that we've got time for a high-protein, low-carb lunch, a little shopping, maybe, if you're good, and then, as promised, a helicopter out to Long Island before sunset. We are going to be fabulous and you need to meet minimum standards: upright, washed and dressed.'

Dixie sat on the bed beside her as Stella watched her suspiciously through one bloodshot and half-closed eye.

'Come on, Stells. And don't forget, tonight we have the surprise to end all surprises. Ana's big moment.'

'What surprise?'

'You remember, the...' And she mimed the words.

Stella sat up quickly, grabbed her head. 'My god, I'd forgotten. She is going to KILL us. Literally.'

'Only by hugging and kissing us to death.'

'Are you sure it's a good idea?'

'Let the cards fall where they may. Come on. That's fifteen minutes now.'

'Breakfast?'

'No. Coffee and car. Come on, what I've got lined up for you is going to melt your labia. Seriously. Sports casual. Go.'

Dixie slapped her leg with a grin and returned to the kitchen/ living room.

'Will I be all right in this?' asked Ana, indicating her light cotton stretch trousers, Adidas pumps and a black long-sleeved Lycra T-shirt.

'Literally, you could have been cut out of a Lululemon catalogue.'

'Where are we going? Are we going to walk the High Line? I read about it on the plane. It sounds amazing.'

'Do you know me at all, Ana? Seriously. Walking, my god, no!'

Slipping into green leggings and a red spaghetti top, Dixie found herself whistling the song Ana had been humming.

'What is that song?' she shouted through the open door.

'What song?'

'That song. The one you're singing. De-de-doop-de-da-de-doop...' She moved to the doorway and watched Ana grimace.

'I have no idea.'

Dixie was pretty sure she was blushing as she turned away.

'And Stella,' she shouted.

'Yes?'

'Wear a sodding bra, you old slag!'

On the corner of Gansevoort and Hudson was an innocuous brownstone frontage that led to a lift that catapulted them to the top floor. There they found a boutique gym and spa. Freddie was a member and had arranged for Dixie's friends to be allowed to join her for the morning.

'You cannot be serious!' said Stella.

'That's about as sporty as you get, isn't it, Stella?' laughed Dixie.

'They better have sunbeds and a pool.'

Dixie checked them in at reception.

'That's awesome. I'm Monique, if you need anything. You are in for such a treat. You're on the sun terrace,' instructed the unfeasibly beautiful receptionist. 'Through the doors to the lift on the right.'

They emerged from the lift onto a hardwood decking with views across Chelsea. It was overlooked in every direction by iconic buildings. A plunge pool in the corner was rippling with what Dixie could only assume were paid extras. They looked like they'd flown in from LA. The men looked like the bastard children of Bradley Cooper and the women the illegitimate daughters of Penelope Cruz.

Dixie gave Ana a poke in the back when she saw her shoulders square, her chin lift and chest pump. 'Later,' she said.

'Thank god I didn't bring my swimmers,' laughed Stella. 'There is no room for me in that bowl of meat soup.'

'Here we are,' said Dixie.

The western half of the terrace was a gazebo. Its walls were fine linen that fluttered in the late summer breeze.

Three pristine yellow yoga mats were laid out in front of a dais where another blue mat, and four bottles of VOSS water, sat, cold enough to condense.

'Take your places, divas,' laughed Dix.

'Yoga? You know I can't see my toes, let alone touch them,' groaned Stella.

'We're not here for the yoga.'

Moments later a tall muscled man appeared. Dixie had met him once before (he was Freddie's personal trainer), but he could only be described as a gift from the gods. He was as hot as hell and as ripped as Patrick Swayze in his *Dirty Dancing* days. He was wearing a white linen shirt, all the buttons undone, white linen trousers that were wafting in the wind, and a gold chain around his neck. His hair was loosely tied into a man-bun.

Normally the chain and the bun would be an issue, but neither Dixie nor the other girls could take their eyes off him. Every time the wind blew against his legs, his packet grew defined against the fabric. He knew it; they knew it. He was hanging freely, no underwear required.

He smiled. 'Bonjour. I am Xavier. I will be your guide for the next hour.'

'Oh my god,' whispered Stella to Dixie, 'I think I might come. That is a cum-fest.'

'Yup,' said Dixie, 'that is hot flesh, ready for consumption! I guess I'll find out how into Freddie I actually am!?'

'Ah, les Ana filles!' said Xavier. 'I am here to teach you all a little bit about mindfulness and how to switch off and relax.' His French accent was ridiculously sexy. It seemed stronger than when Dixie had met him previously.

'Bonjour,' they chorused, followed by some inaudible muttering.

'Before I say anything to you, I would like you to settle down on your knees and close your eyes. I am going to come round and put something in everybody's mouth. I want you to savour it: the taste, the texture, the temperature—'

He was interrupted by an explosive snort. Stella had already collapsed in hysterical giggles. Dixie, who was doing her best to hold herself together, trying to stop the corners of her mouth twitching, felt tears running down her face.

'Sorry,' blurted out Stella. 'Sorry, I didn't mean to laugh.' Then she started again, howling with laughter.

'Was it something I said?' asked Xavier innocently.

'No, not at all,' giggled Stella. 'Please, carry on!'

'D'accord. Alors, please close your eyes and open your mouths.'

Dixie didn't close her eyes. Instead she watched her friends. First Ana, who knelt and raised her chin as if to receive the sacrament. She was hilarious. Her mouth held half open, her perfect teeth in a smile, her hands on her knees, pressing her cleavage up, the dark ponytail. Xavier took something from a jar and dropped it into Ana's mouth. Her lips closed and she sucked with a smile. Dixie was pretty sure she heard a moan.

When Xavier came to Stella, who Dixie now noticed had opted against a bra beneath her faded Ramones T-shirt, Dixie saw that Stella hadn't been able to resist closing her lips around his fingers. Stella's eyes opened and Dixie saw her give him an encouraging wink. Dixie had to fight back the laughter. She closed her eyes as he approached and had a sudden panic that he might be drugging them. This faded when her mouth closed around a fruit, so sweet, but with that hint of acid that makes a perfect strawberry. She couldn't help smiling.

'Oh my god—'

'Shh, silence, enjoy.'

Dixie leaned over to Ana and whispered, 'Will you look at this man! Why settle for a normal like Rex when there are men like this out there, just waiting to be ravaged by women like us. If someone doesn't fuck him, we'll regret it forever!'

'I bet he's wild,' whispered Stella. 'His sheets are satin, and he'll bring you coffee and croissants in bed. Or even better, he's fully into tantric sex, can keep going for hours, so there's no time for pastry!'

'Ladies, is everything OK?' asked Xavier. 'I need you to be quiet, to empty your minds, and it seems like, er, your minds are still very full.'

'Sorry,' said Stella. 'Sorry, you are right, we obviously really do need this. Right, my mind is empty.'

'Good, so I just want you to breathe in the air, to fill your lungs with the fresh air and to feel the ground beneath you. Just enjoy it, the moment you are in, and forget about everything else. This is something we don't do with our busy lives – we never take time to just be in the moment.'

And slowly Dixie began to feel calmer. Xavier's voice sang a song of tranquility and acceptance, of gratitude, of the cessation of desires. To breathe, and one by one, to realise that their lives were all so hectic in their own ways. Dixie drifted, reflecting that each of them was at a major turning point in their lives, which, while exciting, was terrifying.

'And as you feel the warmth of the breeze, you will slowly open your eyes and be ready to deal with all the bumps in the road, reassured, comme toujours, that every moment is in flux, change is constant, everything ends to be replaced by something else. And we can just be, no longer constrained by our desires and our fears. Ça va? Namaste.'

'No, thank you,' gushed Ana. 'You really were amazing, more so than we could possibly have imagined. I feel so much better and clearer after that session. You have such a gift.'

Dixie and Stella burst out laughing.

'It was my absolute pleasure,' he answered. 'Maybe I will see you all later at the chateau. You are all coming, I hope?'

They all nodded, shyly.

'What's it going to be like, Xavier?' asked Stella, putting on her most flirtatious voice. 'It sounds incredible. Will it be *very* glamorous?'

'Glamorous, yes, but people will certainly let loose and enjoy themselves. I have heard some rumour about a special guest taking the stage tonight. But I'll believe it when I see it.'

'I hope very much we will see you there, perhaps on the dance floor?' said Stella.

Xavier grinned, his devilish brown eyes melting them.

'Perhaps,' he said, 'but until then, au revoir, and I will see you lovely zen ladies later.'

After he left they flopped onto an outside sofa and ordered cocktails as they watched Bradley and Penelope's offspring cavorting in the plunge pool. No one spoke. They all took their first sip and sat there and savoured the moment. And then they started to giggle.

'Well, that has to be one of the most enjoyable meditation classes *ever*,' said Ana. 'I think we should all raise a toast to Dixie. The most amazing bit of casting. How the hell did you find him?'

Dixie just giggled. 'As I said, he's Freddie's trainer, but obviously has the same effect on most women. He's a bit notorious. Apparently he's such a target, he can't actually find a girlfriend because everyone wants just one unforgettable night. Freddie assures me he's a very smart guy. He has a degree in philosophy from NYU, but to be fair, I thought you could both do with a bit of eye candy to cheer you up! It's funny, I really can't remember what Freddie looks like, all I can see is that stupendous saucisson!'

'You don't mean that,' screeched Stella. 'You are besotted with Freddie! This is starting to feel like a hen-do. Besides, I'm the one that deserves that. With what I've been through lately.'

'You *deserve* it?!' said Ana. 'I need the meat more than you. I've been on a vegan diet for far too long.'

'But you're pregnant!?' said Stella.

'I've had an egg implanted,' said Ana primly. 'It's too early to call it a pregnancy.'

'Jesus,' said Dixie. 'Will you two look at yourselves? Fighting over the poor French philosopher like he has no free will!'

'Look,' responded Stella. 'We were all created to flirt, and to stray. It's in our DNA to find the optimal mate to impregnate us, and then nurture us, not necessarily in that order and not necessarily with the same person! We all have various needs and to expect one person to meet them all is unrealistic. Name one person you know who hasn't at least thought about playing away from home?'

They each looked from one to the other and laughed.

'No comment,' said Ana.

'Well, I will if I get the chance,' said Stella. 'Once we've done it, we discover that cheating is not the big thing we imagine it is.'

'Is there something you want to tell us?' asked Dixie.

'Is there a man on the side? Has Jake got competition?'

Dixie saw Stella's discomfort and was expecting some admission so was disappointed when she denied it. 'I can promise you there's no man in my life other than Jake. But Xavier, now there's a chocolate lolly I could wrap myself around... more than once!'

'Stella, you are outrageous,' said Ana, 'but I tell you what, it's a good idea. Why don't you have a crack at Xavier tonight and see how you feel about it. If things are tough with Jake, maybe a one-night-stand will clear the head!'

'Or at least a few cobwebs,' laughed Stella.

'Would you really?' asked Dixie.

'Damn straight,' said Stella, serious for the first time. 'First, I never turn down a challenge. Second, Jake has already betrayed me. Third, it's hardly like it's going to be a hardship! Let's get another drink. OK, I know, not you, Ana.'

When the drinks arrived Dixie returned to the subject, 'But Stella, I'm intrigued, going back to what you said earlier, does that mean you've thought about cheating on Jake?'

Stella looked to be blushing.

'Of course I have thought about it, who hasn't?' she answered eventually. 'I've been with Jake for nearly twenty years. Who wouldn't think about straying in that time? I wouldn't be human if I hadn't. But there is no other man in my life.'

'Would you tell us?' pushed Ana.

'Of course I would tell you...'

'So, who have you thought about it with?' asked Dixie. 'Is he hot, do we know him? Is it realistic or just a fantasy? It's one thing to want to screw Brad Pitt, but quite another if it's your next-door neighbour.'

'Well, Brad Pitt is a given... He's had my fingers dancing

more than once. But aside from him, I'm not sure I should tell you – maybe it's a girl...!'

They all burst into laughter again, and Dixie said, 'I think I've known you long enough to know you're not gay. Christ, how would you have resisted us two!'

'Maybe I'm having a midlife crisis,' said Stella. 'It happens you know. Sexual fluidity is all the rage at the moment.'

'Sexual fluidity? What does that even mean?' asked Ana.

'I guess it means that you're drawn to people because of their energy and your chemistry, not because they are male or female. Desire is simply desire, however it shows itself. Perhaps a female friendship develops into something more because that person makes you the happiest.'

'Keep talking...' laughed Dixie.

Stella hesitated then said, 'No, it's just something I was reading a few weeks ago. It's quite interesting though, don't you think? I was considering writing something about it for Slop! There are so many moral issues: like if all us girls started sleeping with each other, which by the way I am not suggesting as that would be super-weird, would you consider that infidelity to your partners? Would you tell them?'

Dixie and Ana looked at each other in silence. Whatever was going on between Jake and Stella, she was deeply unsettled, and the look that passed between them recognised a mutual fear of where the night might go for Stella.

'Shopping. Outfits. Helicopter. Party,' laughed Dixie. 'Tomorrow we can debate the moral ambiguities of bisexual love!'

CHAPTER TWENTY–TWO

Stella

It was exactly 5 p.m. when the car dropped them at West 30th St Heliport. Stella noticed that Dixie could in fact be on time – perhaps only when her boss was involved! Ana and Dixie were both in dresses while Stella'd gone for black velvet flares. She'd bought them in a moment of retro abandon (still glowing from Coco's house call). Her packing had been less than organised so she'd been forced to pair them with a thin, stretchy nude polyester top she'd stolen from Dixie's wardrobe (she hadn't noticed yet), and a feature that she hoped would be picked out by any neon lighting (surely there would be neon lighting, or was that only in strip clubs these days?): a daring pink bra that she'd picked without a second thought, a spontaneous purchase with Coco in mind. At the very least it would draw attention towards her best assets and away from her worst. This was also her intent with the flares.

Stella felt good, she felt confident, she felt angry, and that aggression made her feel hot. Fuck Jake, fuck him and his arsehole bullshit gambling. She was here and she was going to have some fun and she didn't care who knew.

Peter was waiting by the Portakabin, being buffeted by the downdraught of the helicopter's rotors. On the H on the tarmac, a very impressive helicopter was waiting. The tail was marked with the interlinking PP, Peter's private branding.

The three girls ran to join Peter. They were squealing, their hands clamped on their heads as they tried to shield their carefully coiffured locks from the bluster.

'Dixie, Stella, Ana,' boomed Peter. 'Welcome. We can leave in a second. Just getting final clearance. Go ahead. I will join you.'

The driver had piled their three overnight bags behind the seats and they slid in. The pilot, with requisite mirrored shades and salt and pepper moustache, gave them a grin. He even had a gold tooth and military tattoos on his bare forearms. Stella wondered if he was a Vietnam Vet. He indicated they should put on the headsets slung over their headrests.

The warm cans covered Stella's ears. Surprisingly his voice was a rich and rumbling Russian.

'Good evening, ladies. My name is Vlad. I am your pilot today. Our vessel is a Sikorsky MH60 Jayhawk. It's less than two years old so ignore what you have read in the press – we stand a better than 50 per cent chance of making our destination.'

He grinned and waited for them to laugh.

Dixie and Stella gave him a dead stare. Ana tittered nervously. Dixie and Stella were still a little drunk. Ana was sober.

'This is my first time,' said Ana.

'It will not hurrrt. I vill be verrry gentle,' Vlad teased.

Dixie and Stella rolled their eyes.

Peter climbed in and sat beside Dixie, his back to Vlad. He slipped on his headset.

'We have a go, Maverick,' he laughed. His voice was even deeper in the electric static of the headset. He slapped the back of his seat. 'What are you waiting for, Vlad? We go. Now.'

They took a sweeping circuit of Lower Manhattan and Peter pointed out his office in the MetLife Building, the Chrysler Building (Stella's favourite), the Empire State, the Flatiron, and finally the black squares of the World Trade Center memorial. Then they were away, chasing their shadow east as they climbed.

'The journey is only just over thirty miles. We will be there in no time.'

Past Queens, the country opened up and a Legoland of bungalows and tenements gave way to swathes of greens and the pristine landscaping of golf courses, and numerous bays and inlets sparkling with yachts and gin palaces.

The headset crackled and Vlad's voice cut in, 'We will be approaching from the south and landing to the east. The estate has its own helipad. If you now look down to the left you will see the chateau.'

The house comprised three large wings arranged in an H and green-roofed rotunda on the eastern edge. In front of the house were intricately symmetrical gardens arranged like a mandela around a central circle that appeared to be a water feature. To the north the grounds opened onto an inlet.

'The house looks over Cold Harbor Spring. If you get a chance, the sailing is wonderful,' said Vlad.

'You can concentrate, Vlad. I will be the tour guide, yes?'

There was a static click as Vlad acquiesced.

They landed without incident and Stella got to enjoy her 'hero-in-emergency' moment as she jumped down from the helicopter, bag in hand, ducking away from the still rotating blades as she rushed to the emergency. The emergency in this case was a tall butler who awaited them in the doorway of the conservatory with a tray of champagne.

'With the compliments of Mr Eastman. He will join you shortly.'

Stella could not help laughing. His accent was clearly supposed to be English, but his elongation of the vowels was very hammy. She took a glass.

'Cheers, Jeeves. You might want to check those flies.'

She looked down and his eyes followed hers. They all laughed, except Ana, who apologised.

A set of bamboo sofas filled the conservatory and they sat and waited for Freddie.

'Nervous, Dix?' asked Stella provocatively.

'Not a bit. You'd better like him or you'll be walking back to Manhattan.'

Stella laughed. She knew Dixie was bluffing. She was looking forward to meeting him. Anyone who could make Dixie this nervous had to have something about him.

When he appeared she was not disappointed. Well over six feet with an easy charm, a firm handshake, a large, dry hand.

'My pleasure,' said Stella, gripping his hand and pulling him a little closer so she could look up at him. 'I'm Stella. I don't bite unless it's midnight.' She winked.

'Of course, I've heard all about you.'

'All? You haven't, I promise.'

He was attentive and charming to each of them, but with Dixie he was admirable. Stella witnessed a mutual respect that excited her (for Dixie, of course).

'I hope you don't mind, Ana,' he said, 'but I made sure your champagne was alcohol-free.'

'How? Oh. Thank you,' said Ana looking around, a little embarrassed.

Shit, thought Stella, if the sharing of that secret embarrassed her, she was going to implode when she saw what Dixie had arranged for her later!

'Follow me,' said Freddie. 'I can't wait for you to meet my family.'

They headed into the centre of the house where more drinks were being served. Stella was tottering slightly in Dixie and Ana's wake as they entered a busy room with a high ceiling. She stopped and looked around in awe and envy. Wow, she thought, I remember these days! This was like the old days when she got to go to the best parties in town, back when she rubbed shoulders with celebrities on a daily basis, living on Bollinger and canapés, a regular in 3 a.m. columns, and frequently and knowingly tagged as 'overtired and emotional'. She'd left behind all the glamour and glitz that she'd taken for granted, and then quickly forgotten how it felt in the sleepless nights and shitty nappies that followed. She'd certainly never imagined she would be trapped in South London with a gambling, lying bastard of a husband. There was so much more to life than the little world she was living in, and Coco was a part of that realisation. She might have two kids, but she still had many options and no one was going to walk over her ambition. No one. No more. Something in her had switched. She felt like she had years of life to catch up on, all in one night, and an enormous future ahead of her. She'd show Jake.

'Stella, are you with us?' shouted Dixie, looking back. 'Come on!'

'Yes, out of the way,' she said, as she grabbed another glass from a tray. She was already feeling a bit light-headed, and there was a tiny little voice in her head wondering if she should look for something to eat, just to line her stomach, but there was a much louder voice which was actually shouting out of her mouth 'Beyoncé! All the Single Ladies!' and without a second's hesitation, she was dancing, hands on knees, crumping like it was carnival. In her mind at least, she was the spitting image of Beyoncé. There may be a few extra pounds hanging around, but fundamentally the move was identi-equivalent. She was just starting to really feel her rhythm, when she felt a hand on her arm. It was Ana saying, 'Erm, party girl, looks like the dancing hasn't *quite* kicked off yet, shall we go and do some mingling?'

Ana guided her towards the house as onlookers watched. Stella noticed for the first time that no one else was dancing. Not that she really cared, had anyone really even noticed? Who were these losers anyway?

'I was just warming up, you know, getting ready for later. Just checking I still had the moves, you know...'

'Sure,' said Ana patiently. 'So, who do you fancy approaching?

Do you remember when we were younger we used to each pick out someone we wanted to talk to, guess what they did, if they were single or not, and who their partners might be... So, what about those two women over there?'

Stella gave Ana a suspicious look. 'We're looking at women now, are we? Has there been some change? Something you want to say?'

'No, what do you mean?' Ana smirked, perhaps knowingly. 'No! They look interesting. They are stylish, look like they could own this place. Have they just met or are they old friends? What do they know about Freddie? Who are their men? Come on, we can't just get pissed and dance. What would Dixie think!'

And they both belly-laughed.

'Come on,' said Ana and dragged her over to the two women.

Stella could see they'd both been hitting the botox pretty hard. They looked very serious. The tall blonde tried to smile, but only succeeded in revealing her lower teeth, which looked like milk teeth. Laughing and smiling were clearly not their thing. As they approached, Stella saw that everything from their freshly highlighted hair, to their tight glowing skin and immaculate manicures shouted expense... and age. They stood like waxworks, either in their late thirties and badly damaged by shoddy cosmetic work, or in their late fifties and shockingly pre-served. The short, dark-haired one was wearing a silver couture Chanel that Stella estimated at over $10,000, topped off with a diamond tiara. A little OTT. Stella was irritated, and thought a little less of Freddie if this was the company he kept. These were not Dixie's people. Although she was flouncing around in her off-the-peg red Gucci like it was made-to-measure, so maybe you never really know anyone? Stella only had to look at her own life to realise that.

As they neared them, Ana reached out her hand and said, 'Hi, we just wanted to introduce ourselves. We are friends of Dixie's and we don't really know anyone here tonight. I am Ana and this is Stella, so, yeah, hi!'

'Dixie?' said one of the women in a strong Southern accent, 'I'm sorry, should we know her?'

'Well, you would think so,' blurted Stella, 'she's the birthday boy's girlfriend. She pretty much lives with him here in New York.'

She tried to shake a gnarled and liver-spotted hand that felt like a piece of taxidermy, but struggled – it was too cold and brittle. She did a catch-and-release and then warmed her hand against her side as subtly as she could. She now knew how it would feel to shake hands with the dead.

'Oh,' replied the tall blonde with half a sneer, in a slow, considered way, 'Oh *that's* who she is.' This did nothing to endear her to Stella. She found herself staring at the woman's forehead and mouth in fascination. In fact she might have got too close as they both took a step backwards.

'Well, how lovely. Freddie hasn't had the chance to introduce us yet. He really does deserve a little happiness. What a lovely man.'

'A lovely man. So tested. It never ends.'

'Sorely tested. So much compassion.'

They shook their heads, expressionless.

'Tested?' said Stella. 'What do you mean tested?'

No one said anything and Ana touched Stella gently on the arm, saying, 'So, where are you guys from? Have you known Freddie a long time?'

The blonde, who introduced herself as Holly, said, 'Our husbands were at Harvard with Freddie, so you know, we've been here with Freddie through everything. What a ghastly illness. It's so great to see him throwing such a big party, to see so many of the old Harvard faces.'

Jesus, we get it, thought Stella. Your husbands went to Harvard. Well done you. What a massive achievement. You got married.

The blonde was droning on. '... He deserves some fun and this party... and your little friend of, course, are all part of it. Dixie – it was Dixie, wasn't it? – is a very lucky girl.'

'Or rather he's a lucky guy,' smiled Stella through gritted teeth, 'Dixie is one in a million.'

'Well, given what's happened, I don't think anyone would call Freddie *lucky*, but fortitude is the father of resilience.'

At that point, fortuitously, a waiter interrupted them with a tray of irresistible canapés. The Botox bitches just waved them away but Stella grabbed two duck rolls in one hand and declined the offered napkin. She didn't want to have to put her drink down so she shoved both in and chewed with difficulty, cheeks bulging, watching them watch her with what might have been horror or admiration. It was impossible to tell.

At this very moment, another tray of drinks floated by about chest high. Stella followed it and when she returned, Ana had disappeared. She shrugged and, hearing music, followed her ears towards the dance floor. There she knew she would find her people: those who were too drunk to be making polite conversation.

CHAPTER TWENTY-THREE

Ana

The ornamental gardens before her were lit in boulevards like a New World Versailles, and between the low box hedges New York's glitterati buzzed. A jazz band was playing, as Ana stroked her dark, lustrous ponytail and pulled it a little coyly forward over her shoulder and took another sip of champagne, holding it patiently in her mouth so as to savour every molecule. Ana was glowing and it wasn't a pregnancy glow. It was the Perrier Jouet. Being permitted a single drink each day ensured (perhaps it was a hangover from Xavier's mindfulness) that she wrung every microsecond, every mind-accelerating split-second of pleasure from the perfectly chilled coupe.

She'd had to get away from Stella. There was jeopardy in every interaction. She wanted to help her but didn't know how.

Ana's dress choice, a Saturday-prescribed black and white, obviously, was a triumph. The black and white chevrons were stark enough to slow traffic. She was looking superb and she was enjoying that awareness.

A cold hand covered her eyes.

'Guess who?'

'Dix, I can hear you and *smell* you. What have you been doing?'

'That is smoked salmon... FYI! Isn't this amazing?'

They looked down to where a troupe of acrobats had appeared on stilts passing out flowers as they stepped over the hedges and around the partygoers; others were juggling and tumbling, all were dressed as harlequins. One was leading a rather scared-looking giraffe.

'I have never seen anything like it. I keep expecting Leonardo DiCaprio to come round the corner in a tux. Having fun, Freddie?'

Freddie had appeared behind Dixie and was now between them, his arms wrapped comfortably around their waists.

'Let me escort the two most beautiful women in New York State to the music. You, Ana, are going to love this.'

Ana allowed herself to be led down the steps and along the hedgerow, which led them to the side of the house. Ana loved to dance, but her sobriety concerned her. Would she be able to let go without a skinful? She guessed she'd have to learn if she was going to adapt to motherhood.

'What kind of music are we having? I was really enjoying the jazz quartet.'

'Me too, but this is something a little more rock and roll.'

Looking at Freddie, tall and dapper in his tailored dinner suit, a slightly effeminate James Bond figure, Ana picked him for some kind of prog-rock fanatic. He probably felt intensely about Pink Floyd and ELO. Ana liked to grind to Beyoncé.

They followed a trail of tiki torches down a gravel pathway

that led them into a secret garden surrounded by a ten-foot-high hedge. A small stage was set up and the PA was playing Dolly Parton's '9 to 5' and despite herself, Ana felt a little jiggle coming on. She was relieved that Freddie's hand stayed on her waist. Too many of Dixie's men would have stooped to cop a feel. Maybe she had found a good one. Their eyes met and Ana could see that Dix was almost bursting with happiness.

When some of his friends appeared, Freddie pulled Dixie away and they began to dance and sing beside her. Out of the corner of her eye, Ana could see Stella was holding court at the small Waikiki Bar, set up in the corner of the garden, beneath full-sized, up-lit palm trees. She was toasting the crowd with what looked like a piña colada plus all the trimmings: multiple straws and umbrellas, and a dangerous-looking sparkler. She was pleased to see she was having fun, but she couldn't help worrying.

The stage was obscured by the spotlights that shone out over the assembling crowd, but Ana could see silhouettes gathering on the stage. The PA was still playing Dolly Parton, and the dance floor was roaring approval. Ana couldn't tell whether the fun and laughter were ironic or not, but decided it didn't matter: laughter is always good. Then she saw that Stella was weaving towards the dance floor, now with a piña colada in each hand.

The song ended and the crowd gathered, fidgeting as they do between acts. As voices competed to fill the Dolly vacuum, Ana withdrew slightly and was on the point of returning to the big house when she heard a harmony she recognised.

She froze.

She turned.

The harmony continued. The one she'd been humming back in Dixie and Freddie's condo.

She knew that song, but...

The stage was framed by lights and the band were now backlit. To the right was a drummer, to the left a bass player, and to the centre the silhouette of a tall man in a Stetson with an acoustic guitar.

It was a Van Morrison cover. It was *that* Van Morrison cover.

The singer began to sing 'Have I Told You Lately' and something grew inside Ana, filling her with a warm chill. Her spine tingled, her stomach was hollow, and the hairs on her arms and neck stood. She felt sick.

It was him. She was excited and terrified. She was shaking. She didn't know how to clear her head. This could not be happening.

That voice. The husky intimacy. It took her right back to that hotel in Maine as if he were whispering it to her, his breath hot on her ear.

She looked around and saw Dixie to one side of her and Stella to the other, both watching, smiling. Their eyes were gleaming with tears. She realised that hers were too. This was too much.

Her eyes were drawn to the stage as the lights came up on Joel. His stare was on her. He was smiling. He lifted his hat in acknowledgement, and then grabbed the microphone.

She'd forgotten the sheer power and size of him. His voice was crisp like money and as his big brown hands dwarfed the microphone, Ana couldn't help but picture him whole and naked.

He continued to sing to her.

The panic began at her feet. It emptied out her legs. Her stomach tossed and twisted in nausea. Her heart wanted to burst out of her throat. She couldn't breathe. Without looking at Dixie or Stella, she fled from the secret garden, turning left, away from the path of Tiki torches, away from the house, into the darkness.

She headed into the blackness, away from the noise, away from the lights, away from the people. She couldn't contain the volume of emotions. She was freaking out. Her heart was pounding. She stopped in the nothingness, hands on knees, afraid that she was going to hyperventilate. From a distance, he had still looked like the same old Joel – insanely hot, incredibly cool and sooo chilled. But there was something more about him, a confidence, an air of knowing who he was, what he'd done and what he wanted. When she'd known him, he was no one, just a boy with a dream; she had felt the timing wasn't right, and she also felt she needed to go back to England – she never thought they could actually have a future. God, how wrong she was. She let her head drop. She was sweating. Success must have changed him, she thought. She mustn't, she told herself, believe for a second that he was still that kind and foolish young man. Her eyes were adjusting to the moonlight and she could make out a farm track that led towards what looked like the silhouette of an outbuilding. As she drew closer, she saw that it was the conical roof of an old oast house.

A line of hay bales blocked the doors and she sat. She could still hear the muffled sounds of his voice from the secret garden below. She wanted to smoke. That's what people do in movies when they get thrown a curveball.

You bitches, she smiled to herself and shook her head. Of course they'd known. They'd set her up, in spite of knowing that she'd had Rex's seed implanted in her womb. She rubbed her stomach and was baffled at her situation. Poor Rex, she loved him, but was she *in* love with him? This was, she knew, probably his last chance at children and here she was a continent away from him being set up, by her best friends, with her long-lost love. But then she remembered that whilst she'd had very strong emotions for Joel, she'd never actually had his penis inside her. Could you really call it a sexual relation without penetration?

Stop it! she told herself. She was drifting into fantasy. What would Joel want with her other than a bit of flashback fun, some flirtation with 'the one that got away'. She knew better than to fall for the stylised courtship of a global pop star. His brand was selling the possibility of sex. Of course he could play the role, doff his Stetson and sing her the song that made her wetter than a sponge. Resting her head on her hands, her elbows on her knees, she shook her head and laughed. She was 39 going on 25. She wasn't ready for motherhood.

Caressing her stomach, she was mindful of the spark of life inside her. It would grow and it would be the best of her and Rex. He was the kindest man she'd ever dated. She'd picked him after a carefully choreographed process that, if she was honest, had begun at 16. Joel had failed that vetting process.

Rex had passed. Christ, she had the spreadsheet, the columns of must-haves, can't-haves, nice-to-haves, bearables, and her optimal partner was Rex. Grown-ups, mothers, don't base decisions on the mad rush of hormones, but instead on the experience-based, risk-aware, on the rational. She was feeling better. Yes, she was feeling herself again. She sighed deeply, grateful that the infatuation of that designer-romantic moment had passed.

'Hello stranger,' said a voice. 'Of all the barns in all the world...'

'Joel Abelard,' she answered quietly. 'What are you doing here? Honestly, it's like *Candid Camera*, isn't it?'

She looked around theatrically.

'The birthday boy contacted my agent and I spoke to Dixie. She persuaded me that it was a good idea. May I?'

She shifted to her right to make room on the bale.

'Was it?' he said.

She could feel him scrutinising her face in the silvery light.

'If the plan was to give me a heart attack. Then, yes.' She slapped him playfully on the arm with the back of her hand. 'You complete bastard. And as for those bitches... I will *never* trust them again.'

'It was quite the set-up. I didn't know whether you'd be... with someone.'

There was an awkward silence.

'I am. Just not here. He's—'

'I don't want to know.' He straightened and pulled almost imperceptibly away from her, his eyes lifted to the moon. 'Well, the irony is that while before I could barely afford to take you to an island, now I could afford to give you an island.'

'I'm sure you have a million girls to buy a million islands for,' said Ana defensively, 'so I won't get my hopes up.'

'But none as pretty and English and difficult as you,' he answered. Why was he flirting with her? she wondered. She felt weak being so close to him. This wasn't what she wanted, but she felt herself slide towards him. She must tell him about the IVF. She would.

'Shall I buy you a drink? We can talk about the old times. I'd love to hear what's going on with you and your crazy friends. None of you have changed one bit,' he said and slung an arm around her shoulders.

'I'd love to hear how Willy B. Goode got his big break. I just hope you still have your pick-up truck!'

'I actually do. The beast is in my garage, fully restored and only used on *very* special occasions!'

He took her in through the back of the house, down a long, dark gallery room, the walls spotlit with twentieth-century American art. Ana spotted a reproduction *Midnight Ride* of Paul Revere. At least she thought it must be a reproduction.

'I just can't believe this,' said Joel. 'I have thought of looking you up so many times, so when I got the call I was... Well, it felt like fate. Do you believe in fate?'

'You've thought of looking me up?' she laughed uncomfortably. 'I don't believe that, Joel. You, an international superstar, interested in what I am up to, why? I'm sure that ship sailed a long time ago.'

'Oh come on, Ana, you know me better than that. Fame is hard – it might have made me richer, but it hasn't made me many real friends. Everyone is after something, and sometimes it's just *really* hard to know who to trust, who your friends are. You and me, what we had was special. It just wasn't the right time. For you anyway.'

'No, Joel. I don't know you better than... than... anything. Twenty years ago I fell for a penniless singer with guitar and a pick-up truck and now you're a household name. Damn you, I can't even go for a drink with my friends, drive to the gym, take a freaking bus without hearing 'Brown Eyed Girl', or seeing your shiny face on the side of a bus. Damn you, Joel, you're on the side of London buses!'

'You gotta admit that's kind of cool.'

She paused. 'I thought about getting in touch too. Are you still on that pledge thing... with the, you know...'

She mimed a finger going in and out of her fist.

He smiled as he caught her eye.

'Me to know, you to...'

She blushed all over. 'I follow your news, watch your fan sites. I love keeping up to date with what you are doing. Not,' she said hurriedly, 'in a stalkerish way though, just out of interest. I mean, I am absolutely definitely *not* a stalker.' Oh god, she thought, why can't I just shut up!

He laughed.

'Awww, that's a shame, I love the idea of you stalking me.'

'Don't you have hundreds of stalkers?' she asked as they emerged at the front of the house into the bright lights of the ornamental garden. The pathways were quieter now and Ana could hear some heavy beats coming from the secret garden.

'Sounds like it's kicking off now the old country star's stepped aside,' said Joel.

She liked his modesty. It made her wet, which was absolutely *not* what she wanted.

'Is it like *Almost Famous*, when you're actually famous? Has Kate Hudson hit on you? Oh my god, have you met Kate Hudson?'

'I have, she's lovely, but not my type. She's just not uptight enough. I like— What about you? A trail of heartbroken exes who didn't make the grade? No kids, no divorces? Living the middle-class dream you wanted so badly?'

There was a hint of bitterness in his comments that shocked her for a second. Could he really have been pining for her all these years? Could this be anything more than fantasy?

'Not really, no – I am still doing the same job, incredibly, but I love it. It took me a while to settle down. As you know, I'm *very* particular. I spent much of my life thinking there was something better around the corner, that I'd find my baby daddy down the road.'

'Well, maybe there still is?' flirted Joel.

'What, something better around the corner? No, it's too late for all that,' she said, more harshly than she intended. She was feeling a little nauseous and for a panicked second she worried it was morning sickness. But no one, surely, got morning sickness at midnight. She felt slightly dizzy and reached out for Joel's arm.

'I'm not feeling very...' Her head was spinning and Joel wrapped his arm around her and helped her to a bench.

'Let me get you some water,' he said. 'You'll be OK?'

She nodded.

He returned soon with a bottle of sparkling water and a glass, with ice.

'Thank you,' she said smiling. 'I honestly thought I would never see you again. But you look great. Fame obviously agrees with you. So buff...'

Her hand was tiny on his bicep, and his muscled arm was hard through the soft cotton.

'I have to keep the ladies happy. My record label are always telling me to hit the gym and keep myself trim. It's part of the brand. That's the worst bit of it really – you know fitness is not my thing! But you haven't aged a day – still one of the pertest asses I have ever seen.'

He reached over and brushed a strand of hair behind her ear.

'I've really missed you, Ana,' he said. 'I've often thought you were the one who got away.'

'So why didn't you try to find me?' she found herself asking.

'Because you made it clear you didn't want me, that I was just a bit of fun for you. I could never be the city boy you thought you wanted, I was just the rough cowboy you liked having on your arm. I was just part of your story. No one wants their heart broken twice.'

'Well, maybe I was wrong. I was young, I felt too scared to try and break the mould. We all make mistakes,' she said quietly. She knew what was going to happen next. There was nothing she could do. He moved towards her, took her glass and placed it on the paving stone. And then very slowly he started to kiss her. Gently rediscovering her, holding her head in his hands. She let out a gasp. Even the touch of his tongue on her lips sent shivers down her spine. She could feel herself wanting him already, needing him, so she responded to his kisses. She searched his mouth, pulled him closer, wanting him, needing him.

His hands over her breasts, over her nipples. She let out a groan as he kissed down her neck, telling her how beautiful she was, how he had always dreamed of this day, of finding her again. All the memories of when they were first together came flooding back...

She broke away.

'There's something I have to tell you, Joel... I'm trying to have a baby...'

His dark eyes smiled at her.

'Me too, but you know how it happens, right? We'll need to do more than tongues.'

She slapped him on the chest.

'No, Joel, I'm serious,' she said, her voice thick with emotion, her throat tight. 'I'm trying—'

But his mouth closed over hers, muffling her words, and she lost her train of thought as the taste and strength of him flooded over her.

The next thing she knew they'd run, hot and frantic with desire into the shade of the house and through a set of glass double doors inside. They found a library with two antique armchairs and a reading lamp in the window. On the library walls were two murals she recognised by a local painter. One was a swimming pool piece she'd never seen before. In a dark area beneath a mural was a chaise longue. Joel locked the door. She could feel his touch as he unzipped her black and white dress and it fell at her feet. Dropping to his knees, he pulled her underwear down and off her feet in a single motion. Ana smiled, noting how much he'd changed. He had moves. They'd have to talk about that. He was clearly no virgin.

His tongue was soft but insistent. She lay back with her hand on his head, pressing him against her. He was multi-tasking, she noted admirably, and he wrenched at his belt, and wriggled out of his trousers, his tongue never once losing contact with her clitoris in spite of his rush. Rex could learn a lot from Joel, she thought, before she was hit by the cruelty and selfishness of her betrayal.

She moaned and shook her head.

'You are so fucking wet,' he whispered, and as he thrust his fingers into her she let out another guilty cry of pleasure. She knew she wouldn't last long; she remembered his touch, and every part of her body was throbbing and longing for more.

'I want to fuck you so much, Ana, it hurts, years of wanting you, of waiting for you,' he continued as he kissed her belly, her breasts, her neck. The urgency of Ana's desire was rising to meet his, her legs opening wider as she sensed the imminence of penetration.

'Take me,' she gasped. 'Please, I need you, please.' She was begging. She couldn't help herself. She reached down and guided him deftly into her, feeling herself closing around him as she'd imagined a thousand times all those years ago and in all the years since. His penis seemed to swell inside her. Hot and hard. She locked her legs behind his back and tried to pull him even closer. He was pressing against her cervix and it was almost too much. For a second, time stopped and everything went black. Had she passed out? But as her head cleared and he was rhythmically thrusting into her, his stubble rough against her neck, his scent of wood and stone filling her nostrils, she was bitterly reminded of Rex's frenzied humping, his soft hands and milky scent. She felt a surge of resentment that she overcame by pushing herself harder against Joel as she bit into the hard muscles of his shoulder. The pain seemed to inspire him. He throbbed again inside her. He lowered his head to suck her nipples as they fucked harder and harder.

Their breathing was getting heavier, and Ana could feel herself climbing towards the most intense orgasm of her life.

'I'm going to come, Joel, yes, come with me... please,' she said, arching back, thrusting herself harder towards him, wanting him to go deeper and deeper. At that moment both their bodies jerked and climaxed together as they kissed, searching for each other, burying their faces in one another, never wanting to let go. Joel held her tight, their sweat sticking them together, lost in a sea of passion and desire.

As he slowly pulled himself out of her, he glanced at her with a satisfied smile and said, 'Well, that was worth the wait, don't you think?'

She giggled coyly. 'Hmmm, I think so, and maybe you getting some practice in wasn't such a bad thing after all,' and she leaned forward and kissed him again. As her senses returned, she became conscious that they were in a library at a birthday party and that for all the pleasure of their indulgence, she did not wish to be caught *in flagrante delicto*. This guilt triggered a reminder of Rex who was probably asleep at home dreaming of being a father to the foetus she was now coming to be convinced was gestating within. She wriggled away and pulled herself reluctantly into her dress. She couldn't find her underwear but was too sated and soporific to stress.

He pulled her towards him again and kissed her. 'If you don't want this to carry on forever, you'll have to stop me because you really are quite irresistible.'

'Ever the romantic. This is all—' she paused and looked him in the eyes, her hands stroking his face. 'Well, it's a lot to take in, Joel – suddenly everything I have ever wanted is right here in front of me, and I don't even know how I feel. I think overwhelmed, and excited and like I just need to freshen up,' she said with a flirtatious smile, as she kissed him on the lips. 'I'll meet you outside on that bench we were on. I'm just going to take five and I don't want to come back and find you surrounded by groupies. OK?' She stroked his head with a loving tenderness, and then laughed and was surprised to see fear in his eyes.

'I have no intention of losing you again, Ana,' Joel said as he grabbed her hand. 'Never again.' Ana felt her stomach turn as she looked deep into his eyes and felt a depth of trust and longing she'd never felt before. She wished she'd had time to be totally honest about Rex. Oh god. Poor Rex. What was she going to do about Rex? She wanted to confess everything to Joel about him, the baby, her indecision, but she didn't trust herself right then. She was drowning in the aftershock of their sexual union. She didn't feel herself. She didn't trust herself. She felt out of control and she wasn't comfortable.

'You won't,' she said, turning on her heel, her heart pounding, not knowing whether she meant it or not.

CHAPTER TWENTY-FOUR

Dixie

Boom!

They were still in the secret garden when the first fireworks went up over the big house to celebrate the midnight of Freddie's 45th birthday, and the crowd, led by a soprano from the Met finished an a capella version of 'Happy Birthday', before the DJ (one of Freddie's old uni mates) launched into a mildly ironic remix of Destiny's Child's, 'Survivor'. It was a good-humoured singalong.

'Freddie... you're a miracle! This is... I don't know. You are such a dark horse. You never stop surprising me.'

Dixie was draped around Freddie's neck like a scarf. She was a little drunk, and very loved up, but it just felt so good. As he grinned at everyone, his long fingers slid in through the cut-out keyhole on the back of her dress, reaching round, pulling her closer.

'Do you want your birthday present?' she asked.

He nuzzled her neck, inhaling.

'My birthday present?'

'Well, second present. Some presents are things, trinkets,

souvenirs, and others are experiences. I want to give you something you've never had before, something you'll never forget.'

She ground against him, drunk with desire, lost in the moment.

Dixie was having the best night of her life. She thought she'd lived a pretty wild life, been to the high side, walked with some low-lifes, but this was next level, or so it seemed to her lust-heightened, champagne-fuelled consciousness. The chateau was movie-set fantastic. The evening was perfect. The sky clear and the air warm and the people so much fun. Freddie was such a joy to be with. He was funny and attentive, but never needy or cloying. She was having a great time. As, probably, was Ana who'd disappeared, but Dixie had a pretty good idea what she was up to. Little minx.

'What about Rex?' Freddie had asked. 'Isn't he your friend too?'

'Hierarchies, Freddie. My first duty is to Ana, and if Rex and Ana's relationship isn't strong enough to endure a single encounter with Joel, then all we've done is save them both a lifetime of heartache.'

He hadn't looked convinced.

'But you're interfering. It's pretty manipulative. I mean you set them up. Poor Ana.'

'Why do you care so much about Ana? Has Freddie got a little friend crush?'

'Don't be silly. Relationships are always complex. People have to make difficult decisions. What if Ana and Rex are just having a wobble and without your interference they'd be fine?'

Dixie had kissed him and told him how adorable his decency was. He'd turned away.

Stella, fortunately, was on the most incredible form. It was literally like the old days. Late-Nineties-Stella had so many drinks on the go she didn't know which was left and which was right. She looked amazing in a kind of Marianne Faithfull meets Stevie Nicks kind of way. Dixie watched her dancing, perhaps a little too enthusiastically, with Xavier, who was still wearing linen, but an evening wear version of it in layered blacks and blues. Her neon-pink bra shone through the sheer nude T-shirt. Her flares were something people would write about in fashion magazines in years to come. Right on the edge of disaster, they were an era-defining triumph because they so captured her attitude. She was head-banging to Bon Jovi. Luckily Dixie couldn't hear her over the PA, but their eyes met and Stella mouthed, 'You give love a bad name,' before returning to her air guitar.

'Come,' she said to Freddie. 'Let's go join Stella. I want to see your air guitar.' She reached up and nibbled at his earlobe.

'Let's do it.'

They joined Stella, who screamed, dropping to her knees, 'Freddie Fan-Dango, would you like to do the tango!' She stuck out her infeasibly long tongue and mimed some kind of inappropriate cunnilingus. Freddie laughed and helped her to her feet.

'Dix warned me a free bar might be a mistake.'

'I. Have. Only. Just. Started,' hiccuped Stella.

'Come,' said Freddie. 'Let's get some hydration.'

'Champagne! Great idea. You know what, I like you, Freddie. Most of Dixie's men are B-list arseholes, but you're all right. You're A-OK. A as in A-list,' she hiccuped, 'not arsehole.'

Stella folded double in hilarity at herself.

'Is she always like this?' asked Freddie over her head as they wound their way back into the ballroom. The bright lights were a bit of a shock and Dixie felt a tremor of fear as Stella wobbled away with Xavier across the parquet floor.

Dixie slapped Freddie's butt as he disappeared towards the champagne bar, which was still stacked with an impressive pyramid of vintage champagne coupes that glinted and sparkled beneath the enormous chandeliers.

She ducked away into the carpeted quiet of the corridor. Emerging from the washrooms, she ran into Peter.

'You look very happy. This is good. You are very much in love with this boy?'

She moved closer, reached out a hand to touch the silk collar of his evening suit, then to stroke it flat, patting him on the chest.

'He's a good man. It's taken me a long time to find someone who is both exciting and available. I am happy, Boss. Thank you.'

She tilted her head and looked up at him. He growled a little, shuffled from foot to foot, readjusted his groin. He lowered and averted his gaze. Was he blushing?

'You really trust him?'

'As much as I have anyone,' she said, giving him a knowing look.

He nodded. 'I am happy.'

'Good,' said Dixie, relieved. 'Now can we go back to the party?'

Returning to the bar area, Peter left her as she searched for Stella and Ana. Both were absent. She wondered whether to be worried for Stella, or, noting Joel's absence also, excited for Ana. She caught Freddie's eye and he blew her a kiss from the bar. Spotting a gold Starck love seat just behind her, she opted for a moment just to herself. She'd just close her eyes and enjoy the music, just for a minute. Perhaps there was more to Xavier's mindfulness than an eyeful. She slipped her shoes off to allow her throbbing feet to cool and shrink.

She was brought out of her reverie by a snort, followed by a cold hand shaking her shoulder.

'Hello, Dixie? It is Dixie, isn't it? You're Fred's little friend, aren't you? We have heard SO much about you, we just wanted to introduce ourselves.'

She opened her eyes to see two women who looked like they'd been super-dried in a wind tunnel. They were trying to smile but the skin around their temples and beneath their cheekbones was threatening to split. Their faces were hard and smooth, almost ceramic, and their dresses were obviously nothing less than this season's catwalk pieces, with jewels weighing down their tiny frames. Dixie snorted as she realised one was wearing a Barbie-like tiara. Money was obviously not an issue, even if their taste was more kept-trophy-whore than class.

Dixie slid back into her shoes and stood so she could look down at them, sweeping her red hair back over her pale shoulders, and smiled politely.

'Hi,' she said with as much enthusiasm as she could manage. 'It is *so* great to meet you. I am guessing you are *old* friends of Freddie?'

She tilted her head naively.

'Yes,' said the blonde one, 'and his wife. Our husbands all studied together, so we were always quite the gang.'

Dixie was rattled by the mention of the wife, as well as their smug and provocative grins, but she smiled.

'Well, it's great to finally get to meet some of his older friends. Really, isn't this house just so beautiful? I feel very lucky to be here, to share this special day with Freddie. What are your names?'

'I'm Holly,' said the blonde one, poking her chest bone and grimacing. 'My husband is a CFO.'

'And I'm Barbara,' said the Barbie, fittingly, in the tiara. 'And my husband is a COO-stroke-BDO.'

'I'm sure he does,' quipped Dixie. 'Well, as you know, I am Dixie, and I'm the HBB.'

'HB? Head of Business?'

Dixie laughed. 'Hottest Bitch on the Block.'

'I don't get it,' said Holly.

Barbie's eyes moved.

'It was a joke.'

'A joke?'

'A joke.'

'Well, whatever you are, you are SO kind to be helping Freddie through everything,' said Barbie. 'I'm sure you know what a tough time he has had. We all have. I can't even imagine how conflicted he must be feeling tonight. How Daisy would have loved tonight! How she would have shone! Sparkled.'

'Such an elegant woman.'

'Sophisticated.'

'Refined.'

'In fact I am surprised he's seems ready to embark on a new relationship with Daisy still, well, lying there. But then men, they do like to have a woman at their side, however they are feeling. My Matthew Junior would never been seen at a social event without me. He might be the CFO, but we are the TEAM.'

'Losing someone must be unimaginably hard,' said Dixie. 'Such a shock, such unpredictable trauma, but he seems to be adapting. Just because he's a widower doesn't mean his life should stop. I am glad I am bringing him some happiness at least.'

'Widower?' said Barbie. 'Oh darling, that's a bit premature, surely. Daisy is very much alive, not well, but alive.'

They were both grinning, watching and enjoying Dixie's confusion. The words hit Dixie full in the face and the aftershock rolled through her like an ice wave. She was panicking. They saw her weakness, her vulnerability and were about to press in for the kill. They knew something she didn't know; they knew something she'd always feared: everything with Freddie was a lie. Of course it was. People like her didn't deserve nice things. Of course it was too good to be true. Of course it was. She looked up and saw Freddie coming towards her with drinks in his hands, grinning from ear to ear and she thought she might vomit.

'Excuse me for a moment,' she hissed. 'Something I have to do.' She turned and left Freddie staring after her, as the two cold bitches closed around him, cooing gleefully.

She fled towards their room. She had to get her things, get the fuck out of there, fast. She couldn't breathe, she couldn't think straight, she needed space, alcohol, drugs, anything, and she needed the fucking claustrophobic, skin-tight red dress off her body.

Fuck Freddie, fuck this whole charade. She'd always known this was too good to be true. He was a lying bastard just like the rest of them. Just like her no good, non-existent father, and every other bastard with a Y chromosome.

Finding her way to their suite through a tunnel of tears, she ripped off her red dress, grabbed jeans and a T-shirt, gathered her things, and left, slamming the door. She ran to Stella and Ana's room.

Stella was slumped half unconscious on the bed.

Dixie was frantic.

'Stella!' She shook her. Her top was wet and sticky. Just booze, she hoped.

She was trying to open her eyes, but they appeared to be reluctant.

'What?' She sniffed. She'd been crying. She wafted her hand at Dixie. She smelled of sweat and pineapple.

'Stella, I haven't got time for this. We're getting out of here.'

Stella shook her head and smiling stupidly, stroked the satin bedspread.

'No, Stella. I need you up. Where's Ana?'

'Making music with the music man.' She moaned.

There was a vase of carnations on the bedside table. Dixie took a chance and emptied the contents, water and stems over the soporific Stella, who flailed at the interruption, spitting and cursing.

'You selfish bitch! I was sleeping.'

'Precisely. We're getting out of here. Now!'

'What's the drama? You get caught getting high?'

'Freddie's a lying shit. He lied to me, Stella. He's been lying to me all this time, the cheating bastard.'

Stella's eyes narrowed.

'Of course he's a liar. Wake up, Dixie. They all are. Even losers like Jake find a way to fuck you over. Newsflash, Dixie. Men lie. Men cheat. What makes you think that you're so special? Freddie's hot and rich, and at this stage in life he's probably the best you're going to get. Don't be such a princess! You're forty and fading. Get real.'

Dixie recoiled. She couldn't handle this. Stella was sitting up, her chin jutting defiantly. The side of her face was imprinted with the creases from the bed. Her hair a slutty mess. Dixie saw the sadness in her eyes, and she knew this wasn't about her.

'Christ Stella, what is it with you? You think that just because you've got some hot-shot job at Slop! that you can behave like a drunk slut and get away with it? Get a grip. Poor Jake. What did he do to deserve you?' She laughed cruelly, knowing she should stop. 'No wonder he's a gambler. Guy deserves to win something after years of losing. Look at the state of you, drunk and wearing a see-through top and a neon bra. Newsflash,

Grandma, the Nineties are long gone. It's not funny, and it sure as hell isn't sexy.'

'What did you say to me?' shouted Stella. 'At least I'm not a whore. Twenty years as PA to Peter and I suppose you never gave any extras. At least I have a career and the balls to look after myself and sort my own shit out. What have you done? Nothing!! And now you are going to run away at the first sign of trouble. Pathetic!'

Dixie felt the rage burning, sharpened and heightened by her grief. She was sobbing as she went for Stella.

'Peter's like a father to me! How dare you!'

She had Stella's thick hair in her hand and was trying to pull her off the bed. She felt Stella's teeth on her leg, painful even through the denim of her jeans.

'What are you two doing!?' Ana was there. She was trying to pull them apart.

'Will you two STOP! What's going on?'

'She started it,' Dixie hissed.

'Dixie is running scared again, more fear of commitment. And I'm not the one running around in a designer dress on Long Island pretending I am some kind of A-lister. Wake up, sweetheart, it may all be lies but it doesn't get any better than this. I have a husband I can't trust and two kids to worry about. What have you got to worry about? Yourself!' Stella lunged at Dixie again.

'Stop it!' shouted Ana. 'I've done something terrible. I need you! Please...' Her voice tremored.

'Oh piss off, Ana. You going to tell us you fucked your ex. Screwed over your baby Dad. Whatever,' Stella mocked her.

'I didn't mean to,' she cried. 'It just happened.'

'You're 39 years old, Ana,' snapped Dixie. 'Things don't just happen. That's why I invited Joel. You've been living a lie. You needed someone to shock you awake. Now deal with it. You've dodged a bullet, and Rex has a get out of jail free card.'

'I might be pregnant. I can't just walk away. I've got responsibilities. I can't just be a selfish whore. Is my baby going to grow up without a father? I can't— I didn't—'

Stella's face was red and swollen.

'I am gonna rip your clichéd little Lara Croft ponytail right off your pea-sized head,' sneered Stella.

'It's not a clip-on!'

'Oh, I know that.'

'Don't you see that you've wrecked my life! How am I going to tell Rex what's happened? I might be carrying his baby. Will he ever forgive me?'

'Of course he will. You're as good as it gets for someone like Rex. You were always going to mess it up at the finishing line. You can't choose a partner on a spreadsheet. You might be able to hold it together for a while, but biology kicks in in the end.'

'And vanity. A world-famous pop star or a baby-faced accountant. Predictable!'

'He's an account director!'

'Whatever, he's got tiny hands and a flaccid penis. Joel is a proper man.'

'And he's loaded.'

'Yeah, ride the wave. This might be the last one before the

menopause,' Stella said. 'And you might want to think about that, Dixie, before you run out on Freddie.'

'What's Freddie done?' asked Ana.

In the drama, Dixie had almost forgotten, and the recollection overwhelmed her. The world seemed to lose all colour and she had to scrunch her eyes closed to prevent herself screaming. She pulled against Ana's grip on the nape of her neck. The pain made her feel safe.

'What's he done?'

'Cheated or something. Whatever,' Stella slurred.

'His wife's still alive. He's still married. It's all a lie.'

Dixie felt Ana's grip loosen momentarily and took advantage. Ignoring the pain she wrenched herself free and fled the room, not caring where she was going or what was going to happen next. She just had to get away. She'd run to Stella and Ana seeking safety and instead encountered the kind of cruelty that only those closest to us can dish out. She had to find Peter.

CHAPTER TWENTY-FIVE

Stella

Stella arrived home completely exhausted from the flight. She pressed the door closed behind her as quietly as she could. She didn't want to talk to anyone. Jake had left the hall light on, she noticed, feeling grateful on the one hand and caged by her predictability. If he could manage the small things, how could he mess up something as big as gambling away their financial security? At least he never cheated on her. Guiltily recalling Dixie's horrified face as she came to terms with Freddie's betrayal, Stella wondered at the fact that she'd never questioned Jake's fidelity. Even, she was exasperated to note, as she cheated on him with Coco. But for some reason Coco didn't feel like infidelity to her, and she guessed this was because she was another girl, so it felt safe. They had been texting all weekend and Stella enjoyed the banter, but her emotions were hanging by a thread, and she suddenly felt herself feeling needy for Coco, and so she also knew she had to finish it with her to maintain her sanity. Hangovers and fatigue, she recalled, sometimes give us access to uncomfortable truths. Truths, she thought, that we are organised enough to defend ourselves against when we're bolstered by the everyday. She shook her head and momentarily considered opening a bottle of Pinot Grigio to soften her hard landing. No, she thought, I've had my interlude of reality avoidance and the dream had turned into a nightmare. Oh god, she thought. What things had she said to Dixie and Ana? Then she stung with indignation as she recalled the barbs they'd thrown, which had cut deep, close to her heart. Friends make the *worst* enemies. Even gentle Ana. They'd chosen not to speak other than to complete the functional necessities of travelling home together. When the check-in desk had informed them they couldn't sit together, Stella was certain she'd heard Ana mutter 'good' before she strode off with her boarding pass. She'd only seen the back of her head at passport control. She had no idea how Ana had got herself home to Battersea.

Stella's memory of the night was obviously patchy. She'd been very drunk. Specific recollections were rare. But there was a cloud of shame over her memory of events. When Dixie had left, Ana had broken down in tears. Stella was bitterly embarrassed that she couldn't remember what she'd said. Obviously, she'd fucked Joel. That was a given. What Stella and Dixie had obviously underestimated when they initiated the tryst was that Ana was capable of an act of disorganised and poorly considered passion. They'd clearly underestimated how confused and conflicted she'd be by having sex with the ex, Joel, while maybe pregnant with the next ex, Rex. It sounded so absurd. If this were some trashy romance novel there'd be a clear and simple solution that resolved everybody's predicaments in a triumphant wedding scene, everyone would live happily ever after, but this was real life and people were getting hurt. There didn't seem to be a happy ending to their situation. She sighed as she remembered she still had to deal with Jake, and her relationship with Coco needed to be addressed. Her period of happy experimentation prior to the New York trip felt like another life. Or perhaps, more accurately, like a dream or a season finale of a TV show she'd watched months previously. Today's concerns erased everything prior.

Stella opened the fridge and was relieved to see an open bottle of Sauvignon Blanc. One wouldn't hurt. Her thoughts were running at one million miles an hour. She had to switch off. Oh god, what had she said to Ana!? It didn't bear thinking about. She savoured the slightly acidic aftertaste of the week-old Sauv Blanc. At least it was cold. She raided the fridge again. This time for some cocktail sausages that Coco had bought before the trip. She ate them two at a time. OK, maybe one last splurge of indulgence. She didn't deserve it, but she needed it. She'd been an awful friend. OK, she'd been drunk, but that was just a contributing factor. If she was honest, Ana's vulnerability made her envious, as did her skinny prettiness. It always had. She was everything Stella couldn't be. Her anal organisation and frantic need to control everything just served to remind Stella how careless she was about her life. She ate the last sausage, noting, again, that she had no self-control, not like Ana, which was why she was as thin as a stick. Finishing the wine, she lowered her forehead to the table, knocked twice to remind herself she was alive, and allowed her eyes to close. A moment later she heard footsteps, and looked up to see Jake standing in front of her.

'I thought you were sleeping,' said Stella cagily, feeling immediately irritated.

'I couldn't. I've been waiting for you to get home, I wanted to talk, see how you were.'

He sat down opposite her and poured himself a glass of wine. Just like the old times, thought Stella, except when we used to sit and drink bottles of wine that tasted like piss, it was to have fun and shag, not drown our sorrows.

There was a long silence. Elbows resting on the kitchen table, Jake rubbed his hands through his hair as he did when he was under pressure. Stella got up and reached for a pile of leaflets she'd brought home before she headed to New York, and pushed them over to him.

'What are you saying?'

'I am saying you need help. You can't be here in this house doing this, ignoring the consequences of your actions. I don't want the boys to see what is going on. I need to concentrate on being their mother, not your bloody carer.'

'But I *have* stopped gambling, Stella. It won't happen again. Come on, we are strong, we're a team, we've always been a team. You and me, baby, how it's always been. I can make it all go away, make everything right again. I can fix it, please.' His voice was desperate. He reached for her hand and she flinched.

'You lied to me, Jake. You lied day after day, and you risked everything we have. You risked the roof over our children's goddamn heads. You nearly lost us everything! I just can't forgive and forget, not like that.'

'What can I do, Stella? Tell me what I need to do to make you trust me again.'

'I've told you. You are ill. I don't believe you that you won't do it again. You have an addiction. Read the leaflets.'

'What are you talking about? I'm not like these people. I was just acting out. It's under control. I'll pay the money back.'

'The lies, your behaviour, the refusal to admit you have a problem. Until you fix this, Jake, there is no us. We cannot be a family.'

'Are you leaving me? Is that what you mean? Don't you love me?'

'I'm not going anywhere. You are. You need time to think and you need time to get well. This isn't about love. I don't believe in you any more. We lost our way. We used to be young and free, to laugh, to be impulsive. Somewhere we lost all the good stuff and it all just became resentment and obligation. I love Tom and Rory, but when was the last time we were happy as a family? You work every bloody hour God sends. What is the point? It's not just you who got bored. I did too. I just didn't develop an addiction to make the days bearable.'

It looked like the message might be getting through. He was twirling his wine glass in his fingers. His face was flushed.

'I didn't know you felt like this. I'm sorry. I haven't stopped to think. It's all just been too much. I've been trying so hard to give us the life we wanted, but I have never stopped loving you. Gambling has been a distraction, some light relief from everything, and once I started winning I just wanted more and more. And then I couldn't stop. Everything just started to spiral.'

'Why didn't you just tell me, Jake?' spat Stella with tears in her eyes.

She poured herself another glass of wine. She felt torn and disloyal. She knew she should tell him about Coco, but why complicate things. Their marriage was under enough strain. Jake was visibly distraught, but she was angry. She couldn't suddenly tell him she'd had sex with a woman. How would that help? She had to maintain her position. But then she suddenly spat out, 'I've made mistakes too, Jake, I am not a saint, I know that, and maybe some time apart, time for us both to think, will be a good thing in more ways than one.'

He scrutinised her. She held his stare as she prayed he wouldn't cross-examine her.

'I want you to check into that place. Tomorrow. I called them. They have a spot. You have to, Jake. Without it we have no future.'

'OK. What shall we tell the kids?'

'Business trip? Edinburgh?'

'Wow. You've really thought about this.'

'You'll be gone two weeks – initially. You can stay longer, but two weeks is the minimum. You have to commit.'

'And what will you do? How will you cope?'

She snorted. She couldn't help her derision.

'I've been coping without you for longer than I can remember.' She decided not to tell him about the job, she wanted to keep that to herself for now. That was her success, her secret, something she had done on her own. She didn't want it tarred by him.

He nodded guiltily.

'Promise me you'll get some help. I'm sorry about the nanny.'

She narrowed her eyes.

'The nanny?' she asked.

'Pressuring you to get rid of the nanny. I was panicking. The demands were piling up.' He sighed deeply. 'Oh dear, I really fucked this up for us, didn't I?'

'It wasn't just you, Jake, it was me too – we have both played our part.'

He reached out towards her, put his arms around her. At first she froze. Then she realised that she wanted to feel safe there again. His strength, his bulk, his smell, they were as familiar to her as her own, however distraught she was, however angry. She didn't want him to leave on a bad note. She allowed herself to relax into his embrace, and for a moment as she lay her head on his shoulder, she remembered what it had been like when they had really been in love.

★

'Ana, you are not going to work today. Call in sick. I am going to come and pick you up in ten minutes and we are going to go and find Dixie and sort all this out. I cannot let it carry on.'

'Hi, Stella, just so you know, I actually tried to call you both last night, but neither of you answered. But of course, you can take the credit for being the one to sort it all out if you want to.'

'Ana, that's really not relevant right now. Enough with being complete bitches to each other. We need to find Dixie. I think we can both guess where she is.'

'Oh god, all right. But don't think I'm just going to forget about the things you said... This stress and anxiety is bad for my "maybe baby" situation. But any excuse to be away from Rex sounds good.'

'Good, I'm on my way. Make me a coffee for the road... pllleeaasseee.'

'Meet me at The Elm on the corner.'

'Good. Better.'

After a relatively painless chain of traffic lights and tailbacks, Ana jumped into the car, and handed her a cup marked HAG. Stella smiled as Ana studiously ignored her.

'Do we even know if she is there, or is it just a stab in the dark?' asked Ana.

'Her phone is off, but I can't think of where else she would run when the shit hits the fan. Usually I would expect to find her passed out in my spare room with an empty bottle, but she is definitely not there.'

There was a moment's silence, before Ana said with a sigh, 'I am NOT going to forget about what happened in New York. But I mean, there's no real need to discuss the details over and over, is there? I mean, things were said... Perhaps we should leave it at that.'

Stella gave Ana the side eye. 'I agree. Life is complicated. I love you girls more than anything. I wouldn't know what to do without you. Frenemies?'

'Frenemies,' laughed Ana, giving her a friendly nudge. 'Detailed and specific apologies would only serve to open old wounds.'

'We probably all know each other better than we know ourselves. That can be dangerous. Careless truths can hurt.'

She allowed herself to drift off as she tailgated onto the M4.

'Want to tell me about Country Boy? The details I mean. Girth and game?'

Stella glanced over and saw that Ana was crimson.

'Wow. That good.'

'You have no fucking idea, Stella... Whoever he's been training with has taught that boy more than a thing or two. I get wet just thinking about it. It was so...'

'Romantic?'

'Long!' she spluttered. 'And hard. Sooo hard. You know they talk about a throbbing penis? Well, this one was pulsing. Like a freaking lighthouse. But it's done, that was it, it's over. I might be having Rex's baby and that needs to be my focus. Now, talk to me about Dixie, what's our plan? I don't need to tell you that Freddie's wife being alive is like emotional horror porn for her. I've been really worried that she might do something stupid. You know, given her history.'

They were both silent.

'I'm just hoping she's run back to her great aunt Pearl. She's been so much cleaner. She was enjoying a new life. If she's not there, I really don't know. Whenever she doesn't know where to go, she runs there. It is where she feels safe, and she thinks no one can find her. Except us, of course.'

Stella turned on the radio to distract them from the rather dark turn their thoughts had taken.

Her phone rang shrilly through the car speakers. It was

Freddie for the umpteenth time since they had landed the night before.

'Shit,' said Stella. 'I'm going to have to block him. He won't stop bloody ringing!'

'Maybe we should answer it,' said Ana. 'The man must be frantic to find Dixie. We could tell him where we are going—'

'And completely betray Dixie's trust? She would kill us!'

Ana pressed the answer button, and Stella glared.

'What the hell are you doing?'

'Freddie, hi, it's Ana and Stella.'

'Oh thank god you answered. What's going on? Where is she? I have to find her. I have to talk to her. Please!'

'Whoa, Freddie. Calm down. We don't know yet. We're looking for her too,' said Ana as Stella shook her head vehemently.

'Don't,' hissed Stella.

'You mean you don't know where she is? I thought she would be with you!'

'You know Dixie. This will have shaken her to the core, Freddie. You lied about your wife. She thinks that everything she believed in was a lie. She allowed herself to love you and you betrayed her.'

'But I need to explain!' shouted Freddie. 'Please, I love her. I never lied to her.'

'Bullshit, Freddie,' spat Stella, a *lot* angrier than Ana, and annoyed by Ana's cutesy niceness. 'You told her your wife was dead, but she's alive – seems pretty black and white to me. What else is there to discuss?'

'She is alive. But not really. She's in a coma. Has been for eighteen months. And she is not my wife, hasn't been for a while. The courts granted us a divorce due to the situation. Meeting Dixie has given me the courage to take off my wedding ring and look to the future. It's complicated. I didn't want to involve her in it. She didn't seem to want to know details so I left out the details. I see now that I was wrong. I should have been clearer, but... I fell so totally in love with her. I didn't want to scare her off!'

Ana and Stella sat in silence for a few moments. He sounded like he was telling the truth.

'Well, you still lied to her,' said Stella, refusing to let him off the hook that easily.

'Not deliberately. Look, I just want to find her, explain everything to her. Please, let me do that. I love her. I really do.'

'If we find her, we'll let you know, Freddie,' said Ana, 'and I am so sorry about your wife. It sounds awful.'

Stella made a face at Ana, not quite as convinced that they should be being so nice to him. After all, he was still the enemy so she quickly added, '*If* she wants us to let you know where she is, Freddie. This is her life, her call,' and she hung up. She wanted him to know who had the upper hand.

'God, that sounds hideous,' said Ana, as she scraped her still-damp brown hair back into a slick ponytail. 'Imagine your wife being kept alive by machines, that poor man! How do you carry on with your life? Imagine if it was Jake.'

Stella flinched at the thought; maybe there was some hope for them after all.

'Look, we don't even know if it's true,' said Stella. 'Can we really trust him?'

'Oh, come on, Stella, give the man a chance. I like him. I honestly think he was just trying to do what was best for Dixie. Maybe it's time for us to start being nicer to people, trusting people—'

'Like you and your love triangle?'

They both laughed, Ana covering her mouth guiltily.

'Sorry, yes. It's much easier to live other people's lives than your own.'

'That is too fucking true!'

They arrived at the little Cotswold stone cottage. Idyllic pastoral views lay in every direction. Before they had even opened their car doors, Auntie Pearl was outside, clearly in a hurry.

'Pearl, how lovely to see you!' called Stella, jumping from the car, concerned by her body language. 'You remember us, don't you? Stella and Ana.'

'Of course I remember you, girls. How could I forget you? It took me weeks to get this house back in order after the last time you stayed. Was it New Year? Oh, I've never seen such a mess, goodness me! Well Stella, look at you. I'm pleased to see you've got some flesh on those bones! You, Ana, are going to need some cake. It'll never do. You're a bag of bones.'

Stella rolled her eyes. As well as having a heart the size of a mountain, Pearl was one of life's original feeders. According to her definition, all food was comfort food, and anyone who wasn't well-padded was ill.

'We've just popped by to see Dixie,' said Stella, warily, watching Pearl's misty eyes intently. 'Is it all right if we just pop in?'

'She's not here,' said Pearl, too quickly, thought Stella.

'Oh no,' said Ana tearily. 'We can't think where else she might be.'

'Oh dear,' said Pearl. 'Well, she's not here.'

Ana and Stella looked at each other, concern mounting.

'So you have no idea,' mumbled Stella, her thoughts growing darker as all the good options evaporated. 'She's not answering her phone.'

'Oh dear. Well, don't worry,' said Pearl. 'I'm sure she'll be back. You know what she's like. Free spirit that one. Do you want some tea with your cake?'

Pearl was tottering back towards the old wooden door.

Stella and Ana looked at each other.

'We'll just have some cake,' said Stella with a shrug. 'Can't hurt.'

Ana shook her head. 'You are hopeless.'

'We might learn something. I'll text her again.'

The kitchen was low-ceilinged. Wooden beams were hung with pots, pans and plants. Everything had a patina of dust. At the centre of a battered and scarred table was the biggest fruit cake Stella had ever seen.

'Have you heard from her?'

'Heard from who, dear?'

'Dixie?'

'Well, of course I have. She'll be back soon, I'm sure. Ooh, aren't you a little worrier? Cake? Ana?'

'Just a small slice!'

'I know. A slice. There.'

'That's a block, Pearl,' said Ana.

'Oh, eat up, dear. Don't let Stella eat it all.'

'Pearl, when did you hear from Dixie?' said Stella, starting to get irritated.

'There's more cake, dear. Please calm down. Dixie went out for a run a while ago. She told me not to tell anyone she was here, but as it's you, I'm sure it's fine. Oh I hope you can cheer that poor dear up. She's all tears since she arrived, never seen her so unhappy. She's really not eating properly. She won't talk about it, so I hope you girls can help her sort it out.'

Stella and Ana exchanged relieved looks.

It wasn't long before Stella heard the front door slam. There was no way to hide their car. *Shit*, thought Stella. Here goes.

Dixie marched into the kitchen, doled with mud, her flushed cheeks clashing with her fiery hair.

She glared at them.

'What the fuck do you want?'

'Language, dear. We have guests,' said Pearl, cutting another brick from the cake.

Dixie filled a glass at the sink, drained it, wiping her mouth on her muddy arm.

'Nice to see you too, Dixie,' said Stella. That Dixie was still furious was a sign she was coping.

'You two friends again, are you? You sobered up then, Stella? Congrats. That was some performance.'

'Yup, sorry about that,' mumbled Stella. 'I *maybe* got a bit out of hand, but from what I can remember it was a great party... I mean, I really did have a good time... until... well. Yes. I could have behaved better. I could have been a better friend.'

She looked at Dixie to see her reaction, but there was nothing but contempt.

'Things were said... Look, I didn't fully understand what you were going through.'

Dixie exhaled slowly and ominously.

'Things were indeed said. Indeed they were. The truth will out. I guess it's good to know the mutually low opinions we hold of each other. No secrets and no loyalty. One for one and none for all. So why are you here? My phone was switched off. Too subtle? Bit rude to just turn up, don't you think?'

Ana stood up. 'Oh come on, Dixie, it's us. We've been able to forgive and forget and we are hoping you will too. We have bigger things to worry about than a few careless words. We have Freddie and his nearly dead ex-wife to discuss. Stella's got to decide whether to leave her husband, and we have to make a decision on who I am going to choose as my maybe baby daddy. I mean COME ON! Life doesn't get more fun than this...surely? You love this shit. This is why we're friends. It's not just parties, and good times, and cake.' Stella was amazed to see that she'd finished the first block and was onto a second, spraying crumbs as she spoke. 'Friendship isn't all fun and frolics. It's also about being there through the break-ups and betrayals, through the awful boyfriends, tragic fashion choices, bad hair days, and the poorly planned pregnancies.' The cake disappeared, her cheeks swollen. 'I need you girls to help me sort out my life. Without you I might just keep eating until I explode.'

'Well said, dear,' cheered Pearl and handed her a third piece of cake.

Stella watched as Dixie's anger crumbled. 'You're right. Someone is going to have to save you from yourself.'

Dixie took half of Ana's cake and smiled to Stella.

'Eat up, Fattie. This is now officially a team-building exercise. The cake must be eaten.'

Pearl fluttered between them, plying them with cake and tea as they began the process of putting their lives right.

'So what did he say?' asked Dixie as they all sat around the fire that Pearl had lit for them in the sitting room. 'Will I need a drink?'

'I do,' said Stella. 'Besides it's a proven theory that it's easier to understand men when one's drunk.'

'Handicaps us to their bovinely stupid level.'

'Only way I can deal with them,' joined Pearl with a bottle of Prosecco.

'Well,' pushed Dixie, taking a flute, 'tell me.'

'He really does love you,' answered Ana. 'It sounds like—'

'Facts, Ana. Please...'

'He was just trying to protect you. The ex—'

'Daisy.'

'The EX-wife is in a coma. Irrecoverable. She's brain-dead, Dixie. Why didn't you talk to him?'

'Why did he lie to me?'

'Did he?'

'At best he let me believe something that wasn't true.'

'Have you ever been in his situation? How might you act?'

'I'm with you, Dix. He's a lying arse. At best he's weak and way short on integrity. At worst, he's shown his cards. If he'll lie about this, what else will he lie about?'

'Stella, don't bring your shit to this party. Listen, Dixie, it would be easy for me to condemn Freddie. Clearly there are things he could have done differently. But who are we to judge his head state? He's a man who loves deeply. Isn't he? He made you feel loved, didn't he?'

Dixie was silent.

'In fact, I think it makes him seem incredibly selfless when you think about it. I think he really is the amazing person you thought he was. He is just caught up in a very complicated situation.'

'He lied to her, Ana. If he really loved her, he would have been honest. We all know that truth always prevails.'

'No, Stella. Think about your own life. You're not always honest about everything, are you?'

'I—' Stella stopped herself. There was something in Ana's expression that alarmed her.

'Talk to him, Dixie. You made each other so happy. Just allow yourself to have the conversation with him, and if after that you still think you don't want him, then fine. But don't regret not calling him – after all, it's often the things we don't do that we regret the most. I don't want that to happen to you. We all saw how happy he made you.'

'Wow, quite the philosopher, Ana,' smiled Dixie. 'Did Joel's phallus inject some new clarity?'

Stella sighed. 'She's right, Dixie. The man deserves to be

heard out. Act in haste, repent at leisure. If you still think he's a lying bastard then you've lost nothing. You should only make a big decision like this when you know all the facts. It's too easy to act on our prejudices, isn't it?'

'Listen to Stella,' pleaded Ana.

'OK, I get it. I need to talk to Freddie. I am just so angry. It all seemed too good to be true, and then it was. I'd been waiting, I guess, for the bomb to drop. Things are never that good, that's just the way life is... But if he has lied about this, what else has he lied about? Are there more secrets? Maybe I don't know him at all.'

'I say, listen to him, but go with your gut, Dix. Don't give up on it that easily. If you break up with Freddie, where will Ana and I find our excitement?' said Stella as she downed her glass of champagne. She was going to have to ask Jake to sort childcare. Could she still trust him? She knew that she was going to have to: this was going to be a long one.

Ana turned to her.

'Your turn, Stella. Isn't it about time you confessed to Dixie?'

Stella felt herself blush.

'I have nothing to add. You both know about Jake. The gambling and the lying. Tens of thousands thrown away. The—'

'You don't remember, do you?'

Stella felt her throat tightening.

'Remember?'

Ana's eyebrow was arched. A smile played around her lips.

' "Oh Coco, oh my god, Coco, please. Please, Coco." Come on, SPILL!'

Stella's first impulse was to deny it, but she didn't.

'When did I say that?' muttered Stella frantically.

'In New York, when I was putting you to bed so drunk you could barely stand.'

'Coco? You mean the nanny?' hooted Dixie. 'Stella's been supping from the furry cup! Blow me! Actually, don't, I take that back.'

Stella felt the shame rising. She was light-headed. She felt small and weak, like a child caught red-handed stealing cupcakes from the cooling rack. She looked at her friends' faces, so mocking, but so loving.

'Yes,' she said, squaring her shoulders. 'Yes, I have been having an affair with Coco. She's an amazing girl. I don't know why I didn't tell you earlier.'

'You thought we'd be jealous,' laughed Dixie. 'Jeez, Stella, get over yourself, I love you, but your wizened vagina is not on my bucket list.'

'Yeah, seriously,' said Ana. 'She can have you from the neck down.'

They were cracking themselves up.

'Who is Coco?' asked Pearl, refilling her flute.

'Coco is a 25-year-old Latina supermodel I met at the playground.'

'Well that's lovely, dear. Does he speak English?'

'*She* speaks perfect English, Pearl. Her linguistic talents are unsurpassable.'

Then they were all laughing.

'Ooh, when do we get to meet her?'

'Not gonna happen, Ana.'

'I won't steal her, Stella. I promise. I have more than enough to deal with at the moment.'

'I need a quick look. I'm afraid a threesome is out of the question. Ooh, Cunny Coco, click my button.'

Stella should have known that these two ridiculous bitches would turn it into a joke, but she was so happy and relieved to be laughing with them again. It was all worthwhile.

'So you're leaving Jake for the nanny? Could you be any more of a feminist!?'

Dixie was wetting herself and Ana was laughing too, but this barb reminded her of the truth and complexity of her situation. Jake was father to Tom and Rory. Her family was the foundation of her life. She could no more leave them than she could disown her tibia and fibia.

'Sorry, Stella,' said Ana softly. 'Perhaps that was a joke too far.'

Stella found herself speaking without filter or fear.

'I realise Coco is a symptom of my unhappiness. The gambling is a symptom of Jake's. I'm guessing that I was lucky, I got to experience something wonderful – Coco's a fucking wonder. But I also realise I betrayed Jake – it wasn't just him, it was me too. But right now I don't think it's going to help either of us if I tell him about her, it's just all too complicated. For now, he just needs to concentrate on getting better. I don't want him getting distracted by lesbian fantasies!'

They all giggled, and then Dixie said softly, 'Jake needs help. You both need support. You're gonna have to end things with Coco. No matter how sweet that cup.'

It sounded so simple. And she realised that the burden she'd been carrying for as long as she could remember had been lifted by two-thirds now that Dixie and Ana were there to help her.

She stared into the fire in silence and her friends watched respectfully as the tears dried on her cheeks. Eventually she felt strong enough to speak.

'Thank you. Jake is in good hands now, and I will tackle Coco, I promise. Now what about you, Ana?'

It was Ana's turn to gaze into the fire, tears welling in her eyes. 'My gut is telling me one thing, but my head, another. I love Rex, but I don't think that means I am in love with him. It feels like a different thing. But Joel is… If I gave everything up for him, would I regret it and wish I had taken the more well-trodden path with Rex? It's just a fantasy, isn't it? Just because I want it to be true doesn't mean it will be. I mean this would be hard enough even if I wasn't pregnant.'

'Do you know you are pregnant?'

Ana shrugged. 'No, it's too early to take a test, it's not even six weeks yet, but it would be just my luck to be pregnant when I am now not sure what I even want! Imagine if I am pregnant – I mean, it could even be Joel's! After all, I am not the one with the fertility problem… I could be having the child of a rock star!'

'What did you just tell me, Ana? We only regret the things we haven't done and we learn to live with the things we have. I bet Stella isn't sitting here regretting having her pussy seen to by a supermodel.'

'True,' Stella giggled. 'I'm not. But Ana, it has to be what you really want. Long term. Parenthood is a whole new game. Success in procreation doesn't guarantee the future. Don't make this about Joel, don't make it about Rex. Make it about parenthood. Which man do you want to raise a child with? Is it Rex? Do you want to be with him? If you don't, leave him, and then maybe it will work out with Joel, and maybe it won't, but either way you have given yourself options.'

'Frankly I would screw Joel over Rex any day of the week,' added Dixie with a smirk. 'Seriously. Cruel to be kind. Kill the runt to save the tribe.'

'Helpful,' responded Ana, laughing, 'but the thing is I agree with you! I just know I am going to break Rex's heart no matter what I do. And if I am pregnant with his child... I can't believe I'm saying this, but I am prepared to be a single mother, just so that it gives me the chance of maybe having Joel. It's so wrong! It doesn't add up. It's just not me!'

'No,' said Stella. 'You are doing it to give yourself freedom and choice, and that is what you deserve. It's possible you're going to be a mother. You're entitled to do it on your own terms.'

'All so easy to say, all so hard to do. I feel sick at the thought of it all,' said Ana, as a phone pinged. Stella, reaching for more cake, realised it was hers. She grabbed it out of her pocket to see a message from Coco. **'Are you back? I want to see you. I've missed you...'**

Feeling empowered by her promise to the girls, she decided to text straight back. They couldn't continue as they were, and anyway the girls would NEVER stop teasing her about drinking from the furry cup.

'I'm sorry, Coco, you are amazing and kind and wonderful, and you have given me a lot to smile about, but right now I need to focus on my family and my career. Good luck with everything. Sx'

As she pressed send, she felt sad at losing something that had been a lot of fun, but she knew it was the right thing to do. Coco was wonderful, but she needed to be someone else's wonderful. She smiled to herself at how millennial it was to dump someone by text. Now she just wanted to go home to London with a clean slate, ready to start a new chapter. She simply got a text back with three emojis – a heart, a crying face and a pussycat. It made her smile – she thought it was probably the only emoji available for a pussy.

CHAPTER TWENTY-SIX

Dixie

Dixie was curled up on the sofa, fire lit, sketchbook in hand, amusing herself by drawing pictures of the Botox bitches who cruelly crushed her dreams, using an edited version of the truth to bring her world down around her. It was hard to accept how fragile she was, how easy to manipulate. She prided herself on her strength of character, her self-sufficiency. She'd come a long way from the girl who got married at 21, but still, two not especially motivated or Machiavellian women she'd never met were able to find her vulnerability and torture her with it. She was ashamed. Why couldn't she be as tough and resilient as that bitch Stella who could fuck her nanny and never lose her equanimity, never doubt herself. If she could go back in time, what would she do differently? Firstly she'd press Freddie for full disclosure. If he'd been honest, she'd never have been exposed like that. Little weasel. Was it his weakness or hers that was ultimately to blame for her predicament? Well, it was his omission that initiated the 'misunderstanding'. She had to assume that a man as smart as him knew what he was doing. He should have told her everything. Why should she doubt him?

She knew if Freddie had just told her, just trusted enough that she would believe in him, that she would have coped. She'd promised Stella and Ana that she'd talk to Freddie, but she was beginning to doubt the wisdom of that commitment. He'd shown himself economical with the truth when it suited him. He lacked backbone. He lacked integrity. Was that the kind of man she wanted in her life? No, probably not. She sighed and threw aside the sketchpad and drained the gin and tonic. It was getting late. Pearl would be back from bingo soon.

He deserves a chance to tell his story. Hmm. She knew that Stella would be talking to him and she could expect a call. Would she take it? Certainly not the first time he'd called. Nor the second. Nor the third. But she knew you can't just keep running. Life has a way of catching up with you. There are always consequences, and Dixie knew that better than anyone. She had spent her whole life running and look where it had got her. She made another drink and listened to the fire spit and hiss.

What seemed like minutes later she was woken by a banging. She was confused. She was still on the sofa. A blanket over her. The fire was glowing red. The banging was coming from the door. She checked her watch. It was 2 a.m. She must have fallen asleep on the sofa. She was cold and her mouth was dry, and she felt like crap. She had a headache and she'd been dribbling in her sleep. The arm of the sofa was wet. She'd been sweating. Shit. Was she coming down with something? The door was banged again. She was going to have to answer it. Pearl would sleep through the apocalypse after a night at bingo. It was probably one of her hippie friends with a love crisis to be resolved. With the blanket drawn around her cold body, she trudged disgruntedly to the door.

And there he was. His blue eyes, though rimmed with red, were shining with hope. She stared at him. His suit was crumpled, a bag over his shoulder. Behind him a taxi was disappearing down the drive.

'Can I come in?' he asked.

What was she supposed to say? She was angry that he'd cut off her option of sending him away. She couldn't exactly leave him on the doorstep. Or could she? He looked so sad. She'd missed him. She stepped aside and let him in, saying nothing.

He followed her to the kitchen. She slid the kettle onto the Aga, enjoying his discomfort as he carefully pushed aside some dirty glasses, the shopping bags and cookery books and parked his holdall, and looked around the kitchen. He had to step around and beneath the hanging pots and pans.

'I—'

'You woke me up. Apologies if I'm not wearing a tiara and fussing around you.'

'I didn't want to tell you I was coming in case you said no.'

'If you thought I was going to say no, why did you come? Do you really have such a low opinion of me that you think some tragic rom-com midnight stalking is going to compensate for months of wilful lying and evasion? Your ex-wife is alive and you chose to keep that from me, you patronising chauvinist bastard. How dare you?'

She crossed her arms and leaned back against the Aga.

'You're right. I'm sorry,' he said, sitting down. He did look haunted, she noticed with satisfaction.

'That I found out?' she asked, feeling the fury mount up again.

'For everything,' he whispered. 'I was trying to do the right thing, and got it so totally wrong.'

'I don't know who you are, Freddie. Everything I thought I knew about you – your strength, decency, kindness – isn't true. You thought spinning me bullshit was doing the right thing?'

'I am all those things, Dixie, I promise you. Yes, I let you you believe—'

'Oh, own your bullshit, Freddie, or fuck off.'

'OK.' His eyes met hers. 'Yes, it was a daft lie, but it didn't come from a desire to deceive. I didn't know how much you wanted to hear. I didn't know how to talk about her. There's never been anyone else till you. I am learning. I was, at least. I love you more than anything else in the entire world. I cannot bear to lose you. I didn't want you caught up in the past. Daisy is dead, really, inevitably. There's never been a way back for her.'

'Well, that's not what your so-called friends think, Freddie. The ones who think you're not ready for a relationship, that I am nothing more than an emotional crutch to help you deal with the fallout. They seemed to think she might be back on the scene. That she could be saved. Then where would I be? You selfish bastard!'

The anger was gripping her again.

'I couldn't save her. It destroyed me not to be able to cure the person I loved. But I've said goodbye. Eventually life support will be turned off and we can bury her.'

'But how could you love me when you still love her?' she cried. 'I won't play second fiddle to someone else, Freddie.'

'I love what we had, but I am not in love with her. I am in love with you. Everything about you, your temper, your talent, your dreams. I ache for you... Please.'

'Don't, Freddie. I'm not ready to forgive and forget. I was humiliated at your party. There was a massive secret, and I was the only person not in on it. That was your doing. You made your choice. You had your priorities and protecting me was not one. You have hurt me beyond belief. I don't know if I can find a way back. I have spent my life learning to trust. I know all about loss. I can handle being alone. I finally open myself up to someone and this is the thanks I get.'

Dixie was furious to find herself crying. She pulled her hair over her face as he walked towards her. His arms closed around her. He was whispering indistinct words of comfort into her hair. She felt herself weaken. He pushed the hair away from her eyes and tilted her head up towards him.

'Look at me,' he said. 'You are everything I want, and more.' His hand started to stroke her cheek and then he let it fall slightly towards her breast. His hand cupped her, and she didn't stop him, she couldn't. His touch was everything she remembered. It felt so fucking good.

He whispered into her ear, 'I love you, Dixie Dressler,' and she let out a little gasp as he nipped her earlobe. He started to kiss her gently, inevitably. Did she want to stop him? She wanted to want to stop him, but she didn't. 'Don't let this ruin what we have.' He bit her lower lip. She'd forgotten his smell, like granite in a forest. She could feel herself softening, reciprocating, and she knew she was going to compromise, to forgive, and that felt good. It felt like learning, like progress. She realised maybe it was love, and maybe they could make it work, in spite of, or because, it wasn't perfect.

Just as her body was starting to ache for him, as she started to capitulate to her desire, to respond to his touch, he pulled away, and moved across the room.

She was furious, every fibre of her body flared on high alert.

'What now?' she spat at him. 'More games? More fucking surprises? You soften me up, and now what, are you going to tell me you have three children by three different women as well as a half-dead ex-wife?!'

She hated him and was furious with herself for losing control.

He turned his back on her and bent down to get something out of his bag. Great, thought Dixie, it's probably pictures of his other family. Why had she listened to him? That was it, she was done.

Sheepishly, a half smile playing on his lips, he dropped to one knee.

'Dixie Dressler, I am going to ask you to marry me,' he said, the smile spreading. 'So, will you do me the honour of agreeing to be my wife? I mean, if you've finished your fire and ice routine.'

Her mouth fell open. His eyes were shining and his smile was infectious. She found herself reaching out for the most enormous emerald she had ever seen, surrounded by a thousand glistening little diamonds. It was definitely bigger than Kate's.

'How did you get that so fast?' she asked suspiciously.

'Really?' he said. 'That's your answer?'

'Well?' she pushed.

'Well, I was going to ask you that night on Long Island, but you kind of disappeared before I got the chance, so...'

She blushed bright red. She now regretted her wardrobe. Tatty flannel PJs, worn and ripped from age. An old moth-bitten tartan blanket. She hadn't painted her nails in days. They were chipped, torn and war-scarred. These photos were definitely going to need some photoshopping, but first things first.

'Yes, I'll fucking marry you, you bastard! But that doesn't mean I've forgiven you, and that I don't still want a lot of answers, but yes, yes, yes! God, yes.'

She ran into his arms and knocked him over onto the floor, kissing him hungrily with tears in her eyes.

'I can't believe I am actually going to be your wife,' squealed Dixie.

'I promise I will keep you safe forever, Dixie. This is just the beginning of your story,' said Freddie, with tears in his eyes, as his fingers fumbled insider her pyjamas, testing her hot warmth. She was waiting for him.

CHAPTER TWENTY-SEVEN

Ana

Would yellow help? Ana asked herself as she pulled a mustard yellow skirt and daisy yellow blouse from the Monday rail.

'Ana, will you hurry! We really have to go. I'm sure Dr Skinner won't care what you're wearing as long as you're on time and your foo-foo is clean.'

Foo-foo. Ana rolled her eyes. Was Rex becoming more annoying or was she more intolerant? The more attentive and excited he was, the more irksome.

'Darling, you look fabulous. I just hope our baby gets your looks,' said Rex, kissing her paternally on the forehead.

'And your brains,' said Ana awkwardly, trying to join in.

When Ana had left the Cotswolds, she did so with a new personal power: strong and independent. The debrief with the girls had given her a new determination to do the right thing, to end things with Rex, whether she was pregnant or not. She was going to live for herself, trust herself, and hope for the best. She wasn't, she'd thought, the kind of woman who cheats on her man and then lies to him. She wasn't the kind of woman to be trying for a baby with one man and sleeping with another. This was a new beginning. She was excited.

But life has a way of messing with ethical clarity and personal certainty. She let him lead her downstairs to the taxi. Right now, the less thinking she did, the better. London was raining and summer seemed to have passed over to winter without an autumnal pause. The appointment had been in the diary for six weeks, since the day the egg was implanted and since just before she'd slept with Joel. It was still not 8 a.m. and, with the low cloud cover and persistent rain, it was still dark. She cuddled close to Rex, hiding. Was she terrified of the results of today's scan? She didn't know. What's the difference? It was all out of her hands.

Stella had dropped her home that night high on sugar and the solidarity of sisterhood, and she'd bounded up the stairs a strong, independent woman. She would tell Rex everything and she'd get on with her life, embracing a kind of stoic acceptance of what the future might hold, tinged with a desperately romantic hope that she and Joel would find a way to entwine their lives. Rex was at a work thing so Ana channelled her focus into sorting her clothes. Every six months Ana would spend time triaging her wardrobe. She would throw away everything she'd not worn in the past six months. Every type of clothing, all shoes and underwear, every accessory, was examined and if she hadn't worn it, the charity shop received another donation. Humming to herself, she happily sorted everything by colour and age, re-assembling her wardrobe so it resembled a fashionista's periodic table. She found the columns and rows of graduated colours and patterns truly beautiful, calming, uplifting. Her eyes kept returning to the black and white chevron dress she'd stripped off when she and Joel had... She pulled it from its pile and sniffed it, certain she could catch his scent on the silk (even though it had since been dry-cleaned). She went to bed at the normal time, nothing out of the ordinary, but looking forward to the future, to the certainty that tomorrow would bring, to living without secrets and without fear.

She didn't wake when Rex came home. He was very considerate like that. He would undress in the bathroom and creep in, sliding into the bed without a single vibration to disturb her.

But when she woke suddenly in the middle of the night, Rex was cradling her head in his lap, stroking her hair. She'd been crying and crying out in her sleep.

'What's wrong, baby?'

His expression was pale and taut. He looked afraid, but it was nothing compared to the guilt and angst inside Ana. She knew why she was crying. Who was she? What kind of a woman goes through IVF, then travels across the world to sleep with her ex? Only the kind of person who doesn't deserve a baby. She didn't deserve Rex. He was her saviour. He deserved better. She should tell him everything, she'd thought. But what if he left? If he left her, she'd have nothing, and then what if Joel didn't want her either. She felt completely panic-stricken. She should tell him; she couldn't tell him. She wasn't as strong as she thought.

The next couple of weeks passed in a fog. Ana went through the motions, she got dressed and went to work, and she came home and complimented Rex on his cooking. She cried at night and cried on the toilet. She watched reality TV and admired the energy and commitment, the positivity and hopefulness of so many people. She wanted to tell Rex about Joel. She really did, but she couldn't face hurting him and she couldn't talk about it. She hadn't even returned Stella and Dixie's calls, other than to squeal in excitement for Dixie. She was so happy for her. She wondered if she'd ever be as happy as Dixie. Dreams do come true, for some people, but she was paralysed until she knew whether she was pregnant or not. She hoped that knowing that would help her make the right decision, even though she knew it was wrong to be led by that.

Rex held her hand as she waited on the gurney in the exam room. Ana wasn't entirely comfortable with the prospect of superbugs and had insisted that Rex sanitise his hands before touching her. She kept her skin well clear of the metal restraints on the bed. She just had to get through this, she didn't want an infection on top of everything else.

Dr Skinner was waiting and greeted them with a handshake. This surprised Ana, given the well-signposted risks of infection.

'Welcome, welcome. Big day for any couple this. IVF's a difficult road, I know, but let's hope it's a happy destination today. Don't we all, hey? Everything OK? Been behaving yourself?'

Ana looked at him suspiciously. Did he know something? Could he tell just by looking at her? By perhaps the reddish whites of her eyes or the temperature of her palm? Was that why he'd insisted on shaking hands?

'If I may?'

He was pulling up her smock to reveal her stomach. She'd

put on a bit of weight. She rolled her eyes. That would be the comfort eating.

Rex's cheeks were flushed, and there was a dampness, a coolness to his palm. He was terrified, perhaps more terrified than her. He squeezed her hand.

'Here we go.'

The gel was on her belly and the handset circled in cold revolutions.

Dr Skinner moved methodically, sweeping her abdomen, honing in on a point on the right. It seemed a sensitive spot. He peered closer to the screen, adjusted his glasses onto the end of his nose, which was on the point of making contact with the screen.

'Hmm. Yes. Good. There we are. One moment. I just want to...' He checked his notes. 'When was the implantation? Yes. Hmm. One minute...'

Rex's hand froze around hers. 'There's nothing wrong, is there?'

Ana craned around awkwardly to the monitor, which just revealed a patchy fog of white noise.

'Wrong? No, nothing wrong. Just want to check a detail.'

He picked up his notes and disappeared.

'Oh god,' said Rex. 'It's going to be twins, isn't it?' He gulped. 'Or triplets. Yes. Triplets would be... fabulous. Really.'

He was pale and looked close to vomiting. Ana felt sick too. Maybe, thought Ana, they were both succumbing to airborne pathogens.

Dr Skinner returned, brow furrowed, and took a seat.

Ana knew what was coming, somehow he knew she had slept with another man. Rex's hand was slowly tightening around hers. His grip was ice.

'Well, I have good news. You *are* pregnant, albeit very, very early on in the pregnancy.'

Ana froze.

Rex exhaled with a whistle, eyes bulging.

'There were some anomalies on the scan. It wasn't exactly what I was expecting, but there is a gestational sac. It's very unlikely to be the IVF as you are only about four or five weeks' pregnant, but if it was, then it's very behind the curve, and it would be very unusual. No gestation is identical to another. There are numerous explanations. Stress. Diet. Person-specific differences. It is probable that the IVF itself failed and an egg was fertilised naturally.'

Ana could barely breathe; she thought she was going to faint, the room suddenly closing in on her. She and Rex had not had sex since the implantation so there was no way it could be his. It had to be Joel's. But Rex seemed to simply be oblivious to this and carried on chatting in nervous excitement.

'But it's not twins? Not triplets?' asked Rex.

'No,' Dr Skinner smiled and shook his head. 'No, there is a single embryo. We'll start you on a course of vitamins and monitor you closely. We'll need regular check-ups. But congratulations, so far the egg has taken, although of course there is still a long way to go.'

Rex exhaled. He was clearly relieved.

Ana was hollow, shocked, disbelieving and beyond that was a wall of dread.

Rex was on his feet, leaning over and hugging her. He smelled of coffee, stale coffee, and it exacerbated her nausea. His eyes were glassy. He took her face in his hands and kissed her. His lips were dry.

'I'm going to be a father... We're going to be parents. Is it a boy or a girl?'

'I'm afraid it's too early for that. And perhaps that's something you should discuss before the scan. I'm afraid that'll be another three months or so. I want to see you every two weeks until we can establish the embryo's development schedule. We should get a better idea of what's going on soon. Nothing to worry about. You're healthy and there's nothing obvious to explain the anomalies.'

But there was. Ana knew what had happened. She knew exactly what had happened. To avoid Rex's eyes, she pulled him closer. How was she going to tell Joel? Was she going to tell Joel? *What* was she going to tell Joel? And she knew she had to tell Rex. She couldn't let him go on believing this was his child. She felt even worse knowing that it wouldn't cross Rex's mind that she would cheat – he must just think the implantation was a scientific miracle!

'Thank god. Everything's all right,' said Rex.

At home that night in her sweatpants, Rex was waiting on her like an invalid. It was both sweet and suffocating. He made her chicken soup (well, he warmed it), served with some slightly carbonised toast. Her guilt was making her more irritable than usual, and she found herself snapping every time he spoke to her.

'What would you like it to be? I was a very ugly baby. All

long skinny limbs. Like a rag doll. You were a beautiful baby. Your dad showed me photos of you in one of those South American hippy hats with the ear pieces. You were adorable.'

'I was fat.'

'Babies can't be fat. They can only be chubby. It just means they're healthy. No one loves a skinny baby. They look like aliens.'

He reclined next to her. Very close.

'What do you want to watch?'

He flicked through channels. BBC1 was a crime drama. A pregnant Olivia Colman was bumbling around trying to solve a murder. BBC2 was a documentary on gene-editing. ITV was a hospital drama. Channel Four showing one of the *Star Wars* movies. 'I'm your father, Luke. *Wheeze. Wheeze.*'

Ana clamped her eyes shut. Was the god of TV taunting her?

'Ana, darling, are you OK?'

She shook her head.

'Just tired. I'm going to have a bath and go to bed.'

He jumped up.

'Let me run it for you.'

'No!' she said too angrily.

He sat back down, chastened.

'No,' she said, calmer now. 'I'm not made of porcelain. I'll be fine. Just coming to terms...'

Rex looked so hurt that she felt guilty and she leaned down and kissed him.

'Goodnight, sweet Rex. I'm sorry. I'm so sorry.'

From the doorway, she glanced back at Rex. He was staring

at Darth Vader with a look of white terror on his face, she knew she must try to be kinder.

As the bath ran, she stood and scrutinised her profile in the mirror. Was there a baby bump? Were her breasts bigger? Did she feel different? She felt better as she held her belly. She took a deep breath and reached for her phone and scrolled down through her missed calls. She wanted to tell Stella and Dixie, but there was so much going on she didn't know what to say. She sighed and put the phone aside.

Hiding in the hot seclusion of her bath tub, she let the emotions wash over her. She'd run the water very hot and was stewing, but she felt warm and safe, she realised, for the first time since she'd left Joel's arms. She closed her eyes as the sweat ran down her face.

'Is everything all right, babe? Can I get you anything?'

She was so deep in her reverie that she struggled to speak. She coughed to clear her throat.

'I'm fine.'

'I heard splashing.'

'I'm just... washing. I'll be out in a minute.'

He tried the door. She'd forgotten to lock it. He entered.

'You're very red. Let me get you some water.'

'Really, Rex. It's... Thank you.'

She couldn't fault Rex for his loving attentiveness. She had to pull herself together and get her head straight. Sex was one thing. Love was another. But her love for Rex was the wrong love, and her passion for Joel was already nearly love, they just needed a chance to be together. She knew this. She'd always known this, but she also knew it was a risk, and on the whole, Ana was not a risk-taker. But now she had a baby inside her that she had to protect at all costs, and even if was just her and her child, she would be fine. It was all on the spreadsheet – except the baby. There was no column for a baby as a result of a one-night-stand. But what could she trust now? What could she rely on? Eighteen hours earlier, she'd been a woman in a loveless relationship with a kind and gentle man she didn't have the courage to leave, and what was she now?

Rex returned with a glass of cold water and held it to her lips and stroked the damp hair off her forehead. His face glowed in the steam.

'We're going to have a baby,' he said.

She nodded and lowered her eyes.

'Don't stay in there too long.'

'I won't,' she agreed. She closed her eyes and let more fantasies of Joel flood over her, before slowly climbing out of the bath and slipping into bed.

Moments later Rex came into the bedroom where Ana was lying facing the wall, tears in her eyes. She couldn't go on like this. Rex was a good man and he deserved better. She had to tell him. She had to say something.

'I don't get it,' he said, as he stroked her hair tenderly. 'This was meant to be the most exciting day of our lives. This is everything we wanted, Ana, a baby. And yet you are so sad.'

She let out another sob.

'It will be OK, you know... It's probably just shock,' he said. 'I read that the hormones can make you happy and sad, all at once. I just want you to know that I am here for you. Whatever you need.'

'Stop it, Rex, please, just stop!' sobbed Ana, tears pouring down her cheeks. 'It's not hormones, and yes, this was meant to be the happiest day of our lives, but it's not. It's a fucking mess!'

'What do you mean? You're having doubts about the baby? I'm sure that's a totally natural feeling, I mean after all...'

'No, I want the baby, of course I do. It's just... it's just...' She took his hands in hers. 'I'm sorry, I really am. I never wanted this to happen. You've been amazing.'

He pulled away, confusion and hurt flashing through his eyes. 'I don't understand, Ana. What are you saying? What are you talking about?!'

'I slept with Joel. In New York.'

'Who?'

'Joel, my ex.'

'Oh, in New York. Oh, OK.' His whole demeanour changed. His voice became hard. '*That* explains a lot. The Justin Bieber type.'

'Well, more country and western actually.'

Rex snorted, stared for a while at her hands.

'And you tell me this now? After everything we've been through today! You let me— You're carrying our baby... aren't you?' He was pleading.

'I'm sorry, Rex.'

'It could be mine... The doctor said.'

She shook her head and reached out guiltily, but he was out of reach. 'I'm sorry, Rex, I really am, but...'

'OK, OK. Fuck. Fuck you, Ana, for doing this to me – I can't believe I am hearing this! I thought you were different. I thought we loved each other. Obviously that means nothing to you.'

She watched his face set into a determined grimace that held back more rage and shame than she could bear to witness. She lowered her eyes as he stood and left the room. Soon she heard the front door slam and after the reverberations faded, the bedroom was the quietest, loneliest place she'd ever endured.

Ana sat at her desk absentmindedly flicking through the latest auction catalogue. She was meant to be checking the proof before it went to print but her mind was not on her work. She was waiting for morning in New York so she could ring Joel, and all she could think about was what she was going to say to him. It wasn't like she expected him to keep his word and want her. She had no doubt it was all just said in a moment of passion to get laid. Joel had been texting her a lot, sending amazing flowers, singing her little messages down the phone, but she hadn't wanted to indulge her fantasy, but Rex was gone now. Where she didn't know, and she was alone. She felt so guilty about Rex, but he was strong, he was successful, and she hoped at some point he would realise that she had done him a favour. He deserved to be with someone who really loved him for all the right reasons, and that wasn't her. The girls were right: she couldn't stay with him just because he was there and would be an attentive father. She didn't love him in the right way, and whether or not she ended up with Joel, she knew she couldn't have stayed with Rex. Their relationship had just become a habit, and breaking away from one another was ultimately going to be the right call for them both. Anyway, how could she stay with someone who said foo-foo! Joel had just been the catalyst for the break-up. That was what she told herself and she hoped it was true.

Eventually it was 1 p.m. and the alarm pinged on her phone. It would be 7 a.m. in New York and this was a reasonable hour at which to call someone. Wasn't it? She'd been watching the seconds count down, but was still surprised by the alarm. She grabbed her phone from her desk and walked purposefully outside, passing Jan as if on an important call. It was drizzling slightly, and she could feel her clothes starting to get damp, but right now nothing was going to dampen her spirits. She had been preparing to make this call since the door slammed behind Rex.

She pressed call as she settled down on the park bench in the square outside their offices, acting cool, praying a bus with his image on wouldn't pass.

It rang. And rang. And rang. And then went to voicemail.

Ana had not prepared for this. She panicked. What if he was in bed with someone else? What if he was ignoring her call? In her fantasy, he always picked up and whispered something sexy. She hesitated, and then decided to exaggerate her sexy British voice, casually.

'Hey,' she purred, sounding sinister. She changed her voice, to something more chatty. 'So, yup, whatevs, just checking in, to, you know, see how you are. OK, well, I am getting really wet so I am going to hang up now. Oh GOD, not that kind of wet, well, maybe, but it's raining, so that's why I am actually wet. OK, well, bye.'

She hung up and stared at the phone. What, she thought, have I just done? I'm nearly 40 years old and I'm as tongue-tied as a teenager caught shoplifting! I am wet?!

She tried to ring Stella to discuss what she had said. No answer. Then she tried Dixie, no answer. Where was everyone!?

She paced round the square a few times, telling herself that she was fine, it didn't matter. Maybe it was quite funny? Anyway, he was probably with someone else, and wouldn't even listen to the message anyway. Here she found a bitter-sweet consolation and went to get herself some lunch.

She was about to order herself an extra large cheese and ham melt, just in case that was what the baby wanted, when her phone buzzed. It was Joel. She panicked and ran from the shop, leaving behind all thoughts of her sandwich.

'Hey, wet stuff,' said the voice, growly and laughing. 'Does your milkshake bring all the guys to the yard?'

She giggled coyly, feeling slightly sweaty and light-headed.

'I've missed you... I thought you were ghosting me, that you'd gone back to London to forget it all ever happened.'

'Oh I'm sure you don't mind that much, Joel... I'm pretty sure I was just something to pass the time. No doubt there are lots of girls getting Joel-love all the time.'

'Sure, there *might* have been a few, but that excess can't go on forever. It would be exhausting.' He was teasing. At least she hoped he was.

'Well, if you're too busy for little ol'Ana, then I guess I better hang up.'

'You called me, remember? Maybe you want to see me again?'

'I... Yes. There's some things I need to tell you. I need you to know—'

'Are you single yet?'

'Am I— Yes. I told Rex about us and, well, you can imagine.'

'Did you tell him how you feel about me?'

'I... I don't know how I feel about anything right now, Joel. This isn't like when we were in our twenties and it was just a matter of do I want to shag him or not. I have things to deal with.'

'You don't have to come live with me straight away, but do you know where I am? Baja, California. Mexico, baby. Come join me! We can find a deserted island—'

'I'm not joking, Joel. Though I would *love* an island. No, the thing is... I've found out... It's certain that—'

'You want to travel the world with me?'

'No. It's, look, I—'

'If you want to try reverse cowgirl next time, all you gotta do is ask...'

'Joel! I'm pregnant.'

There was silence.

'Joel?' asked Ana. 'Are you there?'

'You're what?'

Then... nothing. The line had gone dead.

Has he hung up on me? Or did the line just go dead? What did she do now, ring him back or leave it? She called him back, but it went straight to voicemail.

Bastard. Why had she said anything? As soon as he heard about the baby, he pulled the dead phone trick. Jeez... did he think she was fifteen? She was a fucking adult. He couldn't treat her like that! She could feel the sobs rising in her chest. Now what was she supposed to do? Of course the weasel ran as soon he found out she was pregnant! She'd known that was a possibility when she'd discussed it with Stella and Dixie. Although it was one thing to have single motherhood as an option, it was quite another to be staring this new future in the eye. She exhaled deeply and took careful steps, walking in circles as she was swamped by waves of panic. She was going to be a single mother, with no partner, and a full-time job – which was fine, she reminded herself, as she was strong and independent, so she could totally cope. Her dad, however, was going to kill her. She was angry at herself. She'd given Joel way too much credit. He was no knight in shining armour. He was the cock-happy country star with neither love nor loyalty.

It was raining harder than before, the rain hiding her tears. She was getting drenched, but she didn't care. Her whole life was falling apart. When she'd spoken to Stella and Dixie, it had all seemed so matter of fact: dump Rex and become Joel's girlfriend, have baby, live happily ever after. If that didn't work out, she'd become an independent woman. The pin-up girl, a single mother who doesn't need a man and can have it all. It hadn't seemed complicated, but she, like Dixie, had discovered, dreams are usually just that. Why did none of them learn that happy endings only ever happen in rom-coms?

She couldn't cope with returning to the office, although she would love nothing more than to share a doughnut and a chat with Jan – she would know what to do. She always knew what to do, but she couldn't face seeing anyone... Neither of the girls had called. She really was all alone. She had her phone and her wallet so she just hailed a taxi and headed for home. She decided she needed to be on her own, with a cup of tea, on the sofa. She needed to work out where it had all gone so wrong. She wished she'd never gone to Freddie's birthday. She wished she'd just trusted the spreadsheet. She missed Rex.

CHAPTER TWENTY-EIGHT

Stella

She was at Slop! at her work station, standing, in her best pair of black fuck-me heels, staring at the Pilates ball that had replaced her chair. She'd taken to wearing trainers to work, telling herself she'd walk more, eat more, NO less, but some days a girl just needs a lift. When she'd asked for her office chair back, the office manager, Charlie, had laughed. 'Live a little, learn a lot,' he'd said. She liked the concept of improving her balance with the ball, but she had no idea where her core was, or if she even had one. Looking down at it in her heels, she had a terrible fear of falling off, surely that couldn't 'empower her creativity' or 'renew her newness', it could only crush her coccyx or fracture her tibia. She shivered and looked around, half expecting a camera to be trained on her, waiting. Not of course that they would laugh at her – they were too millennial for that. They were more likely to send her on a three-hour self-improvement acceleration programme on 'how to sit well on a ball'.

Choosing to stand over her desk, back arched in a hump, and calves and hamstrings at full stretch, she dealt with her inbox. Sorting everything unread by sender, then deleting everything she didn't recognise. One caught her eye. There were three emails from Eliza Dinero, marked 'Confidential: Opportunity'. She didn't think she recognised the name, but thought knowing her luck it was bound to be an intern she had hired at some point and been vile to, who had now decided to sue her for getting her baps out too often or something ridiculous like that. She did have a track record in her heyday – who didn't when you worked eighteen hours a day and every hangover was only ever expunged by a lunch-hour freshener, normally a bottle of Pinot Grigio and a bag of Monster Munch. But Eliza's last message, sent just ten minutes earlier, said, 'Get in touch. I am a friend of Renée and Stef, whom you met recently. I promise you I have something interesting to put to you face-to-face.'

She googled her name. She appeared to work in private equity, for a firm with some dubious, but no doubt profitable, publishing interests. Renée and Stef were the impressive power couple with the lesbian travel blog, Two Birds, One Bed, or something. She decided she had nothing to lose, so she whizzed her back a quick email and got on with her day, losing herself in brainstorming sessions about 'how to save the world from too many carnivores'. She struggled with this issue. Yes, she wanted a sustainable planet; No, she was not prepared to give up meat. She'd already given up plastic straws. One sacrifice at a time. Luckily they established that this was NOT an absolute binary and she was phasing out meat by having one pescatarian and one vegetarian day a week. The kids were struggling. They only ate chicken and things that they thought were chicken. And chocolate.

Leaving work, Stella enjoyed the click-clack of her heels as she strode through the playroom and past the new receptionist, a tall, thin guy with a top-knot who called out, 'Have a great night, Sybil. Every day is a new day.'

She rolled her eyes.

'Night, Dude. Let's hang loose!' She waved and he looked afraid.

Just then her phone buzzed in her pocket, and thinking it was Ana with an update (she was so worried about her), she answered without thinking.

'Stella? Hi, it's Eliza Dinero. We exchanged emails earlier.'

'Eliza, hi! I am just leaving the office,' said Stella slightly more harshly than she had intended.

'I'm not stalking you, yet,' responded Eliza, 'but I might start if I don't get my way. Have you got five minutes to chat?'

Intrigued, though reluctant – because she had two kids at home and the new nanny, a reliable but humourless grandmother, would not be happy if she missed her 6.30 p.m. curfew – Stella said, 'Sure.'

'You were first brought to my attention by Renée and Stef of Two Girls, One Trip. You know them?'

'I have met them, yes.'

'I have a proposition,' continued Eliza. 'Don't worry, not that kind of proposition! I am the CEO of a small venture capital group looking for new markets. We are launching an online social media-led lifestyle magazine targeting metropolitan women, Gen X and Yers, disposable income and big ambitions, in their careers, and in their lives and leisure. The women who want it all and deserve it all. We can't find the right candidate, despite interviewing lots of applicants. Renée and Stef will be content providers and they keep saying I have to meet you. You have a foot in both camps so to speak. You've had a career, and a family, and you're back in the workplace with an open mind. Your experience and more adventurous approach to life sound like a great fit for us.'

Stella worried where all this was coming from. She didn't know Renée and Stef, and she didn't know what they knew about her. How much would Coco have said? Thoughts of Coco added to her confusion. Since their 'text break-up' after New York, she'd deliberately kept her at arm's length. This, combined with her heart-to-heart with Jake, made her nervous about re-engaging with her and her social circle. She'd betrayed Jake enough and even thinking about it made her ashamed of how she'd deceived him.

'That's nice to hear,' said Stella. She was silent for a few moments and then said, 'You know I'm not some kind of militant, feminist, cult figure to lead a lesbian revolution.'

Eliza exploded in laughter. 'No, Stella. Your sexuality is irrelevant to us. We want you for your brain. This could be the opportunity of a lifetime: proper backing, a great team, and an exciting new proposition that you'll get to put your own stamp on.'

Stella's head was spinning. It did sound incredible. There was no doubt Slop! was fun, a stepping stone, a crash course in the online world, but they were NOT her people.

'OK. Perhaps we should meet?'

'How does lunch tomorrow work? Slice of Life by Old Street, one o'clock?'

'Sounds great,' Stella replied with a spring in her step.

She had barely hung up before her phone buzzed again and this time it was Ana.

'Where have you been!?' demanded Stella. 'I have been frantic.'

'Yup, well, it didn't all go quite to plan,' said Ana glumly. 'Rex has gone and I'm pregnant with Joel's baby. It's like a soap opera.'

'Well, that's not all bad,' tried Stella, shocked, desperate to ask more questions, but knowing that Ana needed her to listen. 'Better to have a baby with the man you love rather than the man you used to love. Why do you sound so sad?'

'Because it was horrible, Stella. I have been horrible. I have broken Rex's heart into a million pieces. I betrayed him and now I'm all alone.'

'What about Joel?'

'Joel? I'm such a fool, so naive. I called Joel, and he hung up just after I told him about the baby. I don't know what I expected. He didn't want to know.'

'You sure? Are you absolutely sure? That doesn't sound like Joel, he was SO excited to see you, but then I suppose fame can do weird things to people.'

'I can't believe I thought he would actually really want me. He could have anyone he wants, why would be want a boring old English girl like me. I was just a bit of fun – one more conquest.'

'Maybe he just needs some time,' appealed Stella. 'Maybe he'll call back when he's had time to process. Don't—'

'I called him back and it went straight to voicemail. He's ghosting me. I should have known better. It's probably just another love child to add to his collection. I'm going to have to do this on my own.'

'Oh Ana, you'll never be alone,' sighed Stella, her heart breaking for her. 'Things always look darkest before dawn.'

'Well, they can't get any worse. I trusted that man, I gave up my life for him and he just wanted another notch on his belt and now I have to live with the consequences. My baby won't have a father.'

'Ana, I cannot cope with you like this. I'd normally suggest alcohol, but that's not an advisable idea right now! Have you thought of all the options?'

'All the options?'

'Yeah, you know, you don't have to—'

'I'm 40 years old in January, Stella! I am having this baby whether I want it or not!'

'OK, well, in that case, I command you to come to my house where I will cook you an enormous plate of pasta and let you moan and cry all night!'

Ana was silent and Stella wasn't sure what else she could do.

'Thank you, Stella, I love you and I appreciate the offer, but right now I need to be alone. My head is exploding with so many thoughts. Please don't tell Dixie what is going on. I don't want her worrying. She doesn't need to know that one of the maids of honour at her upcoming nuptials is a tragic, heartbroken single mother!'

As Stella hung up, she wondered why life had to be so hard. It was such a rollercoaster: did having fun always have to have such shit consequences? She longed for the days when all that any of them worried about was how many shots of tequila they could down before they fell off the bar. That's why New York had been so liberating, at least for a little while it had been like the old days, but since then reality had caught up with all of them.

As Stella arrived at Slice of Life, she looked around to see if she could recognise Eliza, whom Stella, after her quick google search, expected to be power-dressed like Alexis Colby with better hair. She was scanning the room when she heard a familiar voice calling her name, and she turned around to see Coco.

'Hola, Stella, over here!' shouted Coco.

Stella waved whilst wishing the ground would swallow her up. What was she doing here? She was never going to be able to focus on her meeting with Coco there, swishing her shiny hair and giggling like a human vibrator. She was suddenly self-conscious about her clothes, her vain bid to look the part of an 'editor'. Seeing Coco's Lycra-stockinged body, she felt like a sausage squeezed into a too-small skin, and she could barely breathe. She was reminded of her first job, work experience in a PR firm. She had to dress as a sausage for the celebration of the launch of the Great British Banger. She had ended up on the 6 o'clock news – to this day it was her father's favourite story.

'Coco,' said Stella, approaching her self-consciously. 'What a lovely surprise to see you! I can't really chat. I'm meeting someone here for lunch about a job.'

'I know,' said Coco, smiling conspiratorially.

'Oh right, great, OK. Why am I suddenly wondering if this is some weird set-up?'

'Stella, always so suspicious,' cooed Coco flirtatiously, grabbing her arm and ushering her into a seat. Her touch was dry and warm and Stella wasn't comfortable with how it made her feel. 'I just started working with Eliza. I'm food blogging. Just like you suggested. It is such an amazing company. Renée and Stef are there too. They're developing the travel section. Imagine the fun we'll have!'

Stella shifted uncomfortably in her seat. This was all very convenient – too convenient. What was she getting herself embroiled in?

'Sorry I'm late,' said Eliza. She wasn't a bit *Dynasty*. Smiling eyes, a firm handshake, late fifties in a no-fuss trouser suit. She was clearly athletic. 'Traffic was awful and I've had the morning from hell. Stella,' she said. 'It's lovely to meet you. I see you have already found Coco. I suggested it might be good if she came along too to tell you more about the company. This isn't entirely my style, but would you object to my ordering a Bloody Mary? Some days. Honestly.'

Stella liked her immediately. This might be more fun than she imagined. Though Coco's presence worried her. What if she wanted more from her? She had already told her it was over, why did she want to work with her? Could Stella work with her? Could they just be friends if they did work together? It all screamed danger to her.

'I know that you two are acquainted, so let's drink to serendipity,' continued Eliza.

Stella didn't know what that meant, and just hoped it didn't have a sexual element.

'Yes,' smiled Stella, going with it. 'We met in the playground with the children and found a kind of solace from the monotony of swinging.' Oh God, what was she saying? 'All those hours watching kids on the swings. You love them, but they can be so boring.' She ignored Coco's smirk.

'I know that feeling,' said Eliza. 'My two are nearly ready to leave home! But I remember the playground years. Park Life.' She laughed easily at her own joke and went on to ask Stella about her family. Stella opted not to mention Jake's present situation in spite of feeling Coco's eyes burning into her.

'So,' said Stella, trying hard to bring it back to a more work-focused conversation, 'I would love to hear a little bit more about what it is you are doing.'

Eliza reached down and got out her laptop, and opened a PowerPoint presentation.

'We want a club, subscription-based and virtual, which builds itself around experts, specifically for women who excel. Women who can lead opinion in the workplace and lifestyles. Influencers have had their time. They've sold out. Most of them have no real experience in their fields. We want to bring together people with real experience and real knowledge. All this starts with finding the right team. Taking all the best of female human capital and making it available. To empower, inform and inspire. A safe space for women. A network and a resource.'

'Wow, I like it, sounds amazing,' said Stella, flattered that such a woman would settle on her. Her stomach was fluttering.

'We have secured significant private equity capital from partners who are invested, financially and morally, in the vision,' said Eliza. 'There are a number of high-profile women. I can't mention any names at this stage, but let's just say that if you leaned into major cultural and sporting events, say Coachella or Wimbledon, you might see some of our partners.

'But why me?' asked Stella. 'You don't know me. This sounds incredible and something I would *love* to be involved in, but I am not exactly experienced in this area. I mean, I've never even been to Glastonbury, and my biggest sporting achievement is retrieving a dropped éclair in less than three seconds.'

Eliza laughed. 'You've got a good track record, Stella. I've done my due diligence. Yes, personal recommendations matter, but I don't rely on that. You'd be surprised how respected you still are in the industry. I have been following your work at Slop!, and although it's been brief, it's been brilliant. I believe you can do this, otherwise you wouldn't be here.'

Stella blushed.

'It's true, Stella,' Eliza continued. 'We are all about female empowerment. We know how hard it is to bounce back after kids. It's a major challenge for women and I was adamant that the best candidate would have dealt with that issue. It defines a central issue for all women. You're a great example. Strong, successful, adaptable. I mean even I can tell Slop! is *so* not you, but you took it on. That's the spirit we want. You don't let other people's expectations define you.'

Stella was not convinced this was a compliment, self-conscious again about her clothing choices. She was silent.

'Listen, I'm not expecting you to make a decision now. I've emailed over the prospectus. Take a look. Any questions, call me. Any time.'

Eliza slid over her card and packed away her laptop. They enjoyed a calorifically respectable lunch and Eliza excused herself.

'Thank you for everything, Eliza. I will consider it all and if I've any questions, I'll be in touch. Thank you for making me feel so wonderful! I might just have a small dessert to celebrate.'

They said their goodbyes, and Eliza left. Stella had wanted to leave with Eliza but she'd seen the dessert menu and found herself incapable of leaving a salted caramel sticky toffee pudding untried. This did of course mean she'd have to stay and talk to Coco.

'Thank you, Coco. I mean it, for all your support on this. She's great. It's a great opportunity.'

Coco gave her enormous smile, her eyes lit up. 'Stella, you are amazing. Sometimes you just need to be reminded of that. You deserve this.'

'I meant what I said on the text – it can't happen again. From here on in, we can only be friends.'

Coco was nodding.

'You know that it's over, right? You promise me you understand what I am saying, that I have to try and make my marriage work, whether I take this position or not?'

Stella's pudding arrived.

Coco nodded sagely.

'Yes. On one condition?'

Stella didn't want to be negotiating on this point. She lifted her spoon and waited.

'Promise me you'll let me have a little taste of your pie?' Coco smiled beguilingly and Stella had to laugh.

'Go ahead, but this is the very last time!'

They both laughed and fell on the salted caramel like rabid wolves.

Afterwards, eyes dilated, lips coated in thick sugar, they mooned at each other.

'Thank you, Coco.'

'Thank *you*, Stella. See you at work soon.'

'I haven't—'

'Yes, you have,' said Coco, and blew her a kiss as she strutted out of the restaurant, turning the head of every man and woman.

CHAPTER TWENTY-NINE

Stella

It was only a few weeks later in early December when Stella woke on the day of the wedding to muffled sounds that indicated snow was falling. She smiled to herself: Dixie would have her white wedding. Dixie's second wedding was to be the antithesis of her first. Where Carlton was a selfish fool and lecherous flake, Freddie was proving himself an upstanding adult and loving partner. Where the first wedding had been a debauched summer affair, all cutesy, English summer clichés – adorable bridesmaids, B-list actors and braying asset managers; a vintage Rolls-Royce and a local parish church in need of a new roof; a plethora of mostly offensive, audacious hats and fascinators more suited to decorating an aviary than adorning a human head; and barely edible mass catering that everyone tried to laud while pushing sullenly around the plate – her second wedding was a chic Christmas affair, instead of a church, a function room at the stylish and well-catered Claridge's, no priest with his hand-out for collections. Instead, Freddie had roped in a friend as celebrant. Stella hoped no one would wear a hat, that there would be no attempt to fascinate by attaching insect or feather-like antennae.

Her first task of the day was to check on Ana.

The girls had all met only once to plan for the wedding, in the Dandelyan Bar at the Mondrian on the South Bank. Dixie had insisted on virgin cocktails: Ana was pregnant and she was de-carbing for optimal wedding day fuckability, so the Dandelyan's renowned mixers were charged with getting them high on two units of alcohol and a clever combination of fruits.

The wedding had been arranged at breakneck speed after Freddie had persuaded Rupert, an old acquaintance and the general manager of Claridge's, to squeeze them in for a wedding before Christmas. It never ceased to amaze Dixie quite how well connected Freddie was. They were both just desperate to get married, move to New York and get on with the rest of their lives. Freddie was all about living in the moment, which Dixie knew was a consequence of Daisy's illness. There was no denying the impact that had had on his life.

Stella arrived to find the girls crying with laughter. They were still floored by her assertion that she was not actually a lesbian, but rather bisexual, or at least bi-curious. Ana was in tears as she tried to express her disappointment at not being able to witness Stella's sexual awakening. It was great to see Ana laugh, especially when she revealed that Rex had apparently recovered within days from his cuckolding and was planning a one-year sabbatical from work and was pursuing his dream (though Ana was certain he'd stolen it off her) of travelling business class anti-clockwise around the world. Ana seemed relieved about Rex, though heartbroken when she revealed she'd heard nothing from Joel. It hadn't been quite a week yet, but she had expected him to ring immediately, or send flowers, or just acknowledge her existence. After all, she had told him she was carrying his baby! He was obviously just an asshole – a day or a week, it was still too long. She was handling it in true Ana style, and Stella thought that this might just be the making of her. Engagement suited Dixie, or perhaps it was just her fake tan; whatever the cause, the dramas in Stella's and Ana's lives gave contrast to her new stability and authority. Dixie and Stella listened with horror and compassion as Ana described her determination to live by her choices and be the best mother she could imagine for her child. Tears of bravery replaced the tears of hilarity as she wore her heart on her sleeve. They fell into an uncomfortable silence, and when Dixie asked, teasing, 'So who would you like as your plus one at the wedding?', Ana could only shrug hopelessly, before saying that as a strong independent woman, she didn't need a plus one.

A toast was made to friends and the future, whatever it might hold for each of them. Their individual plights, thought Stella, revealed how quickly the things we rely on can be taken from us to be replaced by new catastrophes and new opportunities.

*

Water keeps flowing under the bridge, thought Stella, opening her curtains to watch the snow fall silently onto the dark streets. She picked up her phone and texted Ana: **'Do you have crampons for your stilettos? Rushing around, but here if you need me...Sx'**

Stella needed the next few hours to prepare. Her choice of outfit had changed multiple times in the previous few days. For the first time in twenty years, she was dressing to attend a wedding without a man by her side. As Jake was still in rehab there was no one to carry her to bed when she was too drunk to stand. No one to laugh at the fashion disasters, the inappropriate couples, the inebriated media personalities. All she could really hope for was that the Claridge's concierge was trained in the recovery position (at the very least) and would escort her to the room Freddie had kindly booked.

She made a last-minute fashion choice. It was cold and she was likely to be very drunk: the green Diane von Furstenberg velvet jumpsuit, bought from Net-à-Porter with the last few hundred quid on her only working credit card, would be a triumph. It complemented Dixie's hair and could just about contain her enthusiastic bosom, whilst ensuring that in the event of a tumble or other mishap, her vaginal modesty would be protected, and also keep her warm. If people spoke to her tits all day rather than her face, she wouldn't be offended. With the emerald green velvet pretty much glued on (she was dreading needing a wee), she accessorised with bright red killer heels and luminous red Marc Jacobs lipstick. She felt ready for an evening of flirting and fabulousness.

Dixie was staying in one of Peter's investment properties around the corner in Mayfair, while Freddie was already holed up at Claridge's in the wedding suite. When Stella arrived, Dixie was sitting serenely in the corner getting her hair and make-up done, drinking a cup of tea. She looked oddly virginal; very out of character, very calm and peaceful. Through the window the low December sun had an orange glow that softened her freckles and lit up her hair. Stella suddenly felt a tear prick as she realised Dixie was going to be the most beautiful and serene bride she had ever seen. For a brief and sad second, a memory of her own wedding flashed before her; when she was full of hope and love and anticipation, when she thought nothing could ever come between her and Jake. She quickly snapped herself out of it, reminding herself that today was not about her, or Ana's dramas and regrets – it was just about Dixie.

Soon they were hugging and kissing and carrying on as a relatively mild bout of wedding day hysteria overcame them. They might have changed and grown and matured, but there were still times when they were just two best friends who loved and fought and made up and loved again. As if knowing she was missing out, Ana arrived, looking more radiant than ever. Her hair was shining, eyes glistening; in spite of the stress, pregnancy really suited her.

'Wow, Ana, you look good enough to marry!' laughed Dixie. 'How are you feeling? You sure you don't want me to rustle you up a date?'

'I'm good. I have stopped throwing up. I no longer want to kill everyone I meet. Perhaps the next six weeks will be more harmonious than the first! And I even found a designer dress that makes me feel hot as hell!'

Stella noted that she'd ignored Dixie's question about her 'plus one'. Questions would have to wait. She hoped desperately that she really was all right.

Ana's dress, a beautiful, fitted Missoni, glinted metallically and flattered her in every way. The flashing dynamism made everything fluid; unless you knew, there was no way you could tell she was in the early stages of pregnancy. Ana had never looked so elegant and sophisticated. She even wore stunning strappy, gold Louboutins. It was unheard of for Ana to wear one designer piece, let alone two. Stella had to whistle in appreciation.

'Wow girl, you are killing it. You look HOT!'

With Dixie's hair and make-up complete, they helped with the final details of her look. Freddie had sent over some eighteen-carat diamond pendant earrings from Boodles to provide the final bling. Having already done and solidly proven the superstitious pointlessness of something old, something new, something borrowed and something blue from her previous failed marriage, Dixie had instead opted for something bridal (dress), something new (Ana), something old and bitchy (Stella) and something bling (Boodles). They gathered before the wall-to-wall mirror and raised a toast to their friendship, and the bride, obviously.

Dixie's dress was a gorgeous number from a little-known American designer which was just sooo her: a deep V-neck nearly down to her belly button was filled in a light tulle. Beaded all over, with little spaghetti straps, showing off her beautiful elfin-like shoulders and sweeping figure, it was fitted to the ground, and over the top she slipped the most incredible sheer cape covered in more shining beads and gleaming stars.

'You look like the most angelic Christmas fairy, you slut!' laughed Stella.

'Thanks, bitch,' said Dixie, hugging her. 'You get to make every joke you want because we both know I wouldn't be here today without your love and determination.'

Ana joined them both in another hug, before Dixie pulled away.

'I will not fuck with this mascara! Step back, you crazy bitches.'

'Now I'm kind of officially bi-curious, I thought I might introduce an age-fetish into the mix at this wedding,' teased Stella. 'Age-fluidity is the new bi-curiosity. I might turn the tables, check out Freddie's dad, see what he's packing. You know, as I am here alone and all that…'

Dixie gave her a warning look.

'No sexual assault!'

Dixie turned away and tightened her cape around her throat. Stella worried that the cape wasn't going to keep her warm, but it would keep the snow off her shoulders and give her dress a train while she said 'I do'. Her brilliant red hair tumbled down her back, with just a single sparkling clip holding it in place. She was mesmerising – a queen of fire and ice.

'Holy fucking fuck, Dixie Dressler, you look in-fucking-sane! Freddie is the luckiest man alive. If he doesn't gasp when he sees you walk down that aisle, then he's not the man I think he is.'

'I'm feeling a little sick,' squealed Dixie with delight. 'I am in a wedding dress, about to get married! Again! We're just waiting for one more VIP.'

Stella and Ana looked at each other. They read each other's

thoughts: both were hoping that Peter would not be part of the wedding party as he was such a controlling force. Stella wanted to say something but her better instinct ruled that it was Dixie's wedding, and Peter had for many years been the most important man in her life.

Eventually the buzzer rang.

When the door opened, a little shyly, a head peeked around the door.

'Phew, the right place!' said Pearl. 'I brought some snacks.' She opened a pink carton of fairy cakes and, without waiting, snaffled one and held out the box proudly. 'Weddings can be very taxing... calorifically. Eat up!'

CHAPTER THIRTY

Stella

For their arrival at Claridge's, Freddie had insisted they go for something dramatic. After some discussion, ranging from the traditional Bentley to the hackneyed vintage Rolls, they had opted instead for a pseudo-regal arrival: an open-top carriage. Perhaps not the wisest choice for December in London, but they were lucky and the fresh snow had emptied the streets. The flakes fell in orange mounds beneath the street lamps, and the horses' hooves clipped and clopped gently through the streets. With the careful use of dainty umbrellas, warm sheepskin rugs over their legs, and blankets over their shoulders, they arrived outside Claridge's exactly six minutes after 4 p.m. to find a small crowd of onlookers gathered. The hotel had erected red ribbon barriers to allow them unhindered access to the portico.

A footman helped each of them down, Dixie stepping down last, dropping her rug and giving the waiting photographers a few seconds to collect their shots. In the flash of bulbs, Dixie laughed at the drama, loving the attention. As she was helped down to the freshly swept paving stones, Stella heard an insistent American voice behind her.

'You, yes, I insist you let us through. We are guests of Mr Frederick Eastman. We're with them... No, we're not part of the wedding party, we're guests... but surely—'

'If you don't let us through, we're going to miss the—'

'What do you mean that's our problem!'

Stella turned and didn't bother to hide her smirk as her eyes met those of the Botox Bitches. She'd forgotten about them. Her smile broadened mischievously.

Dixie had already begun her royal wedding march into the venue and Stella, taking Ana and Pearl's arms, followed. Every couple of strides she smiled again at the Botoxes, enjoying their increasing indignation. Just before the doorman closed the door behind her, she swung back and allowed them to see her point back as she loudly asked the doorman, 'You see those two awful-looking women in their late fifties? Yes, them, like salamis. Let them in, will you? Today we can afford to share the love.'

Just then, Ana thought she saw a face she recognised, but she decided she was probably just imagining things, and anyway Joel was on the other side of the world. Besides, she was absolutely fine on her own. She had found an inner strength in the last few weeks that she didn't know she had and she felt determined she would be fine. She did not need a man to hold her hand. Even if Joel was the hottest thing she had ever had the pleasure to fuck.

'Sorry it took me so long to get here,' whispered a voice in her ear.

Ana froze, her heart pounding. She felt sick, sure her mind was playing games on her. Hormonal changes maybe?! She turned to see Joel, oozing sex, guitar in hand, standing right in front of her. He was wearing a morning suit, a cowboy hat tilted on the back of his head. He reached for her hand.

'Anything I say right now will sound like a bunch of lying bullshit, but please believe me. I never wanted to hurt you, but I have been on tour and…'

'I can't do this right now, Joel,' whispered Ana, trying to control her breathing.

'Please, Ana, you have to hear me out, please just listen to me.'

She felt the tears welling in her eyes, her heart pounding. 'I have to walk down the aisle with my best friend, and you are going to make me cry, please just let me go.'

'Ana, it's just, I love you… look at you, so goddamn beautiful, radiant as hell,' he said as he grabbed her hand again. 'I lost my phone, all my numbers, I wanted to call you back, I really did. Then I asked my agent to help me contact you via Freddie, and we got Dixie's number, and then she said she needed a wedding singer… and well, here I am… and I'm here for good, if you'll have me…'

She looked at him, searching his eyes for the truth, and turned back to follow Dixie, Stella and Pearl, without saying a word. She didn't know what to think.

The warmth and brightness of the reception area were welcome. Ushers provided by the hotel helped them prepare for the ceremony.

The wedding was to be held in the Drawing Room and they gathered in a side room to make final adjustments. Someone was sent to inform the Master of Ceremonies that they were almost ready. The four girls took a moment to settle themselves.

'You're not having someone to walk you down the aisle?' asked Ana, looking around at Pearl.

'Of course. You guys will be with me, but I think a 40-year-old woman on her second marriage should be capable of walking herself down an aisle, and the idea of anyone giving me away... It's 2019. Ana, I love you, but with the exception of the rather obvious life choice you've made, you're *such* a traditionalist!'

'And no page boys and girls?'

'I might have a few surprises for you, girls,' said Dixie. 'Without you, I wouldn't be here today, so I've taken a few liberties, reached out to a few people to make sure that this isn't just my day, but *our* day, and that all the people who we love, and love us, are here to share it.'

'No kidding,' murmured Ana under her breath, not wanting to have it out with Dixie and ruin the day, but wishing she had been a bit more prepared for the surprise. Someone could have at least told her Joel had been in touch – they all knew what a control freak she was!

Stella felt a lurch of discomfort. 'Dixie, are you OK?'

'Trust me. This is my way of saying thank you,' smiled Dixie.

'What have you done?' said Stella, panic rising.

'Don't worry, Stella, I think Dixie is on a save the world mission, but for today, one day only, we must let her play...' murmured Ana.

'Let's go shall we? All will be revealed... Follow me, ladies. Once more unto the breach! Tally ho!'

Dixie opened the door and led them into the hallway.

Stella's first surprise was to see Tom and Rory, both done

up like little eighteenth-century lords. Ruff collars and long coats. Their faces, all clean and rosy and shining, were almost unrecognisable. They stood either side of a smiling Jake. Stella's first reaction was surprise and slight annoyance, but Jake looked so happy and grateful to be there, and the boys just happy to have their daddy with them. Dixie turned and whispered, 'I'm sorry, Stells, but they had to be here. Jake too. He's promised to leave after the service if that's what you want.'

The sincerity in her voice and tenderness in her eyes forced Stella to relent and relax.

'You're right,' she said, though she wondered whether it was wise for Jake to be cutting short his rehab. He had been supposed to be staying an extra two weeks to complete his recovery. But she felt unexpectedly relieved to see him; after all, they were a family, and seeing what Ana was going through had made her realise that having a wingman who you loved and could trust was something to be cherished.

The doors to the Drawing Room swung open before them. Either side of an aisle were seats for about forty or fifty people. At the end of the aisle the windows were framed in sweeping gold drapes. There was an eighteenth-century vibe increased by the lanterns flickering with candles around the room. The lights dimmed and an electric guitar began to pick out a delicate refrain. Jake directed Tom and Rory to pick up the tail of Dixie's cape.

'Like I showed you. Yes, good luck. You can do it,' he smiled encouragingly.

Stella and Ana followed with Pearl behind them, and then the boys, with Jake standing to the side whispering encouragement to make sure they kept moving – Stella was sure he had bribed them, and then felt a slight hint of panic that they might have inherited his gambling ways. As they moved down the aisle, Stella suddenly nudged Ana.

'Look!'

Seated on the dais, to the groom's side, a black and white Fender Stratocaster on his knee and a small Marshall amp at his feet, was Joel. His eyes sparkled and danced as they met Ana's, searching for the forgiveness and affirmation he so desperately wanted.

'Did you know?' whispered Stella.

Ana nodded her head. She was fighting back tears.

'As of about five minutes ago! Never stop being a bitch, Dixie!'

They both laughed, then cried, then laughed until Dixie turned to scowl.

Freddie was standing in a classic morning suit with a bright red waistcoat that could only be an homage to Dixie. Beside him was a blond-haired celebrant wearing a full priest's regalia: white cassock and detachable collar, gold-rimmed specs propped awkwardly on the end of his crooked nose.

The ceremony passed in a bubble of smiles and tears. The look that passed between Dixie and Freddie as he took her hand was everything Stella could have dreamed of for her friend. She was very aware of Jake's presence behind her and tried hard to blank out any regrets from the last few months. She pulled Rory and Tom closer as they were instructed to stand and sing 'Oh,

What A Beautiful Morning'. Dixie caught Stella's eye briefly as they sang, both remembering school services when they'd stood elbow to elbow and sung 'rhubarb rhubarb' to every hymn. The lip movements required by 'rhubarb' apparently working to cover their teenage refusal to sing-a-long. Stella slipped into an easy 'rhubarb rhubarb' and saw that Dixie was fighting back the giggles as she did the same.

With a pomposity that would have challenged any parish priest, Freddie's friend completed the formalities with aplomb. The moment came, as it did in every wedding, when he asked, dropping his nose and peering over his reading glasses, 'if anyone can show just cause why this couple cannot lawfully be joined together in matrimony, let them speak now or forever hold their peace.' Stella heard a staged cough and there was an awkward shuffling as people leaned and turned to peer at the source of this throat-clearing. Stella saw that it was Peter. She hadn't seen him as they entered as he was seated close to the wall in the row behind hers. His hand was covering his mouth and he coughed again and raised his head as if to speak. Stella looked back to Dixie and she was scowling theatrically. Peter smiled and laughed apologetically. Freddie appeared oblivious to the interaction as he patiently watched Dixie.

'Anyone?' asked the priest again, his eyes roving the assembled, and finished with a final look in the direction of Peter, who had now lowered his eyes.

'Good. Looks like we've got ourselves a happy ending, folks.'

As Freddie and Dixie glided down the aisle after saying their 'I do's, Stella looked sheepishly back at Jake. They'd sat together at many weddings, their hands touching during the vows, unspoken love and trust passing between them. Not any more. That was gone. This time their eyes met, and Stella was searching for a sign, for something. For a moment she was struck by how handsome he looked, but was relieved when a sweaty little hand took hers. She didn't need any more confusion.

The second he could escape, Joel ran over to where they were standing.

'Ana, can I please talk to you for just a minute, before the party?'

'Fine,' she said, her hands shaking, as he led her to an empty seat at the front of the room.

'You lost my number?!' she immediately spat at him, unable to hold her tongue. 'How old are you, 12? You know where I work, it can't be that hard to find me. Jesus, don't treat me like an idiot, Joel!'

'Well actually, you're not that easy to track down, you feisty little firecracker. And yes I do know where you work, but when I rang your office some lady called Jan said you had taken a few days off and she wouldn't give your number out. So then I had to circumnavigate your inner circle to find you!'

'Sodding Jan,' giggled Ana, relieved he knew about her as it certainly added some weight to his story. 'But I still think you are full of crap. Imagine being me, telling you I am pregnant after a one-night-stand when we have not seen each other for years, and then the line goes dead. What am I meant to think? What would you think? And then you just disappear!'

'You're meant to have faith, Ana, that what is meant to be

will be. We were always meant to be together, our worlds have collided once again in the most wonderful way imaginable, and now you tell me, to top it all, we're going to have a baby. We could never have dreamed this up naked in the hot tub.'

'Christ, you've become so poetic and emotionally aware, Joel, I suppose everything is just a song lyric to you.'

'Damn straight it is. Every star needs a muse, baby…'

'It's not a joke, Joel, we barely know each other any more. We can't just pick up where we left off and throw a baby into the mix, this is real life, this…'

'Shh, Ana, please, relax, I promise you, it's all going to be fine. Look at me. We've got this.' And as he leaned in to kiss her, she knew it was pointless even trying to fight it. She was going to go along for the ride, whatever that might bring. But she still needed to have a word with Jan!

As the guests filtered through to the dining room, Stella grabbed the first glass of champagne she could find and found a corner to gather herself. Should she ask Jake to leave the reception? Or should she just see how the evening went? She was torn. She had been excited at the prospect of being at the wedding on her own, and now Jake was there, she felt suffocated. But she also realised she missed him, the comfort of him. Across the room she saw him crouched down talking to Tom and Rory. She sighed as she took in the magnificence of the room. The beautiful white flowers that lined the long tables, so simple and elegant. The green ivy twisted dramatically around every pillar. Somewhere at the other end of the room in a press of unfamiliar faces, she saw Ana and Joel, giggling and laughing, holding each other, happiness radiating from them.

'So what is a man to do when he sees his beautiful wife standing under the mistletoe?' said Jake, who'd appeared beside her. He rested his hand on her lower back and stood beside her. Not too close, but close enough.

'I think the answer is nothing. This "wife" is accidentally standing under the mistletoe while she considers whether or not she even wants her lying husband to stay at the wedding, when it is *her* friend getting married, not his.'

Jake's hand dropped away. 'I'm sorry. I told Dixie it was a risk for me to come today, but she so wanted the boys to be here, and I would have been sad to miss the big day. I'm sorry, Stella. I'll go if you want. I'm not here to fight.'

'No, wait,' said Stella. 'I'm not sure how I feel, whether I want you here or not, whether I even want to speak to you, but your sons need their father, and, for now, we just need you to deal with your problems. I can't think about anything beyond that, and once you are better, then we have a lot to talk about.' She was aware she had her arms folded across her chest and her glass was empty. She felt cruel, but she had to protect herself. She grabbed another glass from a passing waiter.

'It's fine,' said Jake. 'I get it. I am a fucking arsehole and I screwed up our lives. I deserve everything I get. But I want to make amends, and we have to find some way to go on, for them.'

His head indicated Tom and Rory, who were circling the table where the chocolate fountain was churning.

'Yup, damn right you did, but I did too, Jake. We all make

mistakes, we are human, but today is not about us. Today is about Dixie – about the girl who finally found a good man who deserved her. And that is something we *can* celebrate. So are you in?'

She raised her glass in a toast.

Jake looked at her, his eyes twinkling. 'I'd love to, but the programme doesn't allow for drinking. I'm an addict, Stella, I need to steer clear of everything for now. One day at a time.'

Her eyes met his and held them. 'One day at a time. Yes. That. Exactly that.'

CHAPTER THIRTY-ONE

Stella

Stella heard it first, the familiar beat, the sound that could only mean the king and queen of country were about to take the party to the next level. Stella lost all train of thought. Her conversation with a bald, mid-western management consultant was forgotten, and, without warning him, she emptied the flute into the back of her throat and fled in the direction of the music. She knew the others would follow and, like a meerkat, she pushed through the throng towards the double doors, leaping to catch sight of their heads bouncing towards the music. Dixie's height gave her an advantage. Stella saw her already accompanying Kenny and Dolly, with gusto.

They had to reach the dance floor in time to join Dolly's solo. Stella felt two hands trailering her from behind and she knew from the happy laughter that Ana was in position. This was their pre-teen anthem. They'd got 'drunk' on cherry cola and bounced up and down on Stella's bed as they chorused into hairbrushes, hairsprays and nailbrushes, each high on youth, hormones and romance.

The girls were pushing and giggling in overexcitement to get to their positions.

'Make way!' screamed Stella. 'Lady with a Baby coming through!'

They stampeded the dance floor, giddy with collective happiness, and, with the obvious exception of Ana, all pretty drunk. Dixie arrived last – she held her bouquet to her lips as Dolly began her solo.

Her free hand tried to pull Freddie into the circle of love, but his joyful grin was quickly replaced by fear, and he backed away laughing. Stella could feel Jake's eyes on her and wondered for a second if he resented her being the centre of attention, and then realised he just really loved her. Then all three joined in.

Dixie had obviously forgotten the pricey, delicate nature of her bridal gown and fell to her knees. The bouquet was now a guitar and she was playing for the crowd as they gathered in a loose circle around the three girls. Some began to clap, others cheer.

Stella felt a hand pulling at her arm and she tried to shake it off. It was Jake and she saw that he was ushering them onto the dais and offering them the actual, live microphone.

Stella took it and tapped twice. There was a thick electro-static crackle.

'Testing! Testing!'

The girls congregated around the microphone and belted out the chorus.

Stella knew she was drunk, but still, she also knew they sounded and looked amazing. She pulled them all closer. What a group they made, she thought with a laugh. Pregnant Ana with her rock star baby daddy; bi-curious Stella with her boobs cascading onto Dixie, all of them looking just as they had in a thousand teenage Polaroids; the fiery gorgeousness of Dixie, whose curls flared in the wandering red and pink spotlights. Stella felt honoured to belong among them. She saw Jake's smiling face and he picked up both the boys so they could see better. She waved.

Dixie was laughing with her. With a spasm of guilt that was gone before it was acknowledged, she realised that in a certain sense, these girls were her real family. Neither Jake, nor Rory, nor Tom would ever understand who she was, and how she often felt, as well as these girls did. This thought was quickly eclipsed by the communal joy of the chorus.

Together they were strong and they were a team, and, if nothing else, events had shown them over the last few months they were stronger together, and no one, not time, nor misfortune, not an ocean, could fracture the union of their friendship.

They screeched into the microphone, not one of them forgetting a single move of their dance routine. Three 12-year-olds temporarily transported into their 40-year-old bodies. Even the often uptight Ana was pelvic-thrusting like her life depended on it. Stella saw out of the corner of her eye that Joel seemed pretty excited about that too, his eyes shining with delight as he watched.

The girls were all shrieking like teenagers, oblivious to the crowd that had gathered around them cheering and laughing as they delivered the full rendition. And as the final chorus drew to a close, Joel approached Ana, strumming on his guitar, singing up to her.

Ana leaned down to kiss him, then teasingly pulled away, winked, and turned back to her girls shouting, 'Hoes before Bros!' and punching upwards, narrowly missed a lantern.

As the song played out and the crowd sang along, Dixie took the mic, and putting on a masculine voice she hammed it up.

'Thank you very much! My name is Vince Vega, and I'm here all night.'

She held up her bouquet by the base and continued in her fake deep voice.

'Some lucky lady's gonna get herself a bouquet and as surely as winter follows autumn, that lucky little lady's gonna get herself a man. Who wants a new man!?' she shouted. 'Now, I am going to turn my back, so get ready to hustle, ladies! This could be your crowning moment! And you lot, get down there. You too, Stella!'

'Not this time, Dixie, I think I might already have my man!' and she looked over towards Jake, who was looking so handsome and strong. And she knew right then that they were meant to be; they had just got a little bit lost along the way.

'Aaaargh, you soppy old slag, Stella!'

Dixie had her back to the room and was winding up to launch the bouquet. Pearl and Ana were front and centre, leaping up and down like it was 1999. Stella cast another glimpse back at Jake who was grinning at her. In horror, she saw that Tom and Rory had clearly found and explored the chocolate fountain. Their white ruff-collared shirts were muddy with chocolate. Rory had rolled up his sleeves and was brown to the elbow. Tom had obviously taken a more strategic approach and appeared to have dipped his chin into the base and lapped. The lower half of his face was caked. She laughed out loud and pointed to the kids. Jake turned and when he saw the state of them, panicked, swooped them up into his arms and disappeared, quickly mouthing, 'I'm sorry.'

'Everybody ready,' Dixie singsonged with a cheeky glance behind her. 'Not you, Freddie!'

He shuffled to the side with clownish goodwill.

'3–2–1! Jenga!'

The bouquet was lofted high and fast, passing over the priceless chandelier, high over the heads of the gathered hats and fascinators, between the assorted hanging lanterns, and tumbled end over end towards Joel, who, head bowed, and with the concentration of a professional musician, was bent forward packing his Fender into its case. The bouquet of orange, red and yellow roses clipped the front of his Stetson and dropped into his guitar case. He froze.

The guests beneath the trajectory of the bouquet had parted and there was now a clear path between Dixie – and beside her an embarrassed, but stoked Ana, hand on her tummy, and blushing redder than Dixie's roots – and Joel, who was reluctantly lifting the bouquet. He looked around helplessly.

'I didn't do it. It wasn't me,' he pleaded. 'It just flew at me, came at me...'

He stood up, holding the bouquet like it might detonate, and made his way through the parted onlookers towards the girls. Halfway, he stopped, looked down at the bouquet, then lifted his eyes, and lobbed it gently to Ana. 'I think that is where it was meant to go... all being right with the world...'

She caught it and clutched it to her throat, as she reddened further.

He watched her face as she shuffled in joy and embarrassment, and waited for the cheering to quieten. He took off his hat and held it to his chest.

'So… are you ready to go find an island? I promise you won't regret it.'

Acknowledgements

I must thank a few people without whom *No Regrets* would not have become a reality.

The wonderful Lisa Milton at HQ who believed in me from the very first moment we met. Thank you for guiding me through this process.

My gorgeous friend and wonderful agent Alice who is good at helping me to keep it real!

My editor Charlotte who I have horrified on many an occasion, but has always pushed me to do better.

My husband Gav for encouraging me to follow my dreams, for believing in me, and pushing me to write better sex scenes.

My mum for always telling me to say yes, whether I think I can do it or not.

My good friend Sam who has been an excellent sounding board and guidance.

And of course all my awesome sisters and girlfriends – you know who you are. Without *all* the crazy relationships we have been in, this book would never have come to life.

I would like to state that to all of those who know me, I have not researched every aspect of this book.

ONE PLACE. MANY STORIES

Bold, innovative and
empowering publishing.

FOLLOW US ON:

@HQStories